**Here's
Leslie**

"Mixing a deadly sense of humor and plenty of sexy sizzle, Leslie Langtry creates a brilliantly original, laughter-rich mix of contemporary romance and suspense."
- *Chicago Tribune*

"Langtry gets the fun started from page one with a myriad of clever details."
- *Publishers' Weekly*

"The fast-paced romantic suspense chick lit thriller is over the top, but fans will want to follow suit as Leslie Langtry provides a satirical family drama."
-*Midwest Book Review*

"Darkly funny and wildly over the top, this mystery answers the burning question, 'Do assassin skills and Girl Scout merit badges mix...' one truly original and wacky novel!"
-*RT BOOK Reviews*

"Another wicked blend of action, romance, mystery and dark humor, *Guns Will Keep Us Together* gives readers bullets, buff guys and bad boys...I hope the Bombay family continues on with their deadly misadventures.
-*News and Sentinel*

BOOKS BY LESLIE LANGTRY

Greatest Hits Mysteries:

'Scuse Me While I Kill This Guy

Guns Will Keep Us Together

Stand By Your Hitman

I Shot You Babe

Paradise By The Rifle Sights

Snuff The Magic Dragon

My Heroes Have Always Been Hitmen

Four Killing Birds (holiday short story)

Other Works:

The Adulterer's Unofficial Guide to Family Vacations

This book is dedicated to my AMAZING, WONDERFUL, & EXTREMELY TALENTED children - Margaret Lorene and Jack Lawrence. And I'm not just saying that because I'm your mother. I love you both!

TABLE OF CONTENTS

SNUFF THE MAGIC DRAGON: AND OTHER BOMBAY FAMILY BEDTIME STORIES

———

Once Upon A Time, there was a family of Assassins, called the Bombays...

My name is Gin Bombay, and I'm a retired assassin. Because I've retired early and am a bit bored, I decided it was time to write down all the stories that have been passed down in our family for the last few millennia...the Bombay Bedtime Stories, if you will.

First of all, I'd like to make it clear that these stories have been passed down orally. Second, I'm not a historian or writer. So I may get some things wrong here and there. I've decided to write in my own voice, as if I were there, which I was not. If you are some jerk, Ivy League professor bent on pointing out all my mistakes – I may just have to come out of retirement for one more job, if you get my drift.

I'd like to dedicate this book to my wonderful daughter, Romi, who was born (through no fault of her own) into this crazy family.

These stories entertained me when I was growing up. I hope you enjoy them.

- Virginia Bombay

Bombay, The Um, First Bombay—The Minotaur Island of Crete, 1256 BCE

I had to move carefully, I reminded myself as I knocked over a clay pot. Who had clay pots anymore? It was the Bronze Age, for the gods' sake! Clay pottery was useless and would never again be worth more than the dirt it was mixed from.

The pot tottered precariously. My reflexes were pretty quick, though, and I caught it before it hit the stone road. After regaining my breath, I slipped into the shadows, away from the market, toward the outskirts of town.

My contact was nervous. An idiot. An Athenian. He did not like coming to Crete to meet me. But he had no choice. If he wanted me to get the job done, he'd have to come here. I wasn't fond of sailing. Too many sea monsters and that overly sensitive Poseidon. I'll keep my sandals on terra firma, thanks.

Let Codros take the risk. I didn't know what he wanted me to do, but he promised me a *lot* of money. A noise from my left gave me pause. I froze, willing my body to blend in with the wall behind me. Nothing. Probably a bird or something.

At long last I reached the crossroads. Codros was there, twitching nervously, naturally. Fucking Athenians.

"You came," he said as he ran his hand through his thick curls. He'd been my contact for the last year. It took him that long to stop staring at my breasts. Apparently, Athenian girls covered theirs – unlike Cretan women. And also, he'd never seen a pair before. Aside from the fact he was a moron and had no clue as far as Cretan fashion was concerned, he was passable to work with.

"Of course I came," I snapped. "What do you want?"

Codros looked left and right, as if he didn't trust me not to be followed. I rolled my eyes skyward and asked the gods for strength.

"We want to pay you three thousand gold coins to kill the Minotaur."

"Three thousand?" I asked. Surely I misheard him. That was a lot of money. More money than I would ever see in my lifetime. Was this some sort of trap?

Codros nodded. He looked right and left again, which pissed me off, before reaching behind a rock and pulling out a bag loaded with something heavy. He tossed the bag at my feet.

"Here is half," he said quietly. "Once you prove the Minotaur is dead, you will get the rest."

I bent down to examine the bag in the fading light of dusk. My fingers slid past the rough material and closed on a pile of cold coins. I stood, leaving the bag on the ground.

"The Minotaur is a myth," I said. King Minos was always messing with the Athenians. No such half man, half bull existed in real life. Did they really believe that? This had to be a trap.

Codros shook his head violently. "We have been told that we are to send seven Athenian girls and seven boys to be sacrificed in the labyrinth to this beast. If the beast is dead, there will be no sacrifices." He stuck his chin out as if to make his point.

"Okay, say the Minotaur does exist, and I kill him. Why wouldn't Minos just demand the kids anyway and kill them outright?" I mean, that's what I would do. You didn't need a man with a bull's head to kill people.

"If the Minotaur is dead—" Codros slammed his right fist into his left palm. "—Minos will not ask for tribute."

On Crete, we had a lot of jokes about Athenians. Named *ironically* for the Goddess of Wisdom, Athenians were rubes who believed in stuff like flying horses and minotaurs. How many Athenians does it take to milk a goat? Five: one to hold each of the four legs with the fifth one running off to find someone from Crete. Believe me, that's a howler in my village.

"I can't be responsible for what Minos does. If I take your money, kill this Minotaur, and the demand for sacrifice continues, your people will come after me."

"No. You won't be held responsible. And we will pay you once we have proof the monster is dead. Minos won't demand the tributes. If he does, then he's a fool." Codros spat on the ground.

"All right, then." I lifted the very heavy bag from the ground. "I'll do it. And I'll get you your proof. And I won't be responsible for what happens after. We meet back here in four days. I'll have your proof, and you'll have the rest of my money."

He nodded and slipped away into the shadows.

It took me longer to get back home as I dragged an extremely noisy bag of coins through the streets in the darkness. Once inside my little house, I barred the door and dumped the bag on the table. I froze for a moment from the loud sound of coins clanking together, exhaling only after I didn't hear anyone beating on my door.

Why was I worried? I lived alone, with no friends or family on the whole island. People never noticed me. I could slip in and out of anywhere without anyone knowing I was there.

Now, why did I take this job? That confused me a little. I'd been a thief and a spy for most of my sixteen years. But killing? My eyes slid to the bulging sack. Well, clearly that was more lucrative. Besides, I wasn't really going to kill anything.

The Minotaur! Honestly! Those Athenians would fall for anything. There was no Minotaur. What idiots. They couldn't even mess things up properly. Sometimes, those bastards would sneak in and attempt to ruin some festival or another by setting all the goats loose or pouring honey on the streets—you know, the usual Athenian bullshit.

King Minos kept sending our navy to kick their asses, but this crap still happened. He even told the Athenians if they didn't knock it off, he'd demand seven boys and girls every nine years to feed to his weird, made-up, man/bull thing, the Minotaur. But he doesn't have a minotaur. He just says that.

I didn't feel bad in the least for taking their money to kill something that didn't exist. Athens was filled with people who took the "short chariot" to work. Their city state would never last. I give them one more generation before they're completely forgotten.

The only problem would be evidence. How would I prove I killed something that didn't exist? I shook my head and filled a clay cup with water. Damn clay. But with this kind of money, I'd be able to afford a bronze cup or two soon enough.

My parents died when I was two years of age. They were killed in a strange oxcart accident involving a duck and a single olive. This old guy, Deuteronomy, took me in and taught me the fine art of theft. I stole for the two of us while we lived quietly in this house. He died when I was ten. After a while, thieving bored me, and I turned to spying. When I was thirteen, I sold the Athenians a lie that strangely turned out to be true. Who knew Poseidon really *did* have a Kraken? The Athenians believed me, and, as a result, I've been taking their money (and selling them lies) ever since. But this…killing for money, was new.

I wasn't terribly fond of Crete either. People ignored me completely. Maybe after this job, I could disappear—see the world. I was good with a knife and knew my way around poisons—Deuteronomy believed in a well-rounded education. I could take care of myself and had for years.

First things first. I carried the bag of money to my bedroom and yanked the bed away from the wall. After tucking the bag in a hole I had hidden there, I shoved the bed back and lay down on it.

It was hot, and the night was filled with the humid stench of animals, ripe olive groves and people. Yes, leaving after the job was done was a good idea. Wait until after I get paid the rest, and just disappear. I'd probably leave Greece altogether. What would be the point of staying? Maybe I'd even turn faux assassination into a little family business…train the kids and grandkids. Then I threw up in my mouth a little because that would require getting married. Greek boys were gross—always oiling up and wrestling in the nude. What the hell was that all about?

I must have fallen asleep, because the next thing I knew daylight flooded the room and someone was banging on my door.

"Who is it?" I asked in the gruffest voice I could manage.

"Codros sent me," the male voice answered.

I only had two options: open the door and let him in, or keep it barred, grab the money and slip out the window. But I was curious about what kind of moron Codros would send, so I opened the door and dragged the man inside.

"Who are you?" I asked, shutting the door behind him. As I looked him over, my knees grew a little weak. This was an Athenian? He looked more like Apollo. Gold hair, gold skin and eyes as blue as the Aegean. He smiled, and my stomach flipped.

"I'm Sparta." He gave a little bow. I wasn't used to men treating me with respect. Basically, they didn't look at me at all.

"Sparta? Like the city-state?"

He nodded. "Yes. My parents met there. So they named me after that place."

"That's kind of weird," I said before I could stop myself.

"Yes. It is," he agreed. "No one does that."

We stood there, staring at each other for a moment. I motioned to the table and a stool beside it. "Please, sit." I poured him a cup of water and stood back, studying him.

Why did that idiot send someone? And why is he so cute and nice? Is he here to spy on me?

"You said that Codros sent you…"

Adorably, Sparta blushed. "Yeah. I volunteered. I thought I could help you."

"You mean spy on me." I folded my arms across my chest. Sparta didn't seem so cute now. Codros didn't trust me to kill a mythological monster? That bastard!

Sparta rose from the stool and stepped close to me. He was taller than me. And just as gorgeous close up.

"No. I came because I can do things."

It was hard to hear myself over my heart beating. "Really. What exactly can you do?" My guard was up now. Not only did this guy notice me…he actually talked to me. That didn't happen.

"What's your plan for killing the Minotaur?" he asked casually.

"How I kill him is my business." My face was hot, and I could feel that vein pulsing in my forehead. I didn't need some stupid Athenian following me around. I moved to the door and opened it.

"I think you'd better go."

Sparta sighed and made his way out the door, which I may have closed a bit too loudly. He wouldn't last half an hour in the village. Everyone here knew everyone else, and we didn't like strangers. The boy would have to return home or get fed to the goats.

If I had someone spying on me, I'd need to act quickly. Maybe I could just behead a bull and present that to the Athenians? Would they buy it? I could say that he was too large to bring back so I just took the head.

How was I going to behead a bull? I mean, the biggest thing I'd ever killed was a bird, and it wasn't too hard cutting his head off. But a bull? What about the horns? I could get the horns easily enough. But how would that prove anything to people who thought I needed spying upon? Obviously, this wasn't going to be as easy as I thought.

And that stupid Sparta! He probably wouldn't go away. If he had half a brain, he'd hide in the olive groves. His blonde hair would really stand out. I'd have to shake him somehow. Or threaten him.

He'd asked what my plan was. I didn't have one. This job seemed so easy last night. Now it just seemed like a mess…one that would bring the Athenians down on me like a sack of…um…Athenians when I failed.

I could go now. There were fifteen hundred gold coins behind my bed. That would make it easy for me to run away and live fairly comfortably somewhere. All I'd have to do would be to wait until the middle of the night and just slip away. I could bribe a fisherman at the beach to take me across the sea, in the opposite direction of Athens.

In a few days, I'd be in Italy or Africa, and no one would miss me. No one would miss me. Wow. That idea stopped me cold. The only people who knew I even existed were the Athenian morons and Sparta. My neighbors would be hard pressed to identify me as something other than "that weird orphan girl." Even though it would be easy to fade away, I suddenly didn't want to.

I wanted to prove I could do this. For some reason, it mattered that someone out there would remember who I was and what I could do. Slipping away in the night had merit. But it wasn't the right answer. I'd have to go to Minos' palace, Knossos. Then if Sparta was following me, he had to see that I was at least moving toward a plan (one that I really didn't have).

I spent the day preparing for the trip. Deuteronomy had left behind a worn, canvas pack that I filled with dates, olives and bread. Two handfuls of the gold coins and a wine skin filled with water took up the rest of the space. In the early afternoon, I napped. I'd have to move out late at night. By late evening, I'd sharpened my four, bronze throwing knives that I'd stolen from a sailor two years past. They were good knives, and I could throw them with great accuracy. I could use them for self-defense and hunting along the way.

The sounds of the village slowed to a stop as the night grew darker. Finally, I gathered my pack, stuffed my knives in my pockets and headed out the door toward King Minos and his ridiculous, imaginary Minotaur.

The road to Knossos was quiet. There was no moon to highlight my form as I stole along the side of the road, keeping to the trees and shadows. It wasn't very far—just one night's travel on foot. My body slid into a memorized rhythm of soundless flight. I'd been to Knossos before and seen the king's palace. I'd even slipped inside on occasion, unnoticed. I just had to get there. Once I did, I could find an inn and spend the next day in a room, developing a plan.

If Sparta followed me, he would know that I went to pursue my assignment. If he didn't, well, that was fine too. Either way, just getting to Knossos felt like I was actually accomplishing something.

A light breeze stirred the trees around me, and I felt a little peace. Running away in the middle of the night did not frighten me. No one would be traveling at this late hour, and if they were, they would not notice me. It was like being invisible. I liked being invisible.

A twig snapped loudly behind me. On instinct, I slipped around the nearest tree and peered back into the darkness, waiting. He emerged soon after, his blonde hair practically glowing in the dark. Sparta worked his way past me on the road, neither looking right nor left. He seemed completely unfazed at walking alone. I waited to see if he would search for me, but he just kept going, staring straight ahead. If he hadn't been following me, then he'd guessed where I was going. Which meant he expected me to complete the mission.

I smiled and kept to the trees, never taking my eyes off him. I had the advantage. And that made me feel better.

As dawn broke, Knossos was already crowded and busy. I lost sight of Sparta in the maze of people, but that was all right. Turning into a narrow alley, I found an inn that would be suitable, paid the innkeeper a little extra to forget I was there, and once inside my room, I collapsed on the bed.

I awoke hours later and panicked at first. I'd promised Codros four days, and I had less than three left. Getting to Knossos seemed like a big part of the plan, but the truth was I had no plan. None. Whatsoever. And Sparta was waiting out there somewhere. I had to pull it together.

After a quiet dinner of snail stew in a dark corner of the inn's main room, I left the inn to explore the city. My dark hair and skin allowed me to fit in with the people of the city. I wore a gray veil around my head for additional subterfuge—it unnerved me to think there was someone out there looking for me. No one ever looked for me.

The palace walls surrounded the town, and I found myself drawn toward its center. The rumor was that a labyrinth, designed by Daedalus, dominated the grounds. And that was where Minos joked about keeping the Minotaur prisoner. I was hoping that being there would launch some sort of inspiration.

As I wove in and out of the everyday rabble, I heard snatches of conversation about the labyrinth. Workers bragged about working on the structure with such bravado I knew they were all lying. Daedalus was known for carefully selecting his craftsmen.

Still, there was a lot of community pride in the work, and I grew more anxious to see it. The streets were even more crowded now, and I felt like I was wrestling my way through the sea of bodies. At last I found a bench near a bright red wall and sat to gather my thoughts.

"You found it." Sparta joined me on the bench, and I stared at him blankly. Where had he come from? Had he been following me all this time? Impossible! No one followed me.

"This is the opening." He pointed to a sign that said, simply, *Labyrinth*. Huh. I thought it would be more dramatic than that. Oh well.

"I just waited here for you to show up." Sparta smiled and cocked his head to the side. "I knew you would."

I wanted to strangle him. I wanted to drag him inside and beg the gods that there really would be a minotaur inside that would eat him. Maybe bringing back Sparta's gnawed-on carcass with a bull's horn would be proof enough for the Athenians.

"So, let's go," Sparta said.

My jaw dropped open. "You don't just go in! These things require *planning*!" I said as if I really knew. "And it's not a tourist spot—you can't just go in and have someone carve your likeness onto a stone tablet with your arm around the Minotaur!" Okay, I was flustered. This guy found me. Me! Someone who doesn't get found. Someone no one knew or noticed or worried about. I was furious. I was impressed. I was terrified.

He nodded. "You're right. What... are you just checking it out or something?"

"Of course I am!" I recovered quickly. "Why on Olympus did Codros think *you* could help me?"

"I already told you. I have some special skills." Sparta looked a little pissed. And he was so attractive, I struggled with the urge to calm him down and make him happy.

"What skills?" I asked. "I mean, I think I should know, now that we're here and all."

"Soon," he said.

Now I was pissed.

"Fine!" I snapped a little too loudly. "Then you stay here for the rest of the day, doing surveillance. Make note of anyone who comes or goes and what the procedure is. I'll find you tonight." I had no intention of finding him tonight.

"What's *surveillance?*"

I threw my hands up in the air and stomped off dramatically. A few minutes later, I swapped my gray veil for a red one as I faded into the crowd. My thoughts were racing. Did that boy really think you could just walk in and kill a nonexistent creature? No! You needed a plan! You needed to be prepared!

That's when I realized that I really didn't know what I was talking about. Hell, I didn't even know what surveillance was—in fact, I'm pretty sure I made that word up just now. As for planning, I'd never killed anyone for money before. How exactly did one do that? The idea of planning was a nice touch though. And clearly, I'd have to do that once I calmed down.

I skirted the labyrinth wall until I'd put a lot of distance between me and Sparta. Were my eyes playing tricks on me? A small part of the wall seemed to be shaded differently—like it was a fake door from a fresco. It wasn't real...didn't even look real. But I couldn't resist running my hands over the stone.

Except that it wasn't stone. It was fabric painted to look like stone. My hands passed through the material, and I realized that this was some sort of secret door into the maze. After looking around to make sure no one noticed, I slipped behind the curtain to the darkness inside. To my surprise, the curtain drew tight behind me, as if it were a door. How was that possible?

My wonder turned to worry once I realized that it was now pitch dark inside, and I had no idea where the cloth was to get back out. I could chew out Sparta about having a plan when, in reality, I was winging it.

Someone else was in the darkness with me. I could hear them breathing. Did they know I was here? My hands reached the wall, and I frantically slid them around to find the door I'd just stumbled through.

"Hello!" a booming male voice said only inches away. "Nice to have company!"

Uh-oh. There really was a minotaur. And he could talk. And he wanted a playmate. And I'd have to kill him and drag his stupid body all the way back to my village. And that would totally suck because I wasn't sure I could even kill him, let alone get him out of here and get through Knossos with a huge, dead minotaur sight unseen.

"Come this way," said the voice as a hand clamped down on my arm and dragged me away. "It's so nice to have someone to talk to!"

This minotaur seemed a little too happy. But maybe he got that way when some idiot accidentally stumbled into his lair.

I didn't fight as we moved together through the darkness. Mainly because I was in shock. It isn't every day you come face to face with something you thought didn't really exist. Maybe that's how philosophers felt. I just allowed myself to be twisted and turned through a snakelike hallway. We stopped suddenly, and I saw a crack of light glimmering through some sort of door. My captor grunted and pushed, and the sound of stone grinding on stone filled the air.

"Have a seat!" my host said, and I saw to my surprise that it wasn't a minotaur. Actually, I almost would rather it was. Instead, I was in the presence of none other than King Minos himself.

"It's okay!" he laughed, pointing at an ornate chair with cushions on it. Once I sat, he sat and looked at me expectantly.

"Oh! Um, your highness!" I stammered. You didn't just *hang out* with King Minos. That just wasn't *done*. You had to be announced by a guy with a lute or something. Yes, I was pretty sure that was right. "I'm so sorry to have interrupted you! I should be on my way!"

It really was embarrassing. I was the girl no one saw or noticed. Now, in one day, I had this gorgeous Athenian actively looking for me, and I was expected to make conversation with my king—a man who terrorized the Aegean Sea with his navy. A man whose will was so terrible it made the gods tremble. A man who was rumored to be the son of Zeus himself.

I thought I was going to throw up.

Minos frowned. "Are you all right, girl? You've gone green!"

I shook my head vigorously. Throwing up in the presence of such a king would not do. "I'm fine, just, um, surprised to see you here, Your Majesty."

"I guess that would be strange." He stroked his beard before breaking into a huge grin. "Do you play Hide and Seek? The queen won't play with me. And I love that game! Of course, as king, I get to do all the hiding…" Minos nodded his head hopefully.

"I should probably be getting back…" I rose to my feet on shaking legs.

Minos pouted and stuck out his lower lip. "At least talk to me or tell me a story."

"Um, okay?" How could I refuse? "What do you want to talk about?"

"Oh, I don't know…not the weather. That's so boring. Everyone always wants to talk about the weather around me. Why is that?" He seemed genuinely confused, and possibly insane. A little of each, maybe.

"Well, maybe they're intimidated by you and figure that the weather is the safest topic?" He sure intimidated me. I could see how "look at those clouds" or "it might rain" would be preferable to anything that might end up with your head being removed.

"Intimidated?" Minos said, staring off into space thoughtfully. "What does that mean?"

I froze. This wasn't good. You always heard about these tests from the gods and how if you answered the riddle wrong, or cut off the wrong Gorgon's head, you'd end up deformed and guarding a golden fleece or something.

"I like bubbles!" Minos bounced happily into another topic. And that's when I realized that my king, the sovereign of my land, was an imbecile.

"I like bubbles too," I said slowly. "Your highness," I said as an idea came to me, "what about the Minotaur?"

The king burst into laughter, rocking back and forth with glee. I took that to mean he wasn't upset in an "off with your limbs" kind of way.

"Oh, that's good! Really good!" Minos wiped away the tears that streamed down his face. "Minotaur indeed!" He clapped his hands joyfully, and I waited for the laughter to subside.

"So there's really no Minotaur?" I asked carefully.

"No! You mean people really believed that? You must tell me how you heard it!" His breathing was slowing and he was starting to calm down from the laughing fit.

"They do…especially the Athenians." I nodded to show that I really knew stuff.

"Yay!" Minos clapped his hands again. "I hate those stupid Athenians! They're always 'Athena is smarter than Zeus' and 'Our city-state is bigger than yours.' I'm glad they think it's real."

I finally had a plan. "Your Majesty, they believed it so well, they hired me to come and kill it for them."

"Did they?" His eyes were bright. "What did they offer you?"

"Money. A lot of money. But I have to bring back proof that I killed it." On the one hand, I was relieved that there was no Minotaur. On the other hand, proof would be a bitch.

"Bah. I don't want money. I could help you, and it would be great fun! But money is a silly thing to offer." Minos wiggled his fingers in the air. I had no idea what that meant.

"Maybe your highness could help me come up with something...some sort of proof I could take back? If you don't want money in payment, maybe there's something else I could do?" Unfortunately I now was worried what a crazy man would want.

"I know!" he roared. "You can tell me your name! I'll take that as payment!"

"Okaaaay…" For a moment, I weighed the thought that I should give him a fake name. But it was such a simple thing, and if this mad, jolly king was going to help me, it wasn't much to ask at all.

"My name is Bombay."

Minos scowled. "That's a funny name. What does it mean?"

I shook my head. "Nothing, as far as I know. It's just what my parents named me."

The king froze for a moment, and I wondered if I'd been wrong about him. Maybe he was really smart, and there was a man/bull monster. How did I know he wasn't the tyrannical and cruel dictator we'd heard he was? Had I made a horrible mistake?

Minos was still not moving. Was he processing what I was really saying? After all, I'd just admitted to treason with his arch enemy. It felt like my throat was closing, and I began to sweat. I was dead. Really and truly dead…

The king slapped his thigh. "Right! That will have to do, then! Now let's see, what can we use to prove you did your job,

Bombay the slayer of the Minotaur?" He looked around the room, poking cushions, lifting the tapestries, and basically acting crazy. Great. Even the king had nothing in the plan department. You'd think a leader of my known world could come up with something, right?

"Hello?" Sparta's voice called out behind the walls.

Fantastic.

"Who's that?" Minos whispered.

"That's Sparta," I answered.

The king pulled his gown up over his head. And he had nothing on underneath. Great. "The Spartans have breached the maze! What do we do?" Minos quivered like a column of pomegranate jelly.

"I can hear you!" Sparta shouted. "I know you're there, Bombay!" The very next instant, he appeared, holding a torch and a spool of gold thread.

"What are you doing here?" I hissed. This guy could ruin everything! Why didn't I just send him somewhere else?

Sparta shrugged. "I wanted to make sure you were okay." He held up the thread. "I figured this would help me find my way back out." He looked at the man-sized thing with the gown over his head. "Is that the Minotaur?"

Okay. So to sum up, I'm busted hanging with the king—who has the mental capacity of a toddler—while some supposedly stupid Athenian proves he's not so stupid because he's the first person ever to breach the maze. Besides myself, of course. (I thought the gold thread was a nice touch.) There was no way I could get myself out of this mess. I'd have to fess up and hope King Minos ordered Sparta killed on the spot just for starters.

Minos lowered his gown. "Oh. Hello. You don't look like the Spartan army."

"His *name* is Sparta," I replied.

King Minos held out his hand and patted him on the back. "That's almost as bizarre as Bombay here. I'm King Minos."

Sparta looked at me, and I shrugged. He stared at the king for a long time. I waited for him to bolt—to run home and tell everyone in Athens the truth. I'd have to leave Greece altogether. Why didn't I just kill him or trick him or something? Clearly this murder-for-hire thing had gone south.

He sighed. "Well, I guess there really is no Minotaur. Which I always suspected."

I punched him in the arm. "You didn't believe it either? Why did you offer to come along?"

Sparta smiled. "I hate Athens. Those people are morons. I've been following your work with them. Some of that intelligence you sold them was hilarious. That thing about Cretans being cannibals who preferred Athenian meat over all others? That was awesome!"

"Uh, thanks?" I responded weakly.

"I just think you're cool. It was my idea to pay you to kill the Minotaur. The Athenian king is my uncle. He totally bought it."

"Why?" It was the only thing I wanted to know. Why would he fool his countrymen and kin for me?

Sparta shrugged. "I like you. Always have."

I didn't expect that. No one liked me. They didn't dislike me…just didn't know I was there. It hit me like a thousand, worthless clay pots. Here was this handsome guy, and he'd been watching me all this time. He'd learned my tricks, and he liked me. What was happening?

"That's nice!" King Minos stood, clapping us both on the shoulders. "But we still have to come up with your proof."

Sparta laughed. "I told you I had special talents. Here is what we need…"

* * *

One month later, Sparta and I were in Syria, living it up in a house on the beach with a lot of money. I might have fallen for him. I'm not sure. But we had plenty of time. We joked that if we get married, we will have to hide under my name because he's royal and all. We also joked that we'd name our kids after places, like him.

What happened? Well, turns out Sparta did have some special talents. He practices taxidermy. And attaching a bull's head to a man's body was his pièce de résistance. Of course both were dead. I didn't ask Minos where he got the dead guy. It didn't seem like a good idea.

So, Minos dragged the "Minotaur's" carcass into the streets of Knossos and made a decree that the Minotaur was slain by an imaginary Athenian named Theseus who was in love with his daughter. He even threw in the part about Sparta using the gold thread. Spies got back to Athens so fast, Codros was waiting with my money when I got back to the crossroads. Sparta and I fled immediately after.

Syria is still too close. It'll do for a while, but eventually we want to work our way toward Italy. That might be far enough away in case Minos changes his mind about me...or fully loses it. Besides, Italy is a quiet backwater. I don't see it ever becoming an empire or anything like that.

I think Sparta and I have a future together. Turns out he's pretty smart. And he has excellent taste in girls. As long as he doesn't strip down and cover himself in olive oil and want to wrestle other boys, we might just be okay.

Samaria & Assyria Bombay—Draco
620 BCE, Aegina, Greece

"More rope, please, Ria," I said to my twin sister as we slowly strangled the life out of the corrupt politician in front of me. Assyria nodded and loosened her end, which happened to be wrapped around a marble pillar.

Marble was so convenient. It was everywhere in its extremely useful column form. The man turning purple before me probably didn't think so. But then, he shouldn't have enslaved his neighbors and sold his daughters into brothels. Such a bad man. Well, he'd learn his lesson once and for all…the final lesson.

The victim finally turned blue and collapsed. I took up the slack and held it for a few more minutes, just to make sure. Assyria nodded, letting me know he was gone, and we gathered up our things and fled.

My name is Samaria Bombay, and my twin sister Assyria (or Ria as I call her) and I are seventeen years old and assassins. It's all part of the family business, which we had no choice in entering. Not that there are many opportunities for girls around Greece. And it gives us time to work on music and poetry. Ria has mad skills with a lyre, and I write a mean poem.

Back at home, Mom joined us in the music room where Ria was laying down some keen riffs, and I was noshing on a bowl of grapes.

"Girls." Mom looked great—she always looked great. Her hair was perfection, with cascading, shiny onyx curls, and her chiton was always pressed. Ria and I tried to emulate her, but our clothes always seemed more wrinkled and our wild, wiry brown hair did whatever it wanted. Don't even get me started on the pimples...

Mom continued, "You have another assignment." She handed us a sheet of coiled papyrus sealed with wax and paused, waiting for our whining to commence.

"What? No!" I stamped my foot. "We just got done with one!"

"It's not fair!" Ria complained. "They think because we work together that they can give us twice as much!"

Mom rolled her eyes and left the room. She knew there was no way out. As a Bombay herself, she still worked the occasional assignment. Once a Bombay – always an assassin. There was no way out of the family business but death.

Ria pouted as she cracked open the seal. Stupid parchment. Papyrus was so old school. The Bombays were too old-fashioned. She read the instructions and then a devilish grin grew on her face. "OH. MY. GODS! This is soooo cool! You'll like this one!" she said to me.

I snatched the information from her hand and read eagerly. "NO WAY!" I said loudly. "We get to kill Draco? AWESOME!"

Ria nodded, and the two of us held hands and jumped up and down, squealing with joy. Draco was an asshat. We lived in Athens—the home of asshattery, if you ask us—and Draco was the lawgiver and the reason we killed that dude earlier today.

Get this! In Athens, because of this jerk, the penalty for virtually any crime was death. That's right. If you stole a stupid cabbage (although why anyone would steal or even buy a cabbage was beyond me) you were put to death. Why? Because according to Draco, you deserved it. I was personally hoping that once we killed Draco things would get better, right? I mean, who in their right mind would pick up where this jerk left off?

Oh right, back to the dead guy from earlier, Asp...something or other. Well, if you weren't part of the aristocracy, and you were in debt to someone, even for as little as five obols, the person who loaned you the money could enslave you. If you were part of the one-percenters, they couldn't do that to you, because, somehow, you were better than anyone else.

This douchecanoe loaned his neighbor one obol for a loaf of bread when they were at the store so his neighbor wouldn't have to make change on a ten. As soon as they got home, BAM! Asparagus or whatever his name was served his neighbor a summons to be his slave and sold his daughters. And this wasn't the first time Asparagus (I kind of liked calling him that now.) had done it either. But as a member of the upper class, no one could touch him. So he ended up on our assignment roster, and Ria and I happily took him out.

FYI—we'd rescued the daughters earlier and set them up on Crete with their own fashion design business. No girl was going to be a slave on our watch, and they made some awesomely cute sandals...

You might think it unusual that Ria and I can work together. Bombays don't usually do that. But Ria and I are identical twins which is very useful in this field. We'd trained together and could totally read each other's minds. The Council had no problem with us being a team. Unfortunately, that meant we ended up with twice the assignments everyone else did. Whatever.

Draco was a big baddie and a choice assignment! Of course this meant that this was also a tricky job. He was an official legislator and part of the ruling class. It would be impossible to get next to him. Unlike the other guy this morning—in which case we just walked right into his home when his family and slaves were at an outing (that we'd organized).

Ria and I were fantastic organizers! We could throw a party like nobody else. (This one time, we threw a kick-ass school party with gladiator games, a "design your own toga out of toilet paper" contest and we got the coolest singer in Athens—Justinius Beberius—to perform!)! And with two of us handling the hits, we were always successful.

"That rope from this morning ruined my hands!" Ria whined as she examined her skin and fingernails. She was the more fashion-conscious of the two of us. I was a bit more tomboyish. My nails were super short, and I had calluses everywhere. Our hands were the only way you could tell us apart, really.

"So," I said, getting excited now, "how are we going to do it?"

Ria stopped examining her hands and looked at me with arched eyebrows (perfectly plucked, I might add). "Do what?"

I threw my hands in the air and rolled my eyes. "The job! Duh!"

"Oh, right." Ria sprawled on the settee on her stomach, ankles crossed and in the air as her ponytail bobbed. "We need to think about that."

I flopped down beside her. "It has to be an accident or natural causes. I don't want us to end up victims of his stupid laws."

My sister nodded absently. She was already scrolling through ideas in her head. I started munching on grapes. Grapes are my favorite.

After a while, she stood up and shook her head, her ponytail bobbing behind her. She looked good like that (which meant *we* looked good like that). "I've got nothing. Let's head to the market."

"Great idea!" I grabbed my bag and we were off. The market really was the happening place. You could buy anything there—in fact, they had a new shipment of silk chitons coming in this week. Maybe we'd get lucky!

Okay, so it's not all about shopping. The market was also the place where you got the latest news and gossip. We would need to know Draco's latest if we were going to take him out. Anyone who was anyone knew that.

The market was super crowded. It must have been delivery day—which also meant that it was a good news day. Bonus! I browsed the red ochre paste, looking to see if they had anything new for lips. Finding nothing, Ria and I made our way to the olive oil merchants.

We had horrible hair. I know most teens will tell you that, but ours was dark brown and wiry. Ria and I tried everything to tame it with no luck. We were hoping today there might be a new merchant with a miracle cure.

"This is the best oil for your hair!" a short, fat island man barked at us. He was covered with hair that went in every direction. Clearly his oils didn't work.

"I don't think so…" Ria said as we moved on. The next stall had a woman with gorgeous, glossy hair. We stopped.

"I used to have hair like you." The woman was a knockout. She patted her glossy, bouncy curls and nodded. "Use some of my oil." She looked from right to left and then whispered conspiratorially, "I add a special oil from Morocco to it. Works like a dream!"

I sniffed at the jar she handed me. The scent was luscious—and didn't smell like food. I handed over five drachmas for a gallon of the oil. When you found something you liked, you bought in bulk. You might never see the merchant again. Especially under Draco's laws.

"Where are you from?" Ria made small talk with the woman.

"Aegina. Beautiful island!" the woman said through thick, dark pouty lips. I needed to ask where she got her cosmetics. "If you come to the festival next week on Aegina, stop by my shop. I have a lot more than just this." She spread her hands over her small stall.

"Festival?" I asked, my ears perking up. I liked festivals. Basically, they were parties with boys.

The woman nodded and handed us a card with her shop's information. "And the great Draco will be there! He's giving a speech in the Aeginatan Theater!"

Ria and I looked at each other, eyebrows raised. *A party, shopping, boys, and a chance at Draco! Perfect!*

We thanked the woman and headed toward the center of the market. Neither one of us spoke—we didn't need to. We could basically read each other's minds since birth. The important thing now was to head to gossip central to get the deets.

The open square was flooded with people and the smell of roasted lamb, citrus fruits, and wine. I snagged some food while Ria found the perfect spot for us to sit. It was quite a coup to pull off, as you had to find the spot where the "in crowd" was, so you could overhear a number of conversations going on at once.

Ria zoomed in on a couple of legislators chatting to our left, while I focused on the desperate housewives on the right. To look at us, you'd think we were just two teen girls noshing and paying no attention to their surroundings. No one ever gave us a second glance, because they assumed teenage girls didn't care what went on in politics or for the complaints of wealthy, middle-aged women. And I guess they were right about the second part. I mean, these women were really old—like twenty-nine or something. As *if* we'd be interested in them!

"Darling! You simply *must* go to Aegina for the festival! Everyone will be there!" a bored matron dripping in gold snake bracelets said.

"What are you going to wear?" a shrill, skinny woman with huge breasts asked breathlessly. Her hair was blonde, which screamed *fake*! Boy, we think our hair is unruly, but when these rich women used wood ash and lye soap to bleach out their hair, it would eventually have the consistency of straw. Served them right. I stifled a giggle.

"Well, I was thinking of wearing my new, violet cloak! It's the softest wool you'll ever touch!" Bracelets responded.

Fake Blonde nodded. "It will be the season. I wouldn't be caught dead without my scarlet cloak. It's probably heavier than yours."

I continued to listen, rolling my eyes internally, as the group of women grew and chatted about their clothes and who had the best of whatever. Intel gathering can be so dull sometimes.

After an hour, Ria looked at me meaningfully, and we gathered up our things to go. We stopped at a few jewelry stalls, and I bought this fabulous jade broach before we headed home.

At dinner that night, we told our parents about going to the festival.

"It's going to be educational too," Ria said as she stared at a piece of bread shaped like a lyre. Our cook fancied herself a bit of an artist. "Draco will be speaking."

I thought the educational pitch was a nice touch. But Dad wasn't sure.

"I don't know if you should go off alone to a festival on an island…" he said slowly.

"Mom!" I pleaded, "We can stay with Aunt Lydia—she lives on Aegina! And we want to do some shopping!"

Mom couldn't really say no. She knew this was a job. But Dad didn't approve of our entry into the family business even though he didn't have a choice. (Those who married into the Bombays never did.) So we couldn't go at it from that angle.

She laid a hand on Dad's arm. "I'm sure if they stay with my sister it will be okay." Mom used her soothing voice on Dad. "I'll write to her and let her know they are coming. In fact, I'll go with them. It's been a while since I've seen Lydia."

Ria and I tried not to smile. Dad couldn't say no to that. And having Mom and Lydia, both trained assassins themselves, would be an extra bonus.

Dad sighed and shook his head. "You know I can't argue with you. Go and have fun."

"Thanks, Dad!" we said in unison as our cook brought out the fish and fruit. "You're the best!" we threw in simultaneously for good measure.

Mom joined us later that evening in our rooms as we started packing. "You have Draco, don't you?" Her arms were folded across her chest, and she didn't look very happy.

My sister and I nodded.

"I'm not sure about that," Mom said. "Seems dangerous to take out such a public figure."

I rolled my eyes. "It's not like we have a choice, you know."

"You of all people know that," Ria finished.

Mom sighed. "I know. That's why Lydia and I are going to help you."

My sister and I stared at each other. This was a bit of a breach in protocol. We were the rare exception that worked together, but working in a team was a Bombay no-no. The family business had strict rules about working together. The idea was to train us independently as assassins so we didn't have to rely on anyone else.

"And that is the end of the discussion." Mom narrowed her eyes at us. "We leave in the morning." And with that announcement, she left.

"I guess if we don't tell the other Bombays," Ria started.

"Then they won't get upset about it," I finished.

An hour later we were in bed. Staring at the ceiling, I began to think about the concern in Mom's eyes. If she was that worried, I started to worry that we might, in fact, need Mom and Lydia's help. Which worried me even more. At seventeen, Ria and I were supposed to be working on our own.

"Sam?" Ria said quietly. "We'll come up with something. We won't need Mom."

"My thoughts exactly. Night Ria," I said with a great deal less confidence.

* * *

Aegina was a gorgeous little island with full sun and cute boys. Not that we had time for that. After arriving, we made our way to Lydia's house, and after unpacking (you simply cannot have toooo many sandals!) the four of us made our way into town.

Ria and I told Mom and Lydia that we were going to check out the theater where Draco was slated to perform in two days. Only two days! Mom and Lydia decided to do some research.

The theater was the typical round-type arena. Boring. The crowd would enter from two locations, and Draco would already be installed in a dressing room at ground level. At the appropriate time, he would enter the stadium, and the crowd would cheer.

"You never told me what you overheard the other day," I said to Ria as we headed back to the festival (with, I might add, no ideas).

"The big thing," my sister said, "is that they are worried Draco won't get a huge, warm welcome. He's less popular than he was twenty years ago. They want him hailed as a hero."

I nodded. "All I heard was what clothes everyone was wearing. Then they had a bit of a pissing match over who had the most colorful and heaviest woolen cloak for the event." I rolled my eyes for effect.

Ria clutched my arm and stopped suddenly. "That's it!" She threw her arms around me and squeezed. "I know exactly what to do!"

I frowned. What was it? A bunch of talk about how to get the people to honor Draco and the thickness of women's cloaks? And then it dawned on me. Yes!

* * *

It took us a while to find Mom and Lydia, but once we did we dragged them home and told them about our plan.

Lydia and Mom looked at each other and burst out laughing. They weren't twins, but were very close. Maybe they could read each other's minds too?

"That's very imaginative!" Mom said as she wiped her tears of laughter away.

"What makes you think you can pull it off?" Lydia asked between gasps.

Ria shrugged nonchalantly. "You don't have to do it with us."

"We can do this ourselves," I finished. "It's just a matter of marketing."

Mom and Lydia looked at each other, then leaned forward. "What are you planning, specifically?" they asked in unison. I guess they were a lot like us after all.

So we told them. And they started laughing. Again.

In this day and age in Greece, applause is so, so yesterday. The real way to honor someone is to throw your cloaks, tunics and hats onto the floor of the arena when they enter. It's considered one of the biggest props you can show. Yes, it's stupid. And how do you collect your clothing afterward? What if you really, really liked that cloak?

But the wealthy don't care. They will do it to show that they can afford another cloak. And they want everyone to see them throw their cloak. That's the important thing. We'd just use their vanity.

The Aeginian politicians would love this because it would honor Draco's visit, and they want to show all of Greece that they revere the idiot who wrote those stupid laws. We'd just use their need for spin.

And hopefully, we would smother Draco to death under the weight of a thousand wool cloaks and hats before he even uttered a word. It's brilliant really. You're welcome.

It would be expensive. We needed to find a printer to make handbills to hand out to every one of the ten thousand attendees, encouraging them to send their capes to the theater floor. And we needed to volunteer at the theater to hand out the handbills so they went to everyone.

Actually, that was the easy part. Who wouldn't want a pair of cute twins working for them? We told the management we were huge Draco fans (gross!), and they loved the idea. Mostly, they loved the idea that we were encouraging the guests to honor Draco. It would make them look great.

Of course we went to the theater in disguise as blondes. The wigs were pricey, but we'd had them for years just in case something like this came up. We couldn't go as ourselves—what if someone figured it out? Duh!

Mom and Lydia, on the other hand, had their own tasks. As wealthy women, they infiltrated the bored housewives club and spread the word that *the* latest *thing* would be to take your heaviest, most expensive cloak to the theater that night and throw it away on the arena floor. You might think this would be laughed at – but it wasn't. Word spread like wildfire, and outrageous competitions arose to see who would outdo whom.

"I hope this works," Ria said as she paid five hundred drachmas to the printer. Again, we were wearing our blonde wigs and a bit too much makeup.

"If it doesn't, we'll just have to do something else. The great thing about this plan is that it doesn't seem to be what it is." I had to be vague because we were in public. Ria knew what I meant.

Back at the house, Mom and Lydia were drinking wine on the terrace. Lydia had an amazing view of the sea, so we joined them and showed them the handbills.

"In honor of the visit from the Legislator Draco," Mom read slowly, "please show your pride and appreciation by tossing your cloaks out of deference to this great man!"

"Cheesy," Aunt Lydia said. "But the way the society matrons have leaped on the idea means it just might work."

"What I like about it," Mom replied, "is that there's very little risk to you girls. It wasn't like that when we were seventeen, was it Lyd?"

Her sister shook her head vigorously. "No it was not. If we had an assignment back then, we stabbed the guy and ran like Hades!"

Mom laughed. "Ah the good old days! Now—" She pointed at our huge stack of fliers. " —it's all spin and publicity."

Lydia nodded. "Things sure have changed."

Ria and I rolled our eyes. I mean really! Listening to them talk about the "good old days" was nauseating.

* * *

The next morning we were up at dawn and getting ready. Ria and I had to be at the arena early with our fliers. Mom and Aunt Lydia had rounded up everybody they knew and were going to tailgate in front of the stadium. They were even taking extra cloaks. So prepared!

I personally liked the tailgate idea. Mom thought a drunken party before the event would encourage people even more to throw their clothes. It was an epic idea.

It took a little longer for Ria and me to get ready. The wigs were hot and a total pain, but we wanted to make them look like our real hair. We added more makeup than normal to further disguise ourselves and even wore colored chitons. Normally, we just wear white. Two blondes were rare in Greece. Twin blondes would be a huge novelty—which would help with flier distribution. That was what we were counting on.

The tailgate party was in full swing when we set up at the arena. Ria and I each covered an entrance and both looked out at the front. Mom and Lydia really nailed their job. I think everyone attending Draco's event was drinking out there. Good. Drunks made it all better.

Draco arrived with a huge entourage of Aeginian and Athenian lawmakers. He came through my entrance.

"One of the blonde twins." The manager pointed me out, and I bowed in deference. Draco nodded appreciatively and took one of the fliers from my hand.

"What a stroke of genius!" Draco roared with glee.

"Thank you!" The manager bowed and scraped. I didn't mind him taking all the credit. If it worked the way we wanted it to, he would be also saddled with the blame…sort of.

Draco put his hand on my arm and gave me a leering grin. It took all I had not to cringe and pull away. He had to believe I was his biggest fan—that was what we'd told the manager.

So I beamed and nodded. When he took his hand off me, I sighed with relief. I was sure I'd been forgotten moments later as they took Draco to his dressing room.

People began lurching through the doorway a few moments later, and I handed each and every one of them a handbill. I'd never seen so many expensive, brightly colored woolen cloaks! The local society was really doing their part! I made a mental note to thank Mom and Lydia later.

"Don't forget to throw your cloaks out of respect when Draco steps onto the floor!" I called out as I handed out all my thousands of handbills. Everyone was having a pretty good time from the huge tailgate party out front. They rushed past me without giving me a second glance.

As soon as I handed out my last flier, I raced to the other entrance to join Ria, who was just handing out the last of hers. We looked at each other, then raced up into the stands to watch what would happen.

We had stashed our cloaks earlier underneath where we planned to sit. Sitting near Mom and Lydia would not be a good idea. We didn't want anyone to connect us to each other. Besides, Lydia still operated on this island, and we didn't want to endanger her turf.

Our work was done, really. All we could do was sit and wait. Have you ever been a teenage girl who had to sit and wait? It's agonizing torture. Ria and I were so nervous we couldn't even talk. What's that about?

Time was passing slowly, and the audience was growing impatient. A new worry crept in. What if they started to sober up? What if Draco was a total diva and decided to be fashionably late? What if people threw their cloaks too early?

I'd only ever seen a cloak drop once. It was a kindly old poet from Sparta. Because it was the heat of the summer, people only threw light tunics. The poet was so happy he cried, which was cool cuz he seemed nice.

This would be different, if it worked at all, I told myself. I pinched Ria, who was examining her manicure again. She gave me a look that said, *What can we do but wait?*

The trumpets started up, and the crowd was on its feet. The moment had arrived! The fanfare ended, and at the far end of the arena, Draco stepped forward onto the floor, arms raised and a smile on his face. The crowd cheered and a few cloaks began to fall as Draco walked toward the center of the arena.

I held my breath, waiting to see if we pulled it off. The crowd began to roar as Draco stopped in the center of the floor, arms raised as he spun around.

Cloaks and hats rained down on the man like a wool thunderstorm. The sky was blocked by the thousands of huge, heavy rectangles of cloth that fell. It was more than I ever imagined. As more fell, the crowd got louder and rowdier.

On the arena floor, cloaks started to land on Draco. He laughed like a child, delighted in the amount of tribute. What an egomaniac. More and more clothes filled the air and more piled on top of him.

Draco laughed a bit more, crawling out from the cloaks only to be covered by more. He started to struggle with the weight of the material, and his smile began to fade.

The amazing amount of clothing inspired the crowd to roar louder as if they were going for a world record. To my shock, men around me began stripping to the waist, throwing as much as they could. Even sandals were starting to rain down.

"Well this is a bit much," I mumbled to Ria, who seemed hypnotized by the frenzied mob. The smell of half-naked, sweaty and drunken men around us was dizzying, and the air started to fill with fuzz of all things.

On the floor, Draco was seriously struggling. After a moment, I lost sight of him entirely as more and more cloaks, chitons and tunics flew from the stands. The lump beneath the weight of material slowed in its struggling. It was alarming and fascinating at the same time.

The manager seemed to realize what was happening and started to run out onto the floor, shouting for the crowd to stop. They just buried him too—not fatally, I think.

Draco's entourage started to run out to the floor, dodging the capes as they made their way to the middle. More clothing flew, and I worried that the people around me were now completely naked. I didn't even look to see, but I thought I saw Ria turn.

The men on the floor were desperately trying to keep themselves above the material as they tore at the covered body of Draco. The crowd had gone completely berserker, seeming to forget what they were doing there.

Ria tapped me on the arm and I nodded. We fought our way through the crowd until we made it to the ground level. I was covered in bumps and bruises and half deaf before we made it there.

The manager had been knocked unconscious and was being carried out by a few men. Several of the entourage had given up and crawled out past us. The crowd was just starting to calm down. It was as if they were hypnotized, and I thought they looked like they didn't know where they were.

The two remaining members of the entourage had finally managed to uncover Draco's body. One of the men put his ear to Draco's chest. The crowd seemed to sense that something was wrong and became eerily quiet. Within seconds, it had gone from a deafening roar to being able to hear a pin hit the earth below our feet.

Ria and I looked at each other. I felt her hand in mine. We held our breath and waited.

The man looked up at the other member of the entourage and slowly shook his head. Draco was dead. We'd done it! For a moment I almost high-fived my sister, but then I realized that with our job done, it was time to go. We stuffed the wigs and colored chitons in a bag we'd brought and slipped away. And yeah, it was that easy.

* * *

Draco's death had a sobering effect on the rest of the festival. Ria and I stayed at Lydia's with Mom, nursing our many bruises and quietly congratulating ourselves.

"That was a bit more dangerous than I thought it would be," Mom said that first night. "Can you believe how that went down?"

Lydia shook her head. "I have to admit, it was extremely effective. The girls did their job. And it certainly looked like an accident."

"Death by PR," I said slowly.

Ria nodded. "That was an extremely successful hit. But the frenzy was terrifying."

"I know, right?" I asked. "I didn't see that coming. And I don't think I'll be able to wear a cloak again…ever."

* * *

We arrived back in Athens to find Grandma Sicily waiting for us. Mom, Ria and I all exchanged glances. Grandma was not only our mother's mom, but also the head of the Bombay Council. She was tougher than Hercules and shrewder than Hera. A visit from her wasn't usually a good thing.

Dad ushered us into the library and wisely left, shutting the door behind him. We could hear him giving the staff orders to work on something on the other side of the house.

Grandma said nothing for a moment, and Ria and I twitched nervously.

"Mother," Mom said calmly, "what an unexpected surprise."

Grandma nodded and then narrowed her eyes at us before speaking. "A bit of overkill, was it not?"

I nodded. "It did get a bit out of hand."

"And very expensive," Grandma said with a little cough.

Ria chewed her lip, "Yes Grandmama. But we covered it out of our own pockets."

Our grandmother looked away toward the window and sighed. It didn't sound like a good sigh. Clearly we were in trouble.

Grandma cleared her throat. "Best damned laugh I ever had." And then she started to laugh for real. "He was smothered," she said between wheezing giggles, "by his own—" another cough "—self-admiration!" She started to cough so violently Mom went over and patted her on the back until she stopped.

Ria and I were frozen, not daring to say anything.

"You know," Grandma said, "I was a twin too."

Both of our jaws dropped open. We looked to Mom who only nodded with a small smile.

"Back then," Grandma continued, "we weren't allowed to work together. Not like you two. And twins run in the Bombays. Every other generation has a pair."

"We didn't know that, Grandmama," I said. I wondered what happened to her twin. I'd never heard anything about it before.

Grandma rose to her feet very slowly. Mom helped her up.

"Good job girls," she said. "The Council just wanted you to know you can continue to work together for as long as you want." She made her way to the door and turned. "And we expect great things from you."

As she went out the door, we heard her laughing again. "Suffocated by publicity! Hilarious!" And the door closed behind her.

Bavaria Bombay—The Dragon of York
700 CE, Northumbria

"What do you *mean*, I have to kill a magic dragon?" I stared at my mother, hoping she was out of her mind—which was highly possible in this family. She ran her fingers over the elaborately embroidered tapestry.

"Just what I said, Bavaria. Honestly, you shouldn't question me so! The Council knows what it's doing." Mother straightened her long, pointed hat and adjusted her veil. "Besides, we've already been paid. You are to leave for Northumbria tonight." She shooed me away and called for her minstrels. I knew that I'd get nothing further from her. Mother never did anything when she listened to her afternoon "stories."

I nodded and bowed, as was befitting for a man to do toward a woman of my mother's stature, and left the room to ready my things. Great. A magic dragon. Why couldn't it just be a Danish prince or something? Hamlet was driving people nuts in Elsinore. My idiot cousin, Richard, took out Hamlet's father a few months back and the kid was a raving lunatic. It's so much easier to kill someone who sees ghosts. I could make it look self-inflicted while he's all, "Alas, my poor father, blah...blah...blah..." But the Bombays didn't make the contracts—they just carried them out.

There was no point in arguing when you worked in the family business, and that business was assassination. You took your assignment whether you liked it or not and carried it out to its usually bloody conclusion. That was that.

I kicked at a stone with my extremely soft, velvet shoe. The pain was excruciating. Wasn't there a way to make stronger shoes? I didn't want to wear my armor all the time. It was the eighth century, for crying out loud! The only good thing about killing a dragon would be I could use his hide to make some tougher shoes.

A dragon? I mean, sure, we'd all heard about them. There were a lot of dusty books in the library about them. Even part of the Bombay training included dragons and magical creatures. But as far as I knew no one had ever seen one, let alone slain one.

I'd had contracts to kill strange things before. I took out a witch in Wessex. Witches float you know, so if they sink, they aren't witches. Turned out this one wasn't, but you really can't be too careful.

I was contracted to kill a cannibal in the Cotswolds once. He wasn't a very good cannibal. Apparently he thought it rude if he didn't ask permission from his intended meal first. Not surprisingly, they all said, no, so he was basically starving when I killed him, but he still made the peasants nervous, and that still counts. Then there was that giant in Godmundingham who was crushing folks who didn't pay him *not* to crush them. I had to jump off a roof onto his back just to slit his throat. And there was that weird, dog-like thing in East Anglia who'd developed a taste for priests who didn't wash their hands after eating mutton. But a magic dragon? Really?

Still, the tapestries that gave us our orders didn't lie. And considering it takes the Council months and months to embroider them, they clearly have enough time to think about it and change their minds.

Judea was in my room waiting for me. He was my squire, and whether I liked it or not, my nephew. Turns out, I did like him, mostly because he didn't talk much. We all start out as squires during our training. I'd squired for my Aunt Sicily. She was amazing in that she could kill a man with her embroidery needle, and they'd never find a mark on the bodies. I learned a lot from her. It was really too bad she was accidentally murdered by the Welsh with rakes and pitchforks. You really can be in the wrong place at the wrong time.

"We're going to Northumbria tonight," I said as I sat down on a bench with a sigh. "A magic dragon of all things."

Judea (or Jude, as I preferred to call him) nodded as if he heard this every day and began to pack my clothes. I sharpened my sword because I didn't know what else to do. What is the best way to kill a dragon? And a magic dragon at that? What kind of magic did a dragon wield? How would I kill it if I didn't know what it did to defend itself? What if it was invisible and could sneak up on me? Or what if it could set me on fire just by looking at me? I wasn't prepared for that. So much to think about on the road.

I was not partial to Northumbria. They did have a few fetching wenches at the various inns in town. But for the most part, the people were ignorant and cold. If they weren't covered in pox scars, it was some other hideous disease. And they were snooty. I hated that.

Jude helped me dress, and after a quick meal, we rode out. Even the trip was dull. Nothing but a few stiles and muddy fields filled with unimaginative cows. I was tired. And old. At the ripe old age of twenty-four, I was nearing the end of my life outside the castle. My armor creaked on my back. It would need to be oiled when we arrived. I shot a glance at Jude, who ignored me. I was pretty sure he rolled his eyes heavenward—whatever that means.

"How does one kill a magic dragon, Jude?" I asked my page.

"Depends on what kind of magic it has, I guess," Jude answered.

"I'm a little sketchy on this. What kinds of magic are there?"

Jude stared off to his right, his shoulders slouched in a surly manner. "Well, I guess there are the fire-breathers…and I think they all fly…" His gaze slowly turned on me. "I heard of one once who mates with itself to produce more dragons." Jude scratched his nose, slowly.

"That's it?" I asked. "Are you sure that's all they can do?" Because if it was, this might be easier than I thought.

Jude nodded. "One of the minstrels told me there was a dragon in Cornwall who could speak the King's English and liked to tell bawdy jokes." And then, as quickly as his chattiness had begun it ended. And Jude slouched back into silence.

That didn't sound too bad. Flying and fire-breathing could be a problem…if the beast was awake. I'd have to catch it asleep somehow. I wasn't too concerned about the possibility of it mating with itself—in fact, that could be a distraction that would help me kill it. My mind wandered through all the possible positions a dragon would take to mate with itself.

As to the talking, perhaps I could reason with the beast if it did that. If not, I might die laughing listening to its dirty jokes while it fried me. That didn't sound too bad, either.

I rather liked my job, really. There was the travel, the women that came with the travel and a great deal of variety, what with killing a giant one year and a cannibal the next. And I was good with a sword and enjoyed fighting. As Bombays, our loyalties to any one lord were off-limits, and, for the most part, the current ruler understood this. The Bombay Family provided a valuable service.

But because of this, I was unable to join up with any army and fight—something I enjoyed doing. That doesn't mean other family members haven't tried. There are some rather unfortunate chapters of Bombays who fled the family to fight on one side of a war. This never lasted, because Bombays are ruthless at hunting down those in the family who go rogue. Why let an army have the fun of killing us when we will do it ourselves for free?

Still, life wasn't all that great. Marriage was a difficult process. Your intended had to agree to the Bombay 'lifestyle' and to have their children raised as assassins. Men marrying women Bombays had to take on the Bombay Family name. Some were very successful in this. Mother seemed happy. My father was landed gentry and couldn't care less what she or I did. He spent all his time reading books anyway.

I had decided early on that I wasn't going to marry. This was frowned on in the family, because you were supposed to perpetuate the line. But I was getting older and hadn't really met anyone I could marry and introduce to the assassin business.

Or maybe it was that the women I met were so…what's the word? Vapid? They were all giggles and grins, with nothing inside their heads. It could just be that I knew they'd have no problem as long as I left them alone to embroider unicorns. I didn't want a wife who was just… there.

It didn't really matter anyway. Mother was upset, but she finally stopped fixing me up with every Aelfgyth, Beornfled, and Hrothweru. How many times can you take a woman to a Fleece Fair for fun?

We arrived at our destination several hours later. Riding into Northumbria was…anticlimactic. The muddy roads, twisted and charred buildings and the smell! Why would this place even *have* a magic dragon? We rode up to the Broken Man Inn, and while Jude took care of the horses, I checked in.

"So." The fat innkeeper scratched one of his many chins thoughtfully. "It's Bavaria du Bombay, right?"

I sighed and shook my head. "No, it's just Bavaria Bombay. I'm not 'of' Bombay."

"Why is it 'du Bombay' then?" He seemed confused.

"It isn't," I said through clenched teeth. "You made that up. There is no place called Bombay. It's just my name."

His eyes grew wide with understanding. "Ah, so it's descriptive then! Like Beald means 'The Bald,' right? What does Bombay mean?" For a moment I toyed with telling him that Bombay means "kills nosy innkeepers."

"It's not descriptive, and it's not a place. I just have two names. It's a weird, family thing. That's all. Can I see my room now?"

The innkeeper didn't look like he thought it was okay, but wisely decided against arguing with me. Being a Bombay has never been easy. We're an assassins guild, but it includes only family. We are ruled by the Council—a gathering of our family elders who hand down the assignments to kill someone— or in this case, something. It's lucrative, and we have our own money so that we don't owe allegiance to anyone.

"Utta will show you to your room." the innkeeper said. "If she stays, well that's extra." He winked and nodded knowingly. Utta grunted. She looked like a six-foot-tall pig. No, I didn't need company. And I certainly never had to pay for it in Northumbria of all places. Besides, this wasn't the time. I had a job to do.

Jude sullenly joined me in the main room for a late repast. As we tore off chunks of bread to dip into our trenchers of stew, I took in the room. A whole lot of nothing. A few cutthroats and thieves, and I wasn't sure if that thing in the corner was a dwarf or a dog wearing a dress. I needed information and wasn't going to find it here. I toyed with asking Jude to get chummy with the stable boys, but that would be like asking a stack of hay to melt.

"I'm going to bed," I announced to my squire. He nodded. Jude would sleep with the horses. A Bombay never lost sight of his exit strategy. As I drifted off to sleep, I wondered what kind of assassin Jude would make. In this family, you had no choice but to be good. Even my mother killed people back in the day. Her specialty was poison. She was quite good. I didn't want to cross her. When I was a kid and had done something naughty, she'd always give me blood pudding, with a little wink that said, *Eat this, and next time you'll think twice about setting fire to my favorite unicorn pillow*. And then I'd spend two days on the chamber pot.

The next morning I made my way through town. My thoughts were obsessed with the idea of finding and killing this magic dragon. First things first—I needed information. Always know what you are killing, and how to kill it. Our heralds had that put on a coat of arms once, but The Council had not been fond of it. They thought it was too obvious.

I decided it would be best to work the market. People talk if they think you're going to spend money. I dropped a few coins on a table bearing greasy, dead chickens. The squat, filthy old woman took a break from wringing more poultry necks to talk to me.

"Oh, aye then. They've got a dragon up at the castle, they do." She focused her one, cloudy blue eye on me. "That's how they keep us all honest." I noticed that she stuffed the coins inside one of the (what I *hoped* were dead) chickens, making sure her husband didn't notice. Yeah. Honest.

A blacksmith farther down had a little more to offer. "The dragon's magical. He can blow fire out his arse and control you with his mind."

"Why would the Duke keep such a creature?" I asked, throwing down a few more coins.

The smith rubbed his nose, leaving a charred, black smear. "Well, he'd do it to make sure no one messed with his wife and daughter."

This caught my attention. "Wife and daughter? He has a dragon to defend them?" Did whoever paid our Council for this job just want to kill the Duke, marry his wife and take over his lands? That didn't sound like something we'd agree to. If we did that, there'd be new dukes every week, and we'd eventually kill most of them that hired us.

"That's just what I heard," the man said, looking left and right. "And because there's gold up there."

I shook my head as I walked away. That didn't seem right. Bombays didn't get involved in territorial spats. Was there more to this than I was led to believe? It was not like I could do anything about it. Once you unfurled a tapestry, you as good as accepted the assignment.

My mind was foggy, and I wasn't paying any attention, which is how I ended up running into a woman.

"I beg your pardon!" I went down on one knee to apologize. "Please accept my regrets." And then I looked up and swallowed hard.

"It's no bother," the dazzlingly beautiful brunette replied hastily. She looked angry. "I must be on my way, sir."

"Shall I escort you?" I stood and walked with her. "To make sure you don't encounter another misfortune?" This woman looked to be about my age, with icy blue eyes that speared me through the heart. Her hair fell in silken, wavy curtains around her shoulders. I'd never seen anything like her.

"No, really." She pushed me away. "I'll be fine." Before I could stop her, she disappeared into the crowd.

Who was she? I had to know. But how? How could I even describe a beauty such as hers? And intelligence! She was brilliant—I just knew it! The only problem was her haste to get away from me. That might make getting to know her a bit difficult.

Jude appeared at my side. "That's the Duchess." It was the only thing he'd said to me all day. And where had he come from?

"*She's* the Duchess?" No wonder the Duke had a dragon! I would too. Along with a cast iron chastity belt. And a couple of armed eunuchs.

My squire nodded and then lapsed into his usual quiet nature. I wasn't a big believer in love at first sight. And the idea of courtly love always made me snicker. But something about seeing this woman seemed to change all that.

"Am I to kill the Duke too?" I mused. Jude shook his head. Oh, right. I had my assignment. Bombays didn't do anything other than that. If you did, Uncle Essex had a lovely and very pointy iron maiden he kept in the basement.

"Fine." I made my way through the throngs of somber folk, until I came to the door of the castle. It was time to get this over with. I didn't mess with married women—it was a Bombay rule.

Jude sighed heavily and rapped at the door. A very old man answered. He looked...pinched somehow. Jude announced me as the Duke of Sicily (a ruse the family used a lot because who here was ever going to go to Sicily?) and demanded an invitation to dinner later that evening.

If I wasn't going to get the girl, then I might as well just do the job tonight and head back immediately after. No point in lingering. That's another Bombay saying.

That evening, as Jude dressed me, I asked him, "How did you know that was the Duchess?"

"The maid buying bread told me." Jude said this without any emotion or affectation.

"You were gathering information?" This surprised me. But then again, Jude was a Bombay and in training to take over after my generation was either on the Council or dead.

"The Duchess never comes to the market, so the maid was surprised to see her," Jude continued. "And no one's seen the Duke in years. He stays up in the castle all the time."

I graciously ignored the fact that my squire had garnered more information than I and from only one source. Women were known to gossip after all.

We rode our horses to the castle, dismounting as we came to the door. The very old man had been replaced with a very old woman, who looked even more pinched than he had. The woman seemed very surprised to see us and a bit hesitant to let us in. After Jude told her my credentials in a very bored tone, she relented, sending him to the stables before leading me inside.

I was wearing my best armor and clothing. My sword glittered at my side. I'd spent more time cleaning up than was usual and made sure my hair was combed. I tried to tell myself it wasn't because of the lovely Duchess, but because I'm a professional. Still, my heart skipped a beat when the hostess joined me.

"Oh," she said when she saw me. Her perfectly formed lips turned into a frown. "It's you. Again."

"Your Grace." I bowed deeply and kissed her hand. "What a delightful pleasure to see you again! And thank you for inviting me for dinner, I..."

She dropped my hand as if it were on fire. I discreetly looked to see if maybe it was. Women usually liked me.

"I must apologize for this mistake. My servants had no business inviting you to dinner. My husband..." She faltered for a moment, glancing toward the huge, stone staircase. "My husband is not well, I'm afraid." Then she turned and walked away.

I stood there with my mouth hanging open. She walked away from me. Just like that. And how rude to withdraw the invitation she *didn't* make to dinner! What just happened here?

"Sorry about Mummy," a small voice said behind me. I turned to see a rather cute little girl standing behind me. She had long, dark hair like her mother and was missing her two front teeth. She gave me a crooked smile. It gave me an idea.

I knelt beside her. "It's all right, my little lady," I said gently. The child reached out her hand and I kissed the back of it. Unfortunately, she giggled and ran off. What was with the women of this household?

The ride back to the inn had me quieter than Jude. I was so close to the Duchess, and she brushed me off completely. Something seemed wrong. Why not just have the servants explain? It was a tremendous breach of etiquette but still could've been handled by her staff. And where was the Duke? She said he'd been sick. And no one had seen him in a while. Perhaps he had the pox? I shuddered. Even Bombays couldn't fight the pox.

It was time to get this job over with and move on. A castle with disease was just as dangerous as a castle with a dragon, magic or not. I'd have to make my way in covertly— which meant I'd have to go later that night.

Jude helped me remove the armor and change into all-black clothing. I preferred stealth in this sort of situation. I no longer cared about the Duchess or who would want to kill the Duke's dragon and not the Duke. This was none of my concern. I needed to take care of this and go home.

Sheathing my sword on my back, I climbed to the roof and made my way across town by hopping from roof to roof. At the edge of town, I climbed down and kept to the shadows as I made my way around the perimeter of the castle. There was always another way in, used primarily by servants. I might be able to slide inside unnoticed.

My answer came moments later as the cook opened a door and left with a huge bowl. I slipped inside and worked my way slowly through the maze of corridors. There were very few servants about. That was odd. A manor like this should have been packed with staff. Perhaps the illness had taken most of them. On the other hand, this was the Duke's domain. Why weren't the halls filled with servants? Of course, then I realized that it was to my benefit that the castle was largely unattended, and I stopped thinking about it.

The castle was built in the round. I wound around the outer perimeter before I found the entrance to the sub levels. The dungeons. I'd have to start there. That's where I'd keep a dragon.

A dragon. I was supposed to kill a bloody, magic dragon. Unbelievable. Had the Council lost its collective mind? I was the first Bombay with an assignment like this. Why me? I stopped in my tracks. This line of thinking was useless. Just kill the damned dragon and get the hell out of Northumbria. For a moment I grinned. I'd have to have Mother embroider that on a pillow for me.

It was quiet and dark. Water seeped in, dripping noisily and making the walls cold and drafty. A damp and drafty castle…how original. I pulled a torch from the wall and waved it before me as I made my way down a flight of stone steps. My body moved into a mode of operation I was used to when stalking my prey. All of my senses were heightened to a sharpness that would allow me to carry out my mission. It didn't matter anymore if it was a magic dragon, a giant goat or a three-headed cow with a hernia. A job was a job.

At long last, I came upon a huge chamber with two hallways—the one I came in through and another directly opposite. There was light in that hall. Clearly someone was down here and had lit torches to find their way. The chamber had a dirt floor and stone walls. There were two large wooden chairs in the middle of the room, with a small table between them.

A sound came from the hall and I ducked behind one of the chairs. Shadows played on the wall at the end of the hallway. It didn't look human. By God! They really did have a dragon!

The shadow filled the corridor, long like a snake. It had legs in front, with long claws. A ridge of pointed spines ran down its back and as its great mouth opened, a long tongue snaked out. The beast was huge! It moved via its shadow as it grew closer. It didn't look like the dragons I'd seen in books, sitting back on oversized haunches. Instead it had four legs and a long body in between. The tail alone had to be twenty feet long, I estimated as I stared at the shadow.

I drew my sword and stepped in front of the chairs. This was it. The beast was making its way toward me. My senses heightened as I slid easily into kill mode. My plan was to stab it through one of its eyes, driving the blade deep into the brain. I should be able to slay the beast and be back to the inn within the hour. Jude was there, with the horses, waiting.

"What are you doing here?" The little girl from earlier came from behind me and stood at my side. She smiled at me crookedly.

"Get back!" I shouted as I tried to push her away. Didn't she see the shadows? Didn't she know what was coming? The creature was so large it would swallow her in one gulp.

The child looked at my sword, then toward the hallway, and before I could stop her, she ran toward the animal!

"NO!" I called out, "This way! Back to me!"

But she ignored me and disappeared around the corner. I chased her immediately. I was supposed to kill the dragon, not watch it eat a child.

I rounded the corridor and stopped, dead in my tracks. The little girl was holding some sort of lizard in her arms. It was maybe two feet in length and it licked her arm as she giggled.

"You scared Eadgar!" she scolded. "Poor baby!" She stroked the lizard's head gently. Eadgar made a small groaning sound.

"Eadgar?" I asked. Clearly the dragon had young! It must be the kind that mated with itself, like Jude said! And if the little girl was holding the baby, an angry mama could be right behind. "Stand back, behind me!" I shoved the girl and stood in front of her with my sword, ready to strike. We stood there like that for several minutes. Nothing came. Huh.

"But where's the dragon?" I said, mostly to myself.

The girl laughed loudly. "This is him! He's the dragon!"

I continued to hold onto my sword, wondering for a moment whether Eadgar's giant mother would suddenly appear and eat us both. Nothing happened.

"What are you doing here?" The Duchess appeared on my right, and she looked really angry.

"I…" I tried to explain, but found that the words wouldn't come. *I was just here to kill your little lizard, but seeing he's not a dragon nor magical, I'll be on my way*, just didn't sound right. To be honest, this was a bit embarrassing.

"What exactly is going on here?" I asked instead.

The Duchess looked for a moment like she was going to kill me. Then she did something unexpected. She buried her face in her hands. After a moment, she looked back up at me.

"My name is Godgifu and this is my daughter Ebba. I'm the lady of this castle. Come with me, and I can explain."

I followed her back to the room with the two chairs. And then I sat when she pointed to one chair. She looked like she didn't want to tell me, and that she did want to tell me, all at the same time.

"Who sent you?" Godgifu asked. "Was it Alfred of Wessex? One of the other dukes?"

I shook my head. There was no way I could tell her, even if I knew.

The woman nodded, then took a deep breath. She'd decided to tell me something.

"My husband is dead. He has been dead for three years," she said. "My daughter and I live here alone with a few, trusted servants." She motioned to the lizard. "And the dragon."

I couldn't believe my ears. "Your husband is dead? Why the subterfuge? You could be married again and living in a house full of servants, not buried in this castle." It didn't make sense.

She shook her head. "I have no desire to be wed to whomever the king deems acceptable. I don't want to be…anybody."

"What does that mean, exactly?" I wasn't sure. All a woman had was her means and her title. Why didn't she care about that? Her life was comfortable and would be even better once she got out of this tomb.

"I hate running a household. I despise ordering servants around, and I loathe politics." Godgifu said it in one long breath. "My husband was a good man, but he died. I know I won't get another chance at that again. My next husband is likely to be fat, abusive and who knows what. This might seem like a prison, but Ebba and I have real freedom here."

"But it's damp and miserable," I said. "And you can't really go out." What was the point of being a prisoner here? What kind of life was that?

Godgifu nodded. She was beautiful in her sadness. "I know. But I do not want to be sold like cattle to further a king's gains." She reached out to her daughter, who scampered into her arms, while still holding Eadgar.

"It's okay, Mummy," Ebba said. "The strange man here will keep our secret." She turned her big eyes and crooked smile onto me. "Won't you?"

My head was spinning. Someone hired the Bombay Council to kill this dragon. As if he knew I was thinking of him, Eadgar flicked his tongue in my direction. Most likely, it was someone who wanted the Duke's lands and possessions—

including his lovely wife. Once word got out that the dragon was dead, it wouldn't take much for people to discover that the Duke had been dead for years. Godgifu and Ebba would go to the highest bidder.

It was a miracle no one had found out before now, really. Servants gossiped. Maybe these servants were extraordinary, but eventually they'd let it slip.

It was the king's right to distribute and redistribute titled lands at will. There was no way that even a Bombay could prevent that. As I looked at this mother and child, I realized that there had to be a way to help them.

And that's when I got it. That's when I came up with my plan.

* * *

That night, a horrible fire broke out in the castle, burning it to the ground. The people of the town found nothing in what remained but charred stones. I gave the servants a ridiculous amount of money to "relocate" to another region, leaving one servant left behind to tell the town that the dragon had ignited the castle, burning the Duke, Duchess and their little daughter to death.

We did not stay for the funeral. Jude, Godgifu, Ebba and I slipped away on horseback while the castle blazed. We returned home and, after showing Eadgar the Dragon to Mother, explained how the assignment had been a success. Mother was very taken with the lizard and even let him roam freely throughout the castle. Every now and then, you'd hear his feet slapping on the stones as he slowly meandered around.

Godgifu and Ebba were made comfortable as our guests. Mother was concerned about what to do with them. It was possible that someday a visitor from Northumbria might recognize our guests.

We spent weeks trying to decide what to do before an answer emerged. I would take the mother and daughter to another country—maybe Italy or Greece—and get them settled there. It would be far enough away, and I thought these two needed some Mediterranean sun after all those years shut up in a damp castle in the north.

I might've stayed on a bit longer than I was supposed to. We found a lovely villa on a Greek island, and soon our skin turned golden brown. Godgifu and I soon realized we had feelings for each other. Ebba told us—she's a very astute little girl. Being a bachelor in soggy old England wasn't nearly that interesting to me anymore. Being part of a family was.

After a few weeks, I wrote to mother, letting her know that Godgifu and I were married. Months later, I received her reply.

> *My Dearest Bavaria,*
> *Congratulations on your nuptials. The Council knows where to find you, so don't worry about setting down roots in our original home country. There have actually been some interesting developments in your part of the world, so I imagine we will have work for you soon. Please write often and make sure you come to visit with my little granddaughter, Ebba, (and any more grandchildren I'm sure you'll have…soon) now and again. Oh, and I'm keeping Eadgar. He's become very fond of my afternoon minstrels. So if you miss him, you'll just have to find yourself another dragon.*
> *Love,*
> *Mother*

Godgifu laughed as I folded up the letter and threw her arms around me.

"I don't think we'll be in the market for another dragon anytime soon," I told her. Then I kissed her.

"We'll just get Ebba a pet snake and call it a sea serpent."

I could definitely live with that.

Cairo Bombay—Elizabeth of Bathory
August 1614, Cachtice Castle, Kingdom of Hungary

I was in the courtyard, playing with my Dodo birds, when the assignment to kill Elizabeth of Bathory arrived.

"Baggie!" I cried out to my brother as he was escorted to me by my manservant, Julian. I flung my arms around Baghdad Bombay and crushed him in an embrace.

"Good to see you, old boy!" Baggie clapped me on the back and handed me a rolled tube sealed with wax. "From the Council. Mum sends her love, of course!"

I knew immediately that it was an assignment. One I was eager to see as it had been too quiet around here lately.

"Um, say, chap," Baggie said, his eyes focused on the two, squat but large birds in front of us, "what's all this, then?"

I pointed to the two birds that were standing next to each other, eyeing my brother sideways with great suspicion. "This is Tristan and Isolde, my pet Dodo birds."

Tristan grew bored with the introduction and waddled over to Julian with the hopes of securing some more fruit. Isolde flapped her tiny, useless wings indignantly and clacked her enormous bill at us.

"Couldn't you just get a dog like anyone else?" my brother asked, never taking his eyes off the weird animals before him.

"Absolutely not!" I exclaimed. "These are much more interesting than a dog. I got these two on the island of Mauritius just last month. I'm trying to breed more of them. Apparently the Dutch sailors are eating them into extinction. We can't have that." I reached down and patted Isolde on the head, and she squawked at me loudly before waddling over to see if Tristan was receiving more than his fair share of figs from Julian.

"Come inside! It's been ages...absolutely ages!" I steered my brother into the doorway to my sitting room, then removed my sandals at the door. It was hot in Cairo most days, but the brightly colored tiles on the floors and walls cooled the room considerably. I'd had them painted by a local family of artisans. It had taken ages, but as I always say, you can't put a price on creature comforts.

Julian brought us hibiscus tea and couscous as Baggie and I caught up. It was lovely to see my brother again.

"What on Earth were you doing on Mauritius?" Baggie asked.

"I was actually on Madagascar first, collecting Tagena tree nuts. Fascinating poison really! They call it the Ordeal Bean of Madagascar, of all things."

Baggie snorted. "And I thought England cornered the market on all trials by ordeal."

"It's the usual thing, I imagine," I continued. "You see, the kernels of the nut are extremely toxic—disrupting the heart and breathing and causing instant, painful death. Years ago, if you were accused of a crime, you could choose to be speared to death or go through the trial by ordeal." I could feel myself getting more excited as I explained. Rare poisons were my passion—the more exotic the better.

"They would feed you some chicken skin first, and then you would swallow the poisonous kernels. If you vomited them back up, you were innocent. If not, you were guilty, but it didn't matter because you died anyway. Sort of a combined sheriff, magistrate and executioner in one easy step."

My brother laughed, and I realized how much I'd missed my family. Which was strange because I had moved all the way to Egypt to get away from them. My name is Cairo Bombay, and I live in Cairo. Not completely by accident. As a young child, I'd been captivated by photos of my namesake; the vivid colors, the foreign plants, the vibrant zest for life so much the polar opposite to the dull, damp gray of England.

Speaking of which, the heat of the day was becoming oppressive. I had Julian escort Baggie to his room so he could change into the far more comfortable Egyptian cotton clothes I had adopted here. While I knew that Baggie's velvet jacket, silk tunic and large hat were the height of fashion back home, they were ridiculous in a climate like this. While he was doing that, I took the rolled up tube into my office and broke the seal.

Unrolling the parchment, I found the traditional Bombay crest atop the page, a snake and a vial of poison upon two crossed swords with the motto, *Kill With No Mercy, Love With Suspicion*. Sigh. I really missed my family. Good thing Baggie was here.

Countess Elizabeth Bathory was my target. A copy of the most recent painting of her from 1585 was included. Even though this was 1614, her outfit was a bit dated for even 1585. I mean, who wore a cap with a squared, Elizabethan collar anymore? Dreadful!

Her crimes were more ghastly than her clothing. According to court records from several witnesses over a number of years, the woman had killed at least eighty young, Hungarian peasant girls. She lured them to her castle with the promise of gainful employment before imprisoning, torturing and killing these girls. There were those who insisted the number was more like six hundred girls, but I found it difficult to believe that rural Hungarian officials wouldn't notice that many of their population disappearing.

Currently, and for the past four years, the bloody Countess had been a prisoner in her family's castle. According to the Bombay's information—which was rarely if ever wrong— Elizabeth was walled up in a room with no windows and only one door. This door had a slit only large enough to check on the prisoner and to pass food through. She was fifty-four years old which was positively *ancient*.

I leaned back in my chair and sipped my tea. If I had to guess, I'd say that the peasants and the Bathorys' enemies decided she hadn't seen true justice and ordered the job. No matter. Bombays weren't privy to the background of any assignment. We were merely to carry it out.

The real problem would be the language. I did not speak or understand Hungarian. I would need a translator. I called for Julian.

"Sir?" Julian arrived promptly, like a good English manservant. Tall, pale with sharp cheekbones, dark wavy hair and piercing blue eyes, Julian was the perfect Englishman. He'd been with me since we were boys and was the only person in the world besides Baggie whom I trusted. Bombays are not known for trusting anyone—even family.

"Julian, I will be traveling briefly to the Kingdom of Hungary, specifically the area around Cachtice Castle. Could you be a good chap and find me a guide?"

"Of course, sir." He turned and left. If he recognized the name of Cachtice Castle for housing one of the most notorious women in history, he didn't indicate it. Julian was the very definition of discretion.

Baggie joined me, dressed comfortably in a long, cotton shirt, breezy linen trousers and sandals. He looked much more content.

Tristan and Isolde chose this moment to also join us. Tristan probed the corners of the room with his bill in a rather unfortunate attempt to find hidden fruit. Isolde marched straight up to me and squawked, demanding a fig. Clever girl.

I fed the Dodos and asked my brother for the latest news from home.

"Do you remember old Rolfie?" Baggie's eyebrows went up.

I nodded. Of course I did. We were mates together as kids and responsible for several unfortunate pranks that we were frequently caught and punished for. For your own information, it is never a good idea to fill a constable's wig with lice, even if he is a priggish prude.

"What's he up to these days? I thought I'd heard he'd gone to the Americas." I'd always wanted to travel there. I'd heard stories of lush, tropical islands and warm sands. I wasn't like the other members of the Bombay Family who preferred living in Europe. I liked the sandy, dust-swept mystery of Egypt and had lived here for many years. My isolation made it more difficult for the Bombays to get their assignments to me, but I really didn't care.

Western Europe and especially England were just so, so…common. Boring. I don't know what persuaded my relatives to call it home for so long. It was cold and damp, and the food was awful. Egypt on the other hand, was full of warmth, sunshine and fresh fruits. There were adventures and interesting discoveries around every corner, and never had I experienced a dull moment. And the people! Rare, exotic flowers with an enchanting culture! Why would *anyone* live anywhere else?

Of course, it helped that I was wealthy—as all Bombays are. And it helped that I was a man. Women would have difficulty here, although I did have a female cousin in India, and she was fascinating. But the other Bombays were dull beyond comparison.

I'd heard fantastic stories of tropical islands in the Americas. Sounded wonderful. Maybe someday I'd buy one and settle there. We could make it our home base instead of damp, chilly London, and I would name it Santa Muerta de los Bombays. (I had recently been studying the romance language from a Spanish explorer who'd found his way to Cairo.) Wishful thinking I guess. Maybe someday…

Baggie interrupted my thoughts with his reply, bringing me back to the news of my old friend. "Seems Rolfie's married some Indian princess named Pocahontas."

I slapped the desk and laughed. "Well, I never saw that coming! Good for Rolfie! I always thought he was a bit of a stick in the mud, but bravo!"

"And little Stratford has turned five years old. He's beginning his training," Baggie continued. Stratford-Upon-Avon Bombay was my godson. An interesting little boy but entirely too serious. Baggie produced a small portrait of him, and I felt a twinge of guilt. The lad looked like a tiny Greek god with blonde curls and blue eyes. Living in Egypt had made being a proper godfather difficult. I reminded myself to write his mother.

After lunch, Baggie decided to have a lie-down, and I retreated to my office for more thought on the assignment. My study was built on the back of the house, which kept it out of the sun and made it nice and cool in the boiling heat of the Egyptian afternoon.

I wrote a letter to Stratford—well, to his mother anyway—and added a dashing silver cutlass to the package as a gift. Baggie could take it back with him to the boy. Maybe I should have him come out here in a few years for some training? I made a note in my calendar to remember this.

My desk had a secret drawer from where I withdrew my assignment file to study it again in solitude. The language issue was being competently dealt with by the ever-resourceful Julian. I rose from my chair and walked to the armoire in the corner, unlocking it with the tiny gold key I wore on a chain around my neck.

As the doors swung open, vials and jars clinked together on the shelves. I had to find just the right poison. If our intelligence was good (and it always was) that Elizabeth of Bathory was walled up in a room inside the castle where there were no windows and only one door fitted with slits to allow for ventilation and the passing of breakfast, lunch, dinner and I can only *assume*, tea, I would, in fact, have no direct access to her. Strangling her or any other physical methods of death would be impossible. I felt a bit conflicted that her demise would be so swift, considering the torture she had applied to her victims. While I wasn't terribly keen on torture myself, I quite believed in making the punishment match the crime. Pity that wouldn't work in this case.

So it would have to be poison, the easiest means of applying which would be to put it into her food. However, the family and staff would notice a tall, pale Englishman who wasn't supposed to be there, so planting the poison in her food could be a problem.

Luckily, I had another idea. Living on and having traveled throughout the African continent, I'd seen a thing or two. African Bushmen sometimes used a special dart when hunting. The idea was fairly simple. I would employ a poisoned blow dart through the slats of the door. I would just need to lure her near enough to guarantee accuracy.

But what poison? It would have to be very lethal and act quickly enough to kill her, so that I could slip in and out between the delivery of her meals. And because it had to look like a clean death from natural causes, so as not to arouse suspicion, I couldn't use anything that induced vomiting or the release of the bowels.

I tapped the glass jars. The poison would have to be something that would travel well. It couldn't lose its potency over the time it would take me to get there. This was a puzzle.

There was a polite knock at the door. I quickly closed up the cabinet and bade them enter.

Julian opened the door slowly, in case I needed to hide whatever I was doing. Such a thoughtful servant. He entered the room, followed by a young boy I had never seen before. In fact, he bore quite a resemblance to my godson, which immediately tugged at my familial longings again.

"This is Stephen," Julian explained. "The boy is an orphan from Hungary. He's been in the service of Lord Allen's household for six months." He looked at the boy, who in turn nodded to me. "He also speaks French and English."

The child had a head full of gold curls. His blue eyes held mine almost defiantly. How very interesting.

"How old are you, Stephen?" I asked in English.

"I'm twelve years old, sir," the boy answered with a darling tenor voice. Twelve? He was so small! Stephen looked like he was more seven or eight than twelve. He looked more like a small cherub than a young man.

"Lord Allen is abroad for the next several months, and most of his household has gone with him," Julian spoke up. "He is ours on loan, should you choose to take the boy on."

Stephen did not look too sure of this. He sized us up beneath his thick lashes. Clearly he wasn't sure what to make of two Englishmen dressed as Egyptians.

"I'm going to Hungary for a brief visit, and I need a guide and interpreter," I said to the boy. "I will pay you a great deal more than you are making with his Lordship. Are you interested?"

Stephen tried to control his eyes, but the light shining in them at the mention of Hungary was difficult to disguise. The boy clearly wanted to go back home. But he was smart enough to hold out for more information. I liked him immediately.

"You will need to dress differently…" Stephen said. "But yes, I'd be interested."

At that moment, Tristan and Isolde waddled into the room, most likely to pirate some figs. They spotted Stephen, and to my surprise, leaped into his arms and began nuzzling the boy with their bills. Stephen giggled and squealed as Isolde scolded him, then ran her bill through his hair, looking for parasites. From that moment on, the pair of birds followed the boy everywhere, even sleeping with him at night. It was quite charming, really.

I instructed Julian to make the arrangements and to set Stephen up in the guest bedroom. If Julian was surprised that I wasn't putting the boy in the servant's quarters, he did not show it. Of course, Julian occupied the second-largest bedroom in the house, so he'd have no reason to complain.

I was quite pleased that I now had my translator and guide. I just needed a plan—something that would get us into the castle, the correct method for the assassination, and means to escape. And I needed to do it all without Stephen finding out what we were actually doing in Hungary.

Baggie took his leave the very next day. I begged him to stay on, but he said he had an assignment waiting on him back home. Something in France. I did not question him further as it was strictly forbidden to know what other Bombays were working on. I had enough to think of on my own. I embraced my brother and sent him on his way with the package for little Stratford. I promised to visit when Rolfie came home with his new, Indian bride. I was sorry to see my brother go.

While Julian made the necessary arrangements for our journey—travel, packing and so on—I picked Stephen's brain for information on the culture and landscape we would soon be breaching. The boy was very forthcoming with information, and I sensed that he was desperate to go back home.

"How did you come to be orphaned, Stephen?" I asked during one of our discussions a few days later. I was becoming quite fond of the child, and he seemed eager to please.

"My parents were killed in an Ottoman attack when I was seven, sir. I lived here and there until Lord Allen found me and brought me back here with him." Isolde sat in his lap and he petted her. Tristan was nibbling gently on the boy's toes. Maybe he thought they were figs.

"Do you like working for Lord Allen?" I asked. The aristocrat had the reputation of being a hothead. Two wives had died under his care, and two more had abandoned him. He had no children, and I wondered if this was why he'd taken on young Stephen.

The boy squinted warily at me, and I realized that he was worried I might tell Lord Allen what he'd said. Clever boy.

I shook my head. "I have no intention of saying a word to his Lordship. I barely know the man. And you do not have to answer that question."

Stephen was silent for a few moments. "He's all right, I imagine. He has a bit of a temper though." The boy looked at the door, and then back at me. "You really won't tell him I said that?"

"No. I really won't," I promised, wondering what the boy had been through.

Over the course of the next few days, Stephen reviewed maps with me. To my surprise, he was very familiar with Cachtice Castle, where Elizabeth was being held.

"My mother used to work there as a cook," he explained. "I played in the hallways as a boy."

I was about to remind him that he still was, in fact, a boy, but something in his eyes stopped me.

"I don't recall the Ottomans breaching Cachtice. How did your parents fall into their hands?"

Stephen frowned. "My mother got a job on the border with Turkey, cooking for the troops. My father was a soldier there, and she wanted to be near him." He didn't say another word, so I didn't press him.

"Are you familiar with the Bathorys?" I asked as nonchalantly as I could.

Stephen sniffed. "They seemed nice enough. Except for that woman. I knew one of the girls she killed. Her name was Marie, and she used to look after me when I was little." He looked so sad I wanted to stop him from saying another word. "The Countess told her she could be one of her ladies in waiting," Stephen continued, a note of sorrow in his voice. "I never saw her again."

I dismissed Stephen and sat at my desk for a long time, thinking of my method to get to the Countess. It was quite a happy coincidence that the boy knew the inside of the castle well, but the success of this mission still rested on one thing— the delivery of the poison. I had decided on a plant-based poison and narrowed it down to five possibilities: curare, lily of the valley, monkshood, Star of Bethlehem and Tanghinia, otherwise known as the Ordeal Bean of Madagascar.

Julian had managed to acquire for me a small blow dart tube and a couple of tiny darts. You really could find anything in Cairo these days. True, we were no longer on the Silk Road, but merchants came from all over three continents to trade here. The darts and gun would be impossible to trace.

I frowned. But that would mean I'd left something behind to trace. How ignorant of me! I'd found the method and means of delivery, and planned so that it would look as though the Countess died of natural causes, but I'd forgotten that I'd be leaving a dart behind!

This would not do. I needed to remove the dart before the body was found. But how? I couldn't very well walk through walls to go and get it—although that *would* be fabulous. I could wait for the guard to bring Elizabeth her dinner and overpower him—but then there was a witness. And leaving a dead body behind was evidence. Killing an innocent was against the Bombay Code and could bring unpleasant repercussions from the Council.

"Sir?" Julian appeared in the doorway with a platter of figs and wine. I nodded, and he placed the tray on my desk.

"What is for dinner?" I asked absently.

"Sea bass," Julian answered. "Will that be all, sir?"

An idea quickly formed in the recesses of my brain and I smiled. "No. Could you send someone to the market to pick up the strongest silk thread they can find?"

Julian nodded. "Of course, sir. Any particular length or color?"

I shook my head. "Color does not matter, but I would like several yards if possible."

"Very good, sir. I'll have it for you within the hour." And with that, Julian took his leave.

It was the sea bass that gave me the idea. Fishing! I just needed to tether the darts to my person. After deploying, I could then retrieve the dart via the silk thread and—voila! Nothing left behind! I'd use silk because it was the strongest and most durable material, and I was certain it would not break when retrieving it. Brilliant! Once again, Julian had helped me without knowing it. I really must see to his care if something were to happen to me. Not that I planned on that happening, but the Bombays were nothing if not prepared.

Stephen and I made ready to leave the very next morning. Reluctantly we donned traditional Hungarian clothing in hues of blue and saffron, complete with heavily ornate dolman jackets with slit sleeves. The heat was stifling, but once we crossed into Southern Europe the weather would relent somewhat. I wasn't fond of the costume. The Hungarians were a bit dated in their fashion sense. Still, what could I do?

Julian had the carriage ready to take us to the sea, where we would board a boat to cross over to the Ottoman Empire. Tristan and Isolde seemed to sense Stephen was leaving and clutched his feet, squawking their displeasure. I wondered if they thought they were his parents. Stephen seemed sad to part with the Dodos, and Julian gently extracted the fat little birds from his feet.

We didn't say much in the carriage or on the boat. I'd made it clear to Stephen that no one was to know where we were going, and he was very fastidious about keeping up his end of the bargain. Upon entering the Ottoman Empire, I spoke because I knew Turkish. As soon as we made our way into Hungary, Stephen did the talking, and I became mute.

The night before we reached Cachtice Castle, Stephen and I sheltered in a small cave only a short mile away. It was primitive, and I missed my modern conveniences. Sigh. The *things* I do for my job!

"I used to hide in here all the time," Stephen said quietly as we unpacked and set up our dinner for the night. "No one has seen us, so no one knows we are here."

His revelation startled me. The boy was taking to this secret life a bit too easily. And while I admired him for it, it made me uneasy. I worried Stephen might be just too clever for his own good on this mission. I tried to shake off the feelings of discomfort, but as we drew closer to our target, it slowly became clear to me just how much I needed the boy to help me carry out the plan. I didn't speak the language or know the layout of the castle like he did. Which had been fine when he was a simple hired translator. But I suddenly realized that through our discussions I had given far too may clues away as to the nature of my visit to Hungary. And Stephen was far too clever to dismiss them. However, according to the Bombay Code, you couldn't include outsiders in your assignment unless you planned to frame them for the assassination. Or kill them. If I involved Stephen I would have to dispose of him. No loose ends.

I thought about this disconcerting fact as we lay down to sleep that night. Listening to the boy's gentle snoring made me realize with a heavy heart that I would, in fact, have to dispose of him when this was over. He would simply know too much.

This was the main reason that I'd kept Julian in the dark all these years. No one outside the family was supposed to know we were assassins. It had worked quite well for thousands of years. Who was I to break the rules now?

Tears sprang to the corners of my eyes. I didn't want to hurt Stephen. And yet, that was exactly what I had to do. No one would know. No one would care. Lord Allen would certainly understand. Though I was sure Tristan and Isolde wouldn't.

This was truly terrible! I could no sooner kill this sweet boy than I could be happy toiling away in the dull gray of England. My stomach began to ache, and I was working my way up to a violent headache.

Pushing these thoughts from my mind, I focused on the job. My complete lack of knowledge of Hungarian and the castle made it crucial for me to employ Stephen. At this point, I had no choice. Doubt tried to slip through the cracks in my logic, but I shut it down. We were too close to back out on the job, and it wasn't like I could do that anyway. I would have to take this one step at a time. That was the only way I'd make it through this.

In the dark, early hours before dawn, I woke Stephen and explained that I had an assignment for him. I needed him to enter the castle, find Elizabeth of Bathory's prison, observe the movements of the guard throughout the day and report back to me here, in the cave. I made it perfectly clear he was not to be seen, and he was not to mention me or the cave in any way.

To my sorrow, the boy was eagerly excited about the mission. He reminded me of myself and Baggie at that age. This was a lark for him. It was murder for me.

The day passed with agonizing slowness. It was cool and damp in the cave, but no one came near me. I was tormented by grief at the thought that I had to kill young Stephen. He reminded me so of my godson Stratford. If only it were Stratford. Then he'd be a Bombay, and this would merely be a training exercise.

The minutes were achingly long. I ate from our rations for lunch, teatime and dinner in solitude. And for the first time, I felt the sharp pang of loneliness. I tried to head it off by preparing the poison and darts.

The Tagena tree nuts were easy to transport. Using a stone, I smashed the nuts carefully and pounded the kernels into a white mash. Adding a little water to keep the substance together, I scooped the substance into a glass jar and screwed on the lid tightly. The stone, on which I pulverized the nuts, I tossed deeper into the cave.

Carefully I withdrew the darts and tied a few yards of silk thread to the back of each one of them. Back in Cairo I had honed my blow dart skills, and I was certain I could hit the Countess with great accuracy even if she was moving. I packed up my weapons and waited.

I knew I couldn't kill Stephen until we were done. I needed him at least until I came to the border. Whatever I did would have to be quick and painless. The boy would have earned a quiet death. My heart burned at what I had to do.

Sometime after evening had fallen, Stephen returned to my cave and my stomach dropped at the sight of him. He carried a stick with him, and after I offered him some food, he began to draw upon the cave floor.

"The castle wall is circular," he said happily. He drew an inner corridor to a small staircase that went up about twenty steps. At the top, he drew a room. "This is where she's being held. There's only one door and no windows."

Stephen drew a door with one slot about one third of the way down from the top. The slot was the width of a fist, and I was certain I could both aim and hit my target through it.

"There is one guard, but he is only there to serve her food. He doesn't stay between meals. I guess they figure since she's completely bricked in with an iron door that she isn't going anywhere," Stephen said.

"How do we get into the castle unseen?" I asked the boy.

Stephen grinned mischievously. "I know a secret way. There's an old, unused privy tower here." He pointed to a spot on the wall. "It's a short but easy climb to get up and through."

He must have caught the look on my face and he laughed. "Don't worry. I cleaned it while I was there. Not that there was much to clean. It hasn't been used in years."

My heart broke that very instant. He'd cleaned the old privy entrance for me. How was I going to kill him?

"And there's a room here." Stephen pointed to a small indentation inside the wall. "I think it used to be for storage or something, but the wall crumbled a bit, and they don't use it anymore. We can hide there."

"Brilliant," I said without enthusiasm. "When is the best time to go see the Countess?"

Stephen sat back and frowned at this. "You're not going to break her out, are you?" For the first time he realized there must be a reason for this trip.

"No," I said softly. "I have no intention of setting that monster free."

Stephen seemed to accept this as a cue for him to not ask any more questions. Instead, he shrugged and continued on. "I think the best time to go would be soon, since it will be a long time before the guard comes with breakfast. The light is low, but I think we can manage. They keep a torch burning overnight just outside her door."

I nodded and organized my things. We would be taking a small pack with us and leaving the rest behind in the cave, hidden by rocks. Stephen wasn't to speak unless we were confronted. At that point, he was to say that we were mere travelers, looking for a safe place to stop for the night. I didn't think we'd be caught since it was the middle of the night, but you can never be too certain of these things.

Stephen led me to the castle wall. The darkness provided cover as we climbed the wall up to the privy hole and lifted ourselves through. I did everything the boy signaled, and we made our way to the stone stairs where the Countess' prison was above.

The boy motioned for me to stay at the bottom of the staircase while he went up to make sure there was no guard. He re-emerged a moment later with a grin on his face.

"Stephen," I whispered, holding the boy's shoulders. "I need you to stay here. Do you understand?"

He frowned. "But I want to go with you. You're going to kill her, aren't you?"

Icy fear washed over me. He knew. The boy knew. He'd just sealed his fate and didn't even know it.

"You need to stay here and keep a sharp eye out. If someone comes, you have to run up and let me know."

Stephen nodded, and I patted him on the shoulder. He beamed with pride. *Good lad*, I thought sadly.

I slowly made my way up the stairs, careful not to make a sound. At the top of the stairs, a single torch illuminated the dead end. The iron door was on my left. Quickly I assembled my dart gun. After opening the jar of the poison paste, I generously ground the tip of the first dart into it. Carefully, I inserted the dart into the opposite end of the tube, backwards. The silk thread doubled up inside, dropping back out the front of the tube. The other end was tied to my belt.

"Elizabeth…" I called softly into the slot. "Elizabeth…" I repeated and was rewarded by the sound of rustling silk skirts.

"Who is there?" a bitter female voice demanded. Clearly she was not afraid. That was good.

"I've come to help you," I lied. "But you need to come to the door."

Dark eyes flashed in the slot, eyebrows arched into an evil grin. "I knew it! I knew someone would come to fetch me!"

Arrogance seeped out of every pore. I'd have no problem dispatching her.

"Stand up and be ready to run out this door when I get it opened," I said.

Elizabeth nodded and gave a sinister chuckle. She stood, and I found myself face to face with her neck. She was standing and waiting. The slot was the perfect height.

"Just a moment," I said as I prepared the dart. "This will be a bit tricky…"

"Oh hurry up, damn you!" the monster howled.

I pressed my lips to the end of the tube and blew hard, launching the dart straight into her jugular vein. The point went deep, and I had no doubt the poison would work quickly.

Elizabeth choked and clutched at the dart before falling to the floor and clawing at her throat. A quick jerk of the thread and the dart was out. I pulled it through the slot and watched.

My victim writhed on the floor in painful spasms. It only took minutes, but as the paralysis kicked in, her breathing labored, and then her heart came to a complete stop.

I made it back down the stairs in a couple of leaps and grabbed Stephen. The boy nodded, and we raced back through the way we came, ending with a thud on the ground as we dropped through the old privy.

My heartbeat slowed as we made our way to the cave and collected our things. We were at the border of Turkey by morning, and we paused to eat and drink. Stephen grinned broadly at me. My heart sank. Every step closer to that border was one step closer to the boy's impending death. I was completely miserable, but I had no choice. Anger flared inside me as I imagined Stephen's face at the moment of his death… at my hands. I didn't think it was possible to feel such torment and agony. He was only an innocent boy! He'd lost his parents and had a cruel master waiting for him.

"We make a good team!" Stephen grinned as he took a bite of an orange. "What you did back there, whatever it was, I'm sure it was amazing!"

He looked at me with pride and admiration. And I slipped into a deep, dark depression punctuated by an unending headache.

"We have to get going," I said gruffly as I packed things back up. I lifted him roughly to his feet, refusing to look him in the eye. Stephen's face was confused, and hurt. He was trying to imagine what he'd done or said to upset me. The figurative knife in my heart twisted cruelly. Was I really going to act like a bastard to this poor boy? Should his last thoughts be that I betrayed him? This was too painful. Why wasn't there something I could do?

"Wait." I held him back. If I was going to do this, I needed to do it now, before I lost all courage.

Stephen smiled hopefully. "You know, I wish you were my father." His words hit their mark, a bullseye on my soul. I shrank away from him in horror. And then, the most amazing idea came into my mind…

* * *

A few months later, when Lord Allen returned, I visited him. He was very unpleasant, but agreed to my terms and the extremely generous amount of money I gave to him. Within a week I was heading back to England.

"So," Stephen said from the back of his Arabian horse next to mine, "you're my father now?"

I nodded. "You are now Stephen Bombay. And as my adopted son, we are heading back to see my family in England to begin your training." I knew I'd have to change his first name to that of a geographic location, in keeping with tradition. I was thinking of calling him Mauritius, after the island where I got the Dodos. But that could wait. We had left that morning. Julian was staying behind to pack the belongings and sell the house. He would join us later in Oxford.

A large bag tied to the saddle next to Stephen's thigh began to squirm and squawk before two Dodo heads popped out. They cawed at me irritably before nuzzling the boy's leg. Tristan and Isolde were going too. There was no way they were going to be parted from Stephen after the fuss they made when we returned to Cairo. I was bitten several times, and they spent hours combing the lad's hair for possible parasites that undoubtedly attached themselves under my *clearly* neglectful care.

Oddly enough, Stephen, the two Dodos and I were a family now. I would miss Egypt, but having a son seemed to be more of an adventure than just settling down in any old exotic place. Besides, old Rolfie and his new bride, Pocahontas, would be home for a visit soon. Maybe it was time I started thinking about a visit to America. Yes…I thought that was just what we needed.

Stratford-Upon-Avon Bombay—John Billington 1630 Plymouth Colony, The American Colonies

It was dark, like it was every night in this godforsaken colony where no civilized man such as myself should have to set foot. John Billington stumbled around the woods, drunk on beer (sadly, the only spirit we had here) and cursing at the branches. He cursed at people too, in fact, not any differently than he did inanimate objects. I once watched him spend half an hour cursing at a stone. It was quite a creative use of words. Not sure how you can call a rock a "bastard from the bowels of hell," but he did, and he did it with flair.

It was my job to follow him. It was my job to kill him. And I still didn't have any idea how I was going to do that. No matter—a contract was unbreakable. And I would be stuck here, on the other end of the world, until I accomplished it.

Oh, don't get me wrong. I didn't mind traveling for the day job. At the age of twenty-two, I still had all my teeth. That was something. And I'd yet to need a blood-let by leech. So I suppose the travel kept me young. It was just…well, this was way farther than any Bombay had traveled before. My Aunt Persia even offered me some amulet to protect against sea monsters. It looked like a regular stick. Aunt Persia wasn't always right in the head. I took it anyway. Who knows? Maybe it was a magic stick.

I wasn't one of the original pilgrims, or "strangers," who came over on the Mayflower ten years ago. I came a couple of months ago as a laborer on an entirely different ship, bringing supplies to the colony and a secret assignment to carry out from my family back in England. London…what I wouldn't give for those filthy, cobblestone streets right now.

I'd settled into the colony—a single man and laborer. I made sure that I didn't stand out in any way. The rate at which these colonists died from various diseases meant men came and went constantly. The colony had grown in the last ten years. I was a nobody, and no one noticed me. My name was, for all intents and purposes, John Newcomen. I know the Governor thought himself pretty damned clever when he gave me that last name, 'Newcomen.' I didn't complain. It was better than Stratford-Upon-Avon Bombay. Way better. Mum was a bit of a loony about Shakespeare.

I'd spent the last few weeks studying my victim. He was a real asshole before he left England and had made a lot of enemies, incurring a great deal of debt. He'd gotten worse since he arrived here. I guess his first idiot son, Francis, almost blew up the ship. The second one, John Jr., wandered off like a moron and had to be returned by Indians. Indians who laughed at us.

John argued with everyone. He was punished over and over for instigating trouble. His wife was even whipped for her sharp tongue. People avoided them like the plague. Which brings up an interesting point. Typhus tore through the colony the first year, and the Billington Family was one of a very few households that didn't lose anyone to the deadly disease. Maybe assholes were immune, because no one wanted to spend enough time with them to spread the disease. That's my personal theory anyway, and it very possibly could be true. Of course the prevailing theory was that the Billingtons practiced witchcraft. I didn't really believe in witches, but what anyone here thought mattered little.

None of that was important to me. I had to make him pay for his sins in the motherland. John had made some serious mistakes back home, crossing all the wrong people. He owed money to most of them, and, in some cases, had stolen more than coins and more than just mistreated people. It didn't really matter. He pissed off the people who give Bombays assignments.

It wasn't my job to question the assignments. I just had to do them.

So, for the past week, I had followed John around, under the cover of darkness as he stumbled and railed through the woods. He was an angry man. And angry men often died badly—something that was always good for business.

I just wanted to be rid of this contract. I was tired of living here. I should be back in the civilized half of the world, chasing women, sleeping in, and drinking something other than boiled water and stale, warm beer. Not here with a bunch of holier-than-thous taking care of their "problem."

Oh sure, it's considered "glamorous" to be a colonist. Why in the bloody hell was that? The winters are harsh, disease is rampant, there are far too few women (and those who are here won't play footsie in the haystack), and the Indians hate us. I can't blame them. I hate us.

I only had about a week before the next ship sailed for home. And I still had no idea what to do. It's not like you can get a ship out of the colonies anytime. Passages were few and far between. And I didn't want to stay here one moment more than I had to.

There were times when I wished I was more like my godfather, Cairo Bombay. He was such an adventurer. But I hadn't seen him in years—not since he left with his son and Dodo birds to sail to Asia. He'd hoped to find another way to the New World. I hoped he'd at least made it. Maybe they'd already heard from him back home. This was yet another reason for me to finish up the job and go back to England.

"Curse you, John Newcomen!" I froze. Did Billington see me? Could he see in the dark? Maybe I should've brought Aunt Persia's stick.

No, he was just railing about like he always did. He'd been on my case lately over the idea that I'd crossed into his property line. This pissed me off, because he complained about it publicly. Sooner or later he'd file a complaint, and then my name would be on record here. I didn't want that.

Don't get me wrong—this Massachusetts Bay Colony was okay. I just didn't fit in with the work-yourself-to-death-every-day mentality. I kind of enjoyed a little leisure now and then. But the only day of rest was Sunday, and we weren't allowed to do anything but go to church all day, sitting on uncomfortable wooden benches, bored out of our minds, praying for something interesting. Like an ill-timed Indian attack.

And then there was the disease. People fell ill and died all the time. It was ridiculous. Because of my solitary nature and devotion to sanitation and hygiene, I was fine. But this was just silly. If your neighbor has the plague, *don't go visit to see*! But people always did, and they took the disease home with them, infecting everyone around them. I spent a lot of time on burial duty. A *lot* of time.

Of course, if you survived that, there were the Indians. Some were friendly. Most wanted to roast us on a spit and eat us. I was pretty sure I'd feel the same way if I was them. But they were basically screwed. Bows and arrows were nothing against guns. Still, they outnumbered us in ways that could make you lose sleep at night.

Being here was just plain crazy dangerous. I'd give it another ten years at best before everyone here packed it in and went back to England. This whole experiment was doomed to be nothing more than a failed footnote in English history.

I followed John Billington home along the path he always took. I'd have to be more careful. If he caught me following him, he'd really raise a racket—something, again, that I did not need.

As I lay on my straw bed later that night, I realized my risk was becoming greater the more my intended victim railed about me. The more he talked, the more likely I'd be the first suspect in his death. Maybe I could pay some Indians to kidnap him and take him away? Could I convince them that their gods demanded that John Billington should be sacrificed? Probably not. I wasn't the most creative person in the family—in fact, they teased me all the time about being entirely too serious.

The Indians, even the friendly ones, didn't really trust us. And I couldn't guarantee they would kill him. That man weaseled out of everything. He'd been behind several mutinous plots—all of which he denied, and once got out of punishment by begging forgiveness on his knees. The punishment would've had him tied up, ankles to neck. I was kind of rooting for that one out of professional curiosity. You never know when you'll pick up something you can use later.

I was running out of time. If John was calling my name out at night, he was close to saying it out loud in the daytime. And I couldn't have that.

I was up before the rooster crowed. The plan came to me in a dream (and, sadly, not the one about the buxom widow down the lane who always winked at us lads). I now knew what to do.

And so it was that John Billington found me tearing out a tree on the disputed property line. Okay, I was a little more on his property than mine. And it was a tree he liked (I found it amusing he liked a tree, but not people). But I needed to step things up.

"What are you doing, man?" Billington thundered at me.

I gave my most innocent look. "Why, what do you mean, neighbor? I'm just getting rid of this pesky tree."

Billington's face turned purple with rage, and he hopped from one foot to the other, shaking his fists at me. "That tree is on *my* property! I planted it myself when we arrived, ten years ago!"

I knew this. I also knew the tree was the only reminder he had of home. It may have seemed cruel, but 1) I was out of time and 2) I didn't really care.

I stood up and wiped my brow. It was warm for September yet.

"I don't think so." The tree was completely down, and the shattered trunk lay at my feet. "This is my tree, and it's on my land. I want it down, so I can put in a potting shed." Okay, it was a lame excuse, but it was all I had. Potting sheds are no joke in my family. Where else can you grow poisonous plants out of public view?

Billington stepped so close to me I could smell the stale beer on his breath. "I'm going to get you for that, you bastard!" He gathered up the wood in his arms and stormed off.

"Hey!" I called after him. "Where are you going with my wood?"

He did not stop.

With a sigh, I shouldered my axe and walked across the road to the governor's house.

"I cut down that wood with my own two hands," I protested to the governor of the colony. "It took me an hour, and then he took the wood!" I used my most innocent face as I sadly shook my head. "He reeked of beer, too, and threatened me." This wasn't much of an allegation. Everyone here drank beer. They thought it was safer than water. Schmucks.

Governor Bradford pushed back from his chair and let loose a long sigh. He nodded. "It's John Newcomen, isn't it?"

I nodded, pleased that he wasn't entirely sure who I was, and didn't even remember that he gave me that name. The goal was that when this was over, people might remember my name, but no one would be able to remember anything else about me.

The Governor shook his head. "John Billington has been a problem since we set sail."

"I am sorry, Your Lordship." I did not make direct eye contact, trying to make sure he remembered my story but not my face. "But I am frightened for my life."

The official nodded and waved me away. "I'll see what I can do." And that was it. I left the room and made my way back to my one-room house.

Part one of my plan was initiated. Now came the trickier part. I tried to consider all angles as I boiled water in a cauldron in my fireplace. These people didn't trust the water. I tried to explain about boiling out the impurities, but they looked at me like they might start screaming "witchcraft!" so I left it alone. I'm really not fond of being hanged, and slightly less so of being burned alive.

The Bombays have known how to make water safe for centuries. It's just science. We just came through the Age of Reason! Hellllooooooooooo! These people drove me crazy. If you tried to make your own soap or simply brush your teeth with a frayed twig, they'd start imagining that they saw you dancing naked in the woods with demons. No. England, even with its civil war, was much safer. I had to get back there.

I would have to be careful from here on out. In order to make this work, there could be no mistakes. Blowing out the candles, I slipped quietly out the door, bolting it behind me. Within moments, I was sitting behind a haystack outside of Billington's home. Clouds shrouded the moon, making the light spotty at best. I waited. Depending on how early John started drinking, that's when I could move again.

There was a slight breeze, lifting up the scents and sounds of the night. Livestock grunted here and there. A twig snapped in the distance every now and then. But no one came out of the Billington home.

Normally, this would be a good thing. The joke in the colony was no Billington was a good Billington. But I was getting worried. It was late and yet lights still burned through the oilskin windows. Sure, the haystack was comfortable, but I had a task undone. That drove me crazy.

The creak of wood caught my attention. Venturing a peek from behind the hay, I saw John Billington stagger out the door, cursing at someone inside the house. He was carrying his blunderbuss. Swaying violently back and forth, he lurched into the woods, leaning on his weapon for support. He was heading away from my home. Was he so drunk he thought he could hunt at this late hour?

I waited until he was out of sight before following him. It's pretty easy to follow a stumbling drunk through an empty forest at night. People battened down the hatches, worried about getting lost or running into Indians.

Billington muttered to himself as he lurched around trees. I didn't really think he was going anywhere in particular. During the day he was usually clearing his fields, starting fights with neighbors and yelling at his family. But it helped to know his movements.

The clouds began to lift and the moon cast shadows around the trees. This kept me back, farther from him, but by the time I followed him back to his home, I knew what I had to do to complete the next phase of my plan.

To be perfectly clear—I'm not all that into grave robbing. But I was less into killing an innocent person to suit my goals. A young man about the same size as me had perished earlier in the week. He had the same hair color and had died with no marks on his body. I was pretty sure he'd eaten the "wrong" berries, due to the small smudges of red around his fingernails. But I said nothing, because they are suspicious of such things. They pronounced him dead by act of God, and that was it. No one knew him. He was a single guy like me. It was sad but very helpful.

The grave was hidden—we did that so the Indians wouldn't know about our deaths. The Pilgrims had lost so many people since they arrived, they didn't want the Indians to say, "Hey wait just a minute! Look at all those gravestones! I count two hundred at least! Those bastards are fudging their numbers so we won't attack them! Get 'em!"

I didn't follow John Billington the next night. Instead, I dug up the poor, young man, carefully replacing the dirt to look like a reasonably fresh grave and covering the tracks I'd made. The man was not heavy, but the job was disgusting. Working with decaying bodies is not a lot of fun. But his hair was longer than mine and he needed to be wearing my clothes when found. Cutting the hair wasn't a problem. But have you ever undressed and dressed a dead man? I don't really recommend it. Sure, it has its useful applications, but his clothes stank, and his body was stiff as a board.

Rigor mortis. I'd forgotten about that. According to my plan, the body would be found fairly quickly after his "murder." This man's fingers, arms and feet were completely rigid. I'd have to soften him up. Another disgusting job.

Oh, I knew what to do. My family trains us for all kinds of weird stuff that you hope you'll never need to use, and yet somehow always do. Once, back when I was still pretty new to this whole assassin thing, I poisoned my target with arsenic. Unfortunately, I used a bit too much, causing the dead man's skin and lips to turn blue. He was supposed to die of natural causes, so this was a bit of a problem. I won't tell you what I did to make him look in the pink of health, but I will never, ever do something like that again. I still shudder when I think of it.

Basically, fixing rigor mortis boils down to joint and muscle manipulation. It is hard, repetitive work, and I don't recommend it. After a couple of hours of this, I was at last able to finish dressing the poor bastard. Even though it was dark, I could tell that he would pass for me. That almost made it worth it.

I managed to carry the body to the edge of my land, at the very border of John Billington's. It was very late. I waited.

It didn't take John long to stagger my way. He stumbled over roots and rocks, cursing as he went. Clearly, he was far more drunk than usual—which was very useful. Once he got close, I snuck up behind him and pinched a nerve in his neck. It's a secret move, so I can't tell you about it. The man went down like a sack of potatoes.

I took John's gun and aimed it at the dead man's head— close enough to blow his face clean off. I fired. That would be heard. I posed John with the gun and fled back to my cabin. I did not go inside; my belongings would have to stay behind. I rolled up the dead man's putrefying rags and stuffed them into a small pack I'd left hidden in the woods and turned south.

It being an unusually warm September, I was able to spend a few days living in a cave, a mile away from Plymouth. I had stocked the cave with food and clean water and was pretty sure I could live there a few days at least. At dusk, I would hide in the trees near town and listen to the gossiping sentries who guarded the gates. The leaves had not fallen, and they provided me with enough cover to hear that John Billington was going to be tried in the murder of John Newcomen.

Just to make sure, I hung around a little longer until I was certain it was over. Thanks to a couple of women out gathering mushrooms a few days later, I found out that on the thirtieth day of September, John Billington was hanged by his neck until dead. My job was over.

I'd booked passage back to England in Boston, under a new name, and made it there before the ship sailed. After several weeks of horrid autumn weather, the ship docked in England, and I found my way back home. The Council was pleased with my work, which was good, and I even managed a little holiday in Italy.

When I got home I was thrilled to find out that Cairo Bombay had arrived in the New World safely. He'd discovered some small island far south and west of where I'd been. According to his letter, his son Mauritius and he were planning to turn it into a private home for the Bombays. He'd named it Santa Muerta, and there were no other people there. Cairo's letter said the sunsets were *beyond* fabulous—whatever that means.

I should probably write to them. Maybe they needed help fixing the island up. No one would remember that I vowed never to set foot in the New World again…right?

Versailles Bombay—Rasputin December 1916, Petrograd, Russia

"Oh, bugger," I hissed through my clenched teeth as Rasputin staggered into the courtyard of Moika Palace. Please tell me they haven't decided to finish him off here, on the streets, with witnesses. *How did those idiots screw this up now?* Honestly, I should never have asked men to do this. Men were not that smart. Assassination was a woman's game.

Morons. I was working with amateurs. This whole thing could've been wrapped up yesterday, but noooooo. This is what happens when you leave a job up to a room full of drunk, arrogant men. Make that men in general. I was not terribly fond of men as a rule. There had never been a man in my life who had not let me down—and there were no women who had.

I wasn't really a man hater. Just not a man prefer-er. They were silly, puffed-up things who needed their egos stroked constantly. Women were far superior intellectually. There was the women's suffrage movement going mad in England. I was anxious to get home and apply myself. But first, I had to deal with Rasputin—who was, very inconveniently, still alive.

Bloody hell! Women were so much more cooperative. If you killed them, they remained thoughtfully dead.

I slid from my hiding place and raised my Browning pistol to fire. Dmitry emerged from the doorway and began shooting. He acted like a bloody cowboy, firing rapidly—too many shots that didn't hit their mark. I tried not to roll my eyes as I aimed my pistol and fired, hitting Rasputin in the back. This made him stop, and allowed me to drift back into the shadows as Dmitry then shot the bastard in the head.

Dummy Dmi, as I liked to call him, didn't even notice that I was there or had fired. What a git. I watched as the man kicked Rasputin in what was left of his head. *Really?* What good did that do?

Felix came out the door, and I grabbed his wrist. "You fool! Get the Mad Monk inside before the police arrive!" I vanished again and watched as Felix and Dmi dragged the bloody body of Rasputin inside. They forgot to shut the door. Wonderful.

Felix and his servant Buzhinsky came out onto the courtyard and whispered to each other about the possible methods of blood removal (due to the rather unfortunately large stain on the ground), when a policeman came into the courtyard asking about the shots he heard.

Tell him you heard it too, but don't know where it came from, I thought fervently in their direction. I mean, the policeman had already arrived and heard shots. Denying that there was such a sound was sure to look suspicious.

But Felix just shrugged. "I've no idea what you're talking about."

Buzhinsky nodded limply. Idiots.

The policeman identified himself as Vlassiyev and asked again for the source of the noise. He was not convinced.

Both men shrugged, saying nothing. Vlassiyev frowned but didn't move. Bugger.

I slipped around the bushes and approached from the street. Upon seeing the three, I walked over as if I was a stranger.

"An auto backfired," I lied in perfect Russian and pointed south. "Over there."

Felix's eyes bulged at the sight of me. I didn't want to have to give myself away. Only Felix knew about my existence. But the policeman was not leaving, and I still had a body to get rid of.

"Thank you," Vlassiyev laughed. "That makes sense." He left and I went the other way, in the direction I came from, and slid back through the door of the palace.

Felix (who was earning his Twit of the Year status) entered the hall and immediately attacked Rasputin's body with a two-pound cast iron dumbbell. What was he doing? Blood splattered his clothes. Was he nuts? I could do nothing but stare, doing my best not to faint as the sight of all that blood. As far as Dmi and the others were concerned, I was Olga, a mere servant in the household. Most of the others had been sent away for the evening except for me and Buzhinsky. And Buzhinsky just thought I was filling in. I don't think he even noticed that it was me who came up to them a few moments ago.

How did this go so wrong? It was an easy job! Everything should've gone smoothly!

Maybe I should start at the beginning. My name is Versailles Bombay, and I was in Petrograd for an assignment. It was supposed to be simple. Usually, when the Council who hands out the assignments says that, it *isn't* easy and usually requires months of planning and research. But they said this one would be, because everyone hated the victim. I wished they were here now so I could show them how "easy" it really wasn't.

I was chosen because I could speak Russian. My mother was Russian and brilliant. My father was a Bombay and a trained killer. It didn't matter that I was a woman, because in our family those things don't factor into any equation, which is good. And in my humble opinion, with no offense to my father, men weren't as good as women when it came to killing people. They were just too forthright. Stick a sword in him and leave him dead. Where's the finesse? Where's the craftsmanship?

I'd spent three months freezing my arse off in Petrograd (which was three months too many if you asked me), lining this whole thing up. I'd convinced a low-level prince that Rasputin was the devil and had to be disposed of. It wasn't hard. Rasputin was a dirty old man hiding under the robe of a cleric. He slept with every aristocratic woman he could, drank and ate too much and wandered around town with the royals like he was *bloody brilliant*. Russians hated and feared him. It was supposed to be a no-brainer.

All Bombays have a specialty—whether it's poison, ice picks, pistols, whatever. We all have our favorite methods. My specialty is getting others to do the work for me. I had sort of a gift of gab that allowed me to persuade anyone to do almost anything. I didn't usually handle the knife that was plunged into the heart, or even load the dueling pistols with bullets. Not my thing, really.

Okay, to tell you the truth—I'm squeamish. The sight of blood, or even a splinter, makes me faint. Can you imagine growing up, trained by a guild of assassins, and being afraid of blood? Yeah, they thought it was funny too—especially my stupid, male cousin Leeds. The bastard. So I developed another way—the way of persuasion.

In the past this might have been frowned upon by our family, but with the recent introduction of Scotland Yard's ability to pick out a person by reading the prints their fingers left behind on a murder weapon, the Council had shifted their thoughts on just how hands-on a Bombay had to be in their work.

It takes a certain kind of skill to talk others into doing your dirty work for you. The Council thought I was useful, although jealous cousins now and then liked to bring up that I didn't actually kill anyone directly. It didn't matter—the Council liked what I accomplished. That was all that mattered.

Rasputin was a large man with sharp, beady eyes, greasy hair and a tangled forest of beard. What did the empress see in him? I mean, Alexandria was Queen Victoria's granddaughter! She should've been smarter than that. She was part English and a woman, for crying out loud!

Granted, the rumor that Alexandria was an imbecile had floated around for quite a while. My spies said she liked shiny things and couldn't answer simple one-word questions without shouting, "There's a platypus in my pantaloons!" But Rasputin was gross. No, as long as I lived, I'd never understand her interest in him. It was clear the tsarina wasn't going to fire him anytime soon, and according to my contract, it was time for Rasputin to go.

But this team of men I'd organized for the job tonight! Everything might have worked out okay, had they not been stupid enough to let Rasputin walk out the door just now. I had no confidence that they could accomplish the job. If they botched it in front of witnesses, they would end up in prison, and

Rasputin might be saved. While I didn't care about these gits all that much, things were getting messy. I didn't like messy. The Bombays didn't like messy. They were a bit bitchy on that point.

The worst part was that I'd failed at this same mission two years ago. It was a miracle the Council didn't have me killed. But I can be pretty crafty, and I managed to talk them out of it on the condition that I didn't fail this time. It was close. But they agreed, providing I didn't tell the other Bombays. There was no way I'd let my cousins know about the failure. Leeds Bombay is a misogynistic arsehole who'd drop me if he knew the half of it. Doesn't everyone have a cousin like that?

Back in 1914, Rasputin first came across my assignment list. I spent weeks recruiting one of his crazy, female followers, Guseva. Rasputin liked wandering aimlessly about Russia—on foot. Why? Who knows. Of all the countries I'd consider just walking around in, Russia would be at the bottom of the list. It's enormous with thousands of miles between goat farms, and the winters were bloody awful. But since he was considered "mad" I guess it's just who he was.

Anyhoo, he was going to visit his wife and children in Siberia. I set it up so Guseva would jump out and stab him. Guseva was a loon. Totally nuts—but I still thought she could pull it off. Originally a follower of the Mad Monk, she later claimed abuse at his hand. She was the easiest mark I ever turned.

She gleefully gutted Rasputin, then stood there and watched as his intestines spilled out, screaming, "I've killed the Antichrist!" That's right. I'd told her he was the Antichrist. Don't judge me. It worked…somewhat.

Except she hadn't killed him. After stuffing his guts (mmrph—sorry, just threw up in my mouth a little) back in and some miraculous surgery I didn't think even existed in Russia, Grigori Rasputin was just fine. Damn it. That should have been my first clue to be more particular in whom I recruited.

But this was some seriously creepy stuff I could not have anticipated. Rasputin, stuffed his innards back in, was sewn up, and survived. If this didn't add to his spooky factor, nothing could. The man was like a ghost or something. On top of it all, this only added to his claims that he was divine. And that was bad.

This time, he wasn't going to survive. It's bad enough when your target doesn't die the first time, but the second? No Bombay has ever missed his or her mark. I'd go down in family lore as the assassin who screwed up twice. And then they'd hunt and kill me. (Leeds would probably volunteer for the job.) I needed that like I needed a hole in the head…a hole that Rasputin currently sported in his big, smelly head.

So this time I'd recruited Prince Felix Yusupov, and he recruited his loudmouth friend Dmitry Pavlovich to take care of things. Felix was an idiot who liked to dress up like Lillie Langtry, with full makeup, and sing show tunes. Dmitry was a loudmouth member of the Duma—Russia's version of Parliament. They added Dr. Lazavert to the group and a plan was hatched…mostly by me.

Dmitry and Lazavert never knew that. Felix was the only one in contact with me. The others didn't know I existed. Felix's ego immediately seized upon my plan as his (which was the intention, of course), and the other two fell in.

It was such a simple idea. Rasputin had a thing for Felix's gorgeous wife, Irina. Felix would imply that Irina wanted to have sex with Rasputin and that he'd organize it. Once at the house, the doctor would lace food with cyanide, and the evil holy man would drop dead. The boys would drop his body in the river, and that would be the end of that.

Only it wasn't. Not even close. Sigh. The things I do for this job!

Problem number one: the men chose December for the deed. Really? December…in Petrograd? I chose Felix for his palace's proximity to the Moika River. All they had to do was open a window and dump the body in it in the middle of the night. What they hadn't thought of was that because it's *December in Petrograd*, most bodies of water were frozen over.

I tried to get them to wait until summer, but they were so excited about getting the job done that Felix stopped listening. That led to an impromptu drive all over the city this morning where they tried to find a river that wasn't totally iced over. A different river. A not-the-Moika-that-has-easy-access River.

Problem two: Felix Yusupov. Felix was married to the tsar's niece. I thought that was rather hilarious because Felix was a well-known homosexual. But whatever—to each his own, right? Felix got it into his head that he should prepare for the murder. He took it upon himself to arrange a meeting with Rasputin through a close friend under the guise of needing some help with chronic pain. The ditzy socialite happily obliged, and Felix met Rasputin at Rasputin's apartment for some "therapy."

The problem with this was that Rasputin was drawn to Felix's handsome features, and, for whatever reason, Felix was drawn to Rasputin's "methods." And so he became a regular at the Mad Monk's place, acquiring the nickname "Little One," and becoming familiar with Rasputin's daughter, Maria, and the staff.

Word on the street was that he and Rasputin were now lovers. Felix kept seeing him in opposition to my instructions, stating simply, "Nonsense. I always use the *back* stairs."

Which led to problem three: Rasputin. The man was a complete gossip and braggart. He couldn't keep a secret to save his life. The bastard bragged publicly, at length, about the naughty things he'd been up to and with whom. Felix was convinced Rasputin would keep the staged rendezvous with Irina a secret.

Except that he didn't. Rasputin told his daughter, Maria. He informed his servants, "Little One is picking me up at midnight to pleasure his wife." He even called a few friends and let them in on the secret. Hell, for all I know he took out an ad in the papers.

I was working with idiots.

And it didn't get better after that.

The morning started desolate and freezing. I was to hide in a section of the palace that was closed off for the winter. Felix came and reported that the Moika had frozen solid—what should they do?

"Find a spot that isn't frozen," I replied. I didn't like hanging out in the abandoned wing. It was bitterly cold, and the assassination wouldn't even take place until midnight.

Felix nodded. "Okay. Hey, you warm enough?" He cocked his head, and I thought about strangling him.

"I'll slip into the kitchen to warm myself and get something to eat," I assured him, controlling my anger. The simpleton grinned and ran off.

A few hours later, Felix found me in the kitchen, sitting in front of the fire and eating his best caviar. He raised an eyebrow, but the look on my face must have dissuaded him from saying anything. You can't really get good caviar back in England. Since I was here, I might as well help myself.

"We found a spot in the Malaya Nevka River." Felix reached for the caviar, but I slapped his hand away.

"But that's not the plan. You were supposed to find a hole or make one in the Moika!" I sputtered. What was the point of even using this damn place if we couldn't use the river next to it?

"Oh, and, um…there's one other thing…" The prince turned away from me. "Irina won't be here."

"*What*!?" I slapped my hand down hard on the table. "Are you serious? She's the bait! Don't you think Rasputin will notice she's not here and think something's up?" I'd pinned my hopes on Irina—the only other woman in this plot. She didn't have to get horizontal with the disgusting monk, but she did have to be there, smiling prettily and catching him off guard.

Felix raised his hands and shook his head, "Don't worry—Dmi and I have come up with a brilliant plan."

Uh oh. The clock on the wall now showed we were well into the afternoon. I could come up with a plan on short notice, but I wasn't sure these guys could. I wondered if we should cancel the attempt.

Felix motioned for me to follow him out of the kitchen, down the hallway and a set of stairs to a private dining room. The room was tiny, with windows high up at street level. One end held a small, round table and wooden chairs, and the other end seemed to be some sort of area for entertaining.

"What's this?" I asked.

"Oh, this is where various Yusupovs have entertained lovers over the years. It'll be perfect."

I sighed. "And just how will this be perfect without the potential lover?"

Felix nodded. "I know what you are thinking. But we have it figured out! Dmi and the doctor will be upstairs making noise in a parlor. I'll tell Rasputin that Irina is entertaining unexpected guests, and while we are waiting for them to leave, he will eat the poisoned food and drink!" He grinned like an idiot who thought he had it all figured out.

I wasn't sure if it was false hope or temporary insanity. But I thought this might work.

Felix pointed to a screen halfway across the room. "You can hide here to make sure it works out. And it will. Dmi is a genius at these things."

I was about to ask him how many assassinations Dmi had planned and successfully executed (my personal record was forty-seven) but changed my mind. It was getting late, and there was work to be done.

Back in the kitchen, I started to make the tarts and cakes that would hide the potassium cyanide. After a few hours, the sun had gone down, and I had several platters of various sweets. I added a bottle of red wine to the tray with two glasses and made my way down to the small dining room.

Dr. Lazavert barely noticed me. And why should he? Servants were ignored, and this was part of the plan. The doctor would add the cyanide to the baked goods and wine, making sure to add enough poison to kill a man without it tasting obviously of poison. I set the napkins and cutlery, watching the doctor work.

He was nervous and wearing rubber gloves. I stoked the fire and stood aside, presumably awaiting instructions, but actually observing. The doc seemed to know what he was doing, even though he was perspiring heavily. He added poison to all the platters but one and told Felix to make sure only to eat from that tray. Then, the man stripped off his rubber gloves, and, to my absolute shock, tossed them into the fireplace.

The smell hit first, followed by an unnatural smoke that quickly filled the low-ceilinged room. I grabbed the fireplace tongs and removed the burning gloves. The doc was trying to open the tiny windows.

I couldn't chastise the idiot doctor—I was merely a servant. I wanted to kill him, but I didn't do that either because we still needed him. Instead I merely seethed as I tried to fan the smoke out of the room. The smell of burning rubber would be very hard to explain to anyone, let alone a suspicious Rasputin. Rumor had it that he had foreseen his own death recently and had become quite paranoid. I silently cursed the doctor and vowed never to take a job in Russia again. Was it possible to suddenly forget a language I'd known my whole life? I'd have to give some serious thought to that one.

"What's that smell?" Felix entered, holding his nose. I didn't answer, so the doctor nervously explained what had happened—except in his version, I was the one who had thrown the gloves in the fireplace. I steeled myself and gave Felix a deadly look.

"Um, okay, that's fine," the prince said as he waved away the stench. "We have to leave soon, Doc, to pick up our special guest for tonight." He actually wiggled his eyebrows suggestively.

Dr. Lazavert nodded and fled the room, leaving me to deal with the mess. Sigh. How typical.

The smell of burnt rubber is certainly a force to reckon with. The windows were open and the fire was blazing but that horrible smell hung in the air, refusing to budge. I raced upstairs to the kitchen and searched the cupboards until I found some sage branches. Returning to the small dining room downstairs, I burned the ends in the fireplace and waved the smoking branches around the room, feeling a bit silly. It worked though. I'd used burning sage before to mask other odors during my assignments, but to use it to erase such a strong, chemical smell was new. I was just closing up the windows when Felix led Rasputin down the stairs and into the room.

"Irina is entertaining some guests from America!" Felix said way too loudly. "She will join us when they leave. Aren't Americans tiresome?" The prince gave a garish smile. What was he doing?

Rasputin said nothing. He grunted and turned his attention to me. His eyes were truly hypnotic and a bit crazy. I cast my gaze to the floor and curtseyed like a good maid.

"That's Olga," Felix shouted. The Mad Monk wasn't hard of hearing. "She'll fetch us whatever we need."

I nodded and curtseyed again, and after both men were seated, I stepped behind the screen. It was a Chinese screen with a lot of complicated carvings on it. There were spaces that I could see through, so I could observe what was going on unnoticed.

"How about a pastry?" Felix practically screamed as he slid one of the poisoned platters toward his guest.

Rasputin did not move. "No," he said. Maybe he was unnerved by Felix's shouting.

"*What*?" The prince's voice went up an octave. "Why? I...I thought you liked these..." he sputtered. The man was losing it already. All he had to do was be patient. Rasputin would eat, I was sure of that.

"Too sweet," Rasputin grunted.

Felix stood and poured his guest a glass of poisoned claret. Then he filled his glass. With the poisoned claret. I wondered if he would drink it.

"No." Rasputin pushed away the glass. Apparently, he didn't want to eat or drink yet.

Assassination is basically a game of hurry-up-and-wait. I understood this. In the case of poisoning someone at dinner, especially, you don't want to push your victim into it. Let him decide when to drink and eat. Being pushy would only raise suspicions.

Unfortunately, Felix Yusupov had the patience of a fruit fly. He started to perspire. His face turned red and, again, he loudly insisted Rasputin eat and drink.

"No," was all Rasputin said. I was starting to wonder if that was the only word he knew.

"Um, I'll just...check on things..." Felix stammered and vanished up the staircase. Smooth. If I was Rasputin, I'd find this suspicious. What was that stupid prince doing?

I stepped out from behind the screen and tidied up the table a bit, even though nothing had been touched. Something told me that my presence might allay Rasputin's suspicions. Unfortunately, it did.

I felt a sharp pinch on my arse. Son of a bitch. That nasty bastard was flirting with me! I had to keep it together.

Turning and deftly stepping out of Rasputin's reach, I tried to giggle flirtatiously.

"You are pretty," he grunted and reached for me again. I giggled unenthusiastically and stepped out of his way. Upstairs, someone put a record on the phonograph and "Yankee Doodle Dandy" blasted. For the first time, I heard laughter and murmurs. I guessed they were finally getting started on the Irina-entertaining-Americans ruse.

Felix returned back down the stairs, looking pale but acting gracious. "Irina's guests are upstairs," he managed weakly, his loud voice now gone. He sat down at the table and picked up a pastry from the non-poisoned tray and started nibbling at it. My guess was Dmitry told him if he ate something, Rasputin would. Felix then raised his glass of the poisoned wine. I moved quickly to stand behind Rasputin and shook my head vigorously.

Felix's eyes bulged as he remembered the poison in his glass and replaced it on the table without taking so much as a sip. For a moment I thought I should've let him drink it. But while potassium cyanide took a few moments to work, Rasputin would certainly become suspicious if his host clutched his chest and fell to the floor.

Rasputin grunted and finally reached for one of the pastries. He took a large bite and seemed to swallow without chewing. Pale, flaky crumbs littered his dark beard. One more bite and he finished the pastry and reached for another. A few minutes passed and he'd eaten four, washing it down with a gulp of wine.

I slid behind the screen and allowed myself a small smile. The amount of poison he'd just ingested would've killed an ox. We just had to wait now for it to kick in.

Felix relaxed somewhat and began chatting amiably. He did most of the talking, and most of it was silly gossip about the most beautiful ladies in the court—one of Rasputin's favorite subjects. The monk grunted his agreement here and there but said little. He seemed comfortable and at ease.

Time passed. A lot of time. Rasputin ate four more poisoned pastries and drank two more full glasses of poisoned wine. Nothing happened. Did the doctor screw up? I could swear

I saw him load the pastries with the poison. The bag he used was clearly labeled cyanide. He was a doctor and surely knew where to get the real stuff.

My heart began to pound. Yes, assassination is a waiting game, but it had been half an hour. Rasputin had ingested more poison than you'd use to kill off a dinner party of twenty people. (And, yes, I speak from experience.) And yet here he sat, perfectly fine. That weird, creepiness he exuded worried me. Was he immune to potassium cyanide? I'd never heard of such a thing.

Rasputin pointed at a guitar in the corner. "Little One, do you play?"

Felix nodded shakily. Clearly he was anxious about the fact that Rasputin wasn't dead yet. I was inclined to agree.

"Play something for me!" Rasputin ordered. I stepped from behind the screen, and after retrieving the guitar, I handed it to Felix. He searched my face with a what-the-hell look, but I gave him nothing and returned to my spot behind the screen.

The prince found his courage and began to play one of several Russian folk songs. The music clashed with the constant, loud, repetitive playing of "Yankee Doodle Dandy" upstairs (Seriously? Did they only have one song?), but Rasputin didn't seem to mind as he began to hum along to the music, closing his eyes and tapping his feet.

After several songs, Felix stopped, rose to his feet and after setting the guitar down said, "I think I'll see what's keeping Irina." He vanished up the stairs.

I emerged from the screen and returned the guitar to its spot in the corner. Rasputin rose to his feet so I could clear the now dried-out pastries from the table. He wandered over to an ebony cabinet against the south wall and began to examine it.

Rasputin had eaten two trays full of poisoned food and drunk an entire bottle of poisoned wine. He should be dead and writhing on the floor. Instead, he seemed completely and unnaturally healthy. Footsteps came down the stairs, and I wondered if I had a second to warn Felix to calm down a little. All these disappearances were suspicious.

Rasputin ignored the sounds, fascinated with the cabinet. To my shock, I saw that Felix was now carrying Dmitry's gun.

Was he insane? The police station was down the street! We'd agreed no guns because that might cause some unwanted attention.

Before I could cross the room, Felix Yusupov stepped up behind Rasputin and aimed the gun at his back. "Grigory," Felix said as he saw the monk studying a crucifix in the cabinet, "you would do better to look at the crucifix and pray to it." Felix then fired the pistol into Rasputin's back and watched as he fell to the floor.

Dmitry and Dr. Lazavert came flying down the stairs to see Rasputin lying on the floor. I wanted to strangle all of them—, Dmitry for giving Felix his weapon and Lazavert for screwing up the poison somehow. I also wanted to beat Felix for his stupid little monologue. We have a strict rule in the Bombay family—don't give speeches, just kill them. You'd be surprised how many times the bad guy gets away because some moron decides to give a speech.

"The rug!" Felix howled. For a moment, I thought he'd regained his senses. Yes, we should roll him up in the rug and move him before a bloodstain forms.

"Get him off the rug!" Felix shrieked. "It's polar bear!"

I stared at these idiots as they moved the body off the rug so that *it wouldn't get stained.*

Rasputin's body began to twitch, convulsing on the carpet, before going completely still.

"That'll do it then," Dr. Lazavert confirmed—without checking the body. I watched in surprise as the men patted each other on the back and celebrated.

"Come on!" Felix roared with the first shadow of confidence I'd seen all night. "Let's go upstairs and toast the death of the monster!"

The three men left the room, laughing as they mounted the stairs. I heard them call for Buzhinsky and champagne. I examined the body, trying not to look at the blood. Rasputin was stiff and cold. I couldn't find a heartbeat. This was good news. While the men waited for it to get later and dark enough to dump the body, I took the trays of poisoned crumbs, the wine glasses and empty bottle upstairs to dispose of them.

It was finally done, I thought. I cleaned the platters thoroughly three times, the last time with bleach. I did the same with the wine glasses and bottle before taking it all out to the garbage.

The wind whistled through the bare branches outside, and I slid back into the shadows of the trees in the courtyard, letting out a huge sigh of relief. It had been a very long night. We still needed to get rid of the body, but that should be the easiest part of the plan. Rasputin was dead. I'd finally gotten the job done. And it wasn't easy.

Maybe I needed to rethink this idea of getting others to do the work. We barely made it through this murder. Maybe the other Bombays were right to just do the job themselves. If anything, the screw-ups this evening were a good sign that it was time to go solo.

To my amazement, even though nearly every aspect of the plan had gone wrong, these guys actually did what Guseva couldn't a few years ago. They had managed to kill Rasputin. The Mad Monk was dead. And he was running into the courtyard...wait, what?

Which brings us back to where I started...with Rasputin's caved-in face and bullet in the head on the carpet in the hall, Felix holding cast iron dumbbells in each hand, splattered with blood.

I helped the men roll the carpet around the now *certainly* dead Rasputin. We secured it with rope. Dr. Lazavert assured us this time the man was dead. I watched as the men, with the servant Buzhinsky, carried the body to the trunk of Felix's car and drove off into the night.

I was mopping the blood up from the foyer, pretending it was wine so as not to get lightheaded, when I heard Buzhinsky re-enter the room with Dmitry.

"Do you think the policeman believed the story of a backfiring automobile?" Dmitry said somewhat sarcastically.

Buzhinsky nodded. "Maybe."

Dmitry said nothing for a moment as I wrung the last of the blood—er, *wine*—into the bucket and went into the kitchen to pour it out. When I returned with a cloth to dry the floor, I found the policeman Vlassiyev standing in the foyer with

Dmitry. What was he doing here? Maybe he didn't buy the story and had returned?

"Thank you for coming," Dmitry said as he rose to his full height and puffed out his chest. "I appreciate it at such a late hour."

Wait…what? Dmitry had called him? To come here??

The policeman nodded and waited.

I stared openly at Dmitry. What was he thinking? I had Vlassiyev convinced it was nothing! But Dummy Dmi summoned him back? Did he not notice the *huge pool of blood in the courtyard*!?

Dmitry introduced himself to the policeman and asked if Vlassiyev had heard of him. Of all the egotistical bullshit! This was not the time to throw your weight around as some sort of political celebrity, Dmi!

"I have heard of you," Vlassiyev replied.

"Have you ever heard of Rasputin?" Dmitry waited for the policeman to nod—which he did. I broke out in a cold sweat. What was happening?

"Well," Dmitry continued in a proud voice, "Rasputin is dead. And if you love our mother Russia, you'll keep quiet about it."

My mouth hung completely open. This idiot just told the police that we'd murdered the tsarina's favorite Russian!

"Yes, sir." Vlassiyev nodded and left.

Dmitry clapped his hands and laughed. "Well, that's that! We won't have to worry about him!" His tone was smug and self-congratulatory. I had just witnessed the stupidest thing I'd ever seen. If I moved quickly, I could kill Dmitry before the others got back. I didn't care if anyone saw me do it. I could get out of Russia before they even looked for me. Maybe I should kill Felix, Dr. Lazavert and Buzhinsky too. My mind was whirling, and I was lightheaded, unable to think straight. Maybe I could make it look like they all committed suicide so they wouldn't get caught? I took a step toward Dmitry just as Felix and the doctor burst through the door in a triumphant mood.

"We did it!" Felix said as he raised one of the bloody dumbbells into the air. "We threw him in the river!" He handed the bloody dumbbells to me for cleaning and smiled dopily.

I stared at the weights. The weights that were supposed to be tucked inside the carpet just before they tossed Rasputin into the water. The weights that were supposed to make the body sink so it wouldn't be found. The weights I held in my hands.

I closed my eyes and used every ounce of will that I had to not attack Felix with them.

When I regained my senses, I heard Dmitry finishing his story about how he masterfully handled the policeman. Felix clapped his friends on the back, and they decided the deed was done, and they all went their separate ways.

I was sitting in the kitchen an hour later, still trying to wrap my head around the events. By now, Rasputin, if he wasn't dead before, would have been dead almost an hour from hypothermia. I felt fairly confident about that.

Didn't I?

The bottle of very expensive champagne was empty next to me; I'd just finished the last glass. Two empty tins of Felix's best caviar sat beside me. I spared no expense. Fuck Felix if he was pissed. The man barely pulled it off.

He hadn't come down to see me—choosing instead to take Buzhinsky with him to help clean himself up. I'd waited in the kitchen, so I could yell at him or kill him. But he never came down. I'd like to think that's because he knew he'd screwed up and that I'd be mad. I was more certain that it was because he thought he'd done a great job and went to bed.

How had everything gone so wrong? And by everything, I mean *everything*! It was as if the prince and his merry band of misfits went out of their way to make every comic error they could think of.

I shook my head. Maybe the policeman really did decide not to tell anyone. Rasputin was vastly unpopular. And the policeman would have blackmail material enough to make himself a very rich man. Perhaps I was over-thinking it. I was definitely tired and starting to feel the results of the champagne.

I left everything out so Felix could see what I'd done, and, instead of the chilly west wing, found a nice, warm guest room and passed out.

I awoke a few hours later to find Felix shaking me. My head was spinning. What time was it? Why was he waking me up?

"Um…" he said slowly, as if that would help. "...we may have a problem."

Somehow I pulled myself together. My mouth tasted like the Dead Sea, but I managed to show up dressed downstairs. Buzhinsky met me and led me into the courtyard, where I found the prince standing next to a dead dog. A gun gleamed in his hand. My gun. How did he get my gun?

The poor dog was clearly dead, shot once through the head. My heart ached for it.

"You shot a dog?" I said, my anger barely contained.

Felix handed the gun to Buzhinsky, who spirited it back into the house. I didn't even want it back. I would never have shot a dog.

"I had to. We couldn't get rid of all the blood." Felix looked at me like I was an idiot.

"So," I hissed through clenched teeth, "you shot a dog?" I was furious! I loved dogs! How could he do that? And with my gun?

Bombays weren't supposed to kill anyone we weren't assigned to kill, but I thought I might scrape by with an exception here.

Felix rolled his eyes. "Of course! I had to make it look like one of my guests from last night shot a dog! That would explain the blood."

Oh sure. That made perfect sense. Of course.

I knelt down to touch the poor beast. It was one of Felix's own Borzois. What a bastard.

"And what on earth made you think that one shot to a dog would cause this much blood?" I tried to control the rage that bubbled up inside of me. I was interrupted by the arrival of the police. Perfect.

Vlassiyev arrived with four other officers. Clearly he never meant to "not tell anyone." I stepped behind Felix and kept my face down.

"We are investigating the murder of Rasputin, sir," Vlassiyev said. "What do you have to say to that?"

Felix shrugged. "I have no idea what you mean."

The five policemen looked at the enormous pool of blood and at the pitiful body of the dog lying in the middle of it.

"Would you care to explain this?" Vlassiyev pointed at the ground.

"I had a party last night. One of my guests thought it would be funny to shoot one of my dogs." He didn't say any more.

Vlassiyev knelt down and examined the dog. "Only one shot to the head." He straightened up. "That would not account for this much blood."

Felix shrugged again. I realized that this had been his defense most of his life.

"And we've had a call from Rasputin's daughter," Vlassiyev continued. "She said her father never came home last night. She said you picked him up and brought him to your house, and he hasn't been seen since."

Felix nodded smugly. "Rasputin was not one of my guests. I've never met the man."

My fingers curled into fists. Was he kidding? The police just said Rasputin left with him last night. It wouldn't take much to find out Felix had been one of his patients for the last two months. Was he insane?

Vlassiyev cleared his throat. "And one of your guests summoned me to the house last night to tell me Rasputin was murdered here and not to say a word about it."

"I'm sure you misheard him," Felix said simply. "Was Rasputin murdered?" His voice dripped with hope.

"Yes," the officer said, "we found his body this morning. He is dead."

I braced myself in case Felix did a little jig in front of the officers. At that moment, a Count Something-or-Other appeared in the courtyard and, completely ignoring the police, walked over and shook Felix's hand.

"Just heard! Well done, my fellow! I always hated that damned monk!"

I went inside and gathered my things. Before anyone noticed, I'd packed up and fled Moika Palace through a side door. It took days to catch a train to Finland. I'd read a newspaper in Sweden that said the tsar hushed the whole thing up and sent Dmitry and Felix to the Western Front. Whatever.

The Rasputin Assignment became famous in the Bombay Family. For years, my relatives expressed sympathy for the job, and they all said they were grateful it wasn't assigned to them, which made me feel a little bit better.

After all we went through with this greasy bastard—the poison, the shooting, and the bludgeoning—the autopsy showed that Rasputin had died of the one thing I hadn't planned on...hadn't even considered as a means of execution.

Rasputin was poisoned with potassium cyanide in his food and wine. He was shot in the back and shot in the head. His face was bashed in with weights. But that wasn't what got him in the end.

Rasputin died...of drowning.

But at least this time, he really was, totally and completely, dead.

MY HEROES HAVE ALWAYS BEEN HITMEN: AND OTHER BOMBAY FAMILY BEDTIME STORIES

From the Bombay Family of assassins' vault...

These tales are the bedtime stories and family histories of the Bombay Family. Because of the oral tradition in which they've been handed down all these years, I'm writing these in my own voice. Well, because of that and the fact that I'm very lazy, and apparently there are four cassowaries in Australia who are a bit impatient for this next book. By the way—this is for you, Bulvai, Hrothgar, Beowulf, and Kevin!

I've had some requests to include at least one story about how one of our strange family rules got started, so I've included one. See if you can spot it. Hint—it's a bit darker than the others. Being a Bombay isn't easy my friends.

Since publishing the first collection: *SNUFF THE MAGIC DRAGON: And Other Bombay Bedtime Stories*, I've had a few critics complaining about voice, historical accuracy, etc. And I'd just like to say that there are now a few less critics in the world.

You're welcome.

I hope you enjoy the stories. I know I did.

- Gin Bombay

Rio Bombay
Felony, Texas—1870

It was dawn, and it was dusty the morning I rode into Felony, Texas. There was something romantic about that because I was in town to kill a man. Not just any man—the corrupt Marshal Beauregarde Figgins. My name is Rio. Rio Bombay.

Norbert, my horse, slumped between my legs. He was tired. But we were here, and he could have oats, a good rubdown, and a nice, dry stable for the night. Norbert didn't have to kill anybody. He could just hang out and wait until I was done. Then, I rather hoped we'd be able to ride off into the sunset or something poetic like that.

Chances were pretty good I could arrange that sunset thing. It didn't really matter when I killed Figgins. I was my own boss, so I thought I could make this happen.

Alright, I'll admit right now that I was a bit of a Wild West nut. Actually, I grew up in Newport, Rhode Island. But I spent all my time reading about cowboys and lawmen and gunslingers. When this opportunity came up, I jumped at it. Even bought a horse and everything. It was just unfortunate his name was Norbert. I'd envisioned a name like Duke or Trigger when I got my first horse. But he was a trick horse from the circus and only knew how to respond to 'Norbert,' so that's what I had to deal with.

Oh yeah, Rio really is my name. Rio de Janeiro Bombay. As a kid I shortened it and told everyone it was because of the Rio Grande. I wished it was. I really, really did.

"Why are you so quiet?" Jeb asked.

"Just thinking," I answered a bit sheepishly.

"Okay, Colonel," Jeb said as he continued riding next to me.

Did I forget to mention I wasn't alone? Jebediah Smith was a man from my infantry unit in the war. I'd come across him just outside of St. Louis. He was headed this way and thought we could ride together. A good man in a fight, I liked him when he served with me. Besides, a little company made the long trip to West Texas a bit easier. Unfortunately, his horse was named Cochise. I thought that was a bit unfair. But no matter. Jeb was just looking to homestead somewhere in Texas. Once he found that place, we'd be parting ways.

I slowly rode Norbert up what passed for a Main Street in this backwater town. Townspeople walked through the dirt, looking at me warily. It had to be the hat. I'd bought a black, ten-gallon hat in Oklahoma, much to Jeb's amusement. I thought it was most appropriate. I tipped it to several of the ladies who I passed. They ignored me. I hadn't expected that.

We found the hotel and tied up Norbert and Cochise. Norbert gave me a look that said he'd rather go directly to the stables. I stroked his ears and made my way into the two-story clapboard building.

"I need two rooms," I tried to say with a gruff, cowboyish snarl. In all those stories, cowboys were men of few words and had deep, crackling voices. Jeb turned away to hide his grin. I'd really have to talk to him about that.

"Okay." A bored matron shoved the register toward me and asked me to sign for both rooms. I wrote Rio Bombay in big, dark letters and a sharp, sloping hand. I was admiring my new gunslinger style signature when she tossed me two keys and snapped the book shut without even looking at my name. That was disappointing.

"Fifty cents a night. Dinner's at six. Stables around back." She frowned at us. Ah, the old spinster who ran the hotel, I thought, imagining her coming out here as a bride for sale, but having found no takers, she chose to run the local hotel. She would have a 'no frills' name, like Prudence and a sour attitude to match.

I paid her and tipped my hat and said, "Ma'am." I'm not sure she heard me because she turned away as soon as she had my money. I looked at my key—Room Four. Yes, that sounded like a good number for the room of a gunman. I tossed Jeb his key, and he caught it mid-air, which I thought looked good. He went up to his room while I checked on the horses.

Norbert looked a bit unimpressed with our new status as the savvy, sage lone rider and his trusty steed. I led him and Cochise around back to the stables. Once I was sure they were taken care of, I headed up to my room and dropped my satchel on the bed.

The room was neat and clean. There was an iron-framed bed with two pillows and a clean, simple quilt. In the corner was a table with a bowl and pitcher and small mirror. Perfect. Exactly what I wanted.

I practiced my quick draw in the mirror for a little while and must admit, I looked very cool doing that. Truth be told, I was pretty fast. When six-shooters first came on the scene, the Bombays started training on them immediately. I was good with one—the best in my family. That's probably why they sent me on this assignment. Maybe they saw cowboy potential in me.

Back home in Newport, there was little need for quick draw contests. Even though I came from a family of deadly assassins, my sister and mother were far more interested in the social seasons. Don't get me wrong. Both women were lethal and good at their jobs. But they preferred quieter methods, like a well-placed hatpin in the eardrum or a tincture of arsenic during a six-course dinner on 5th Avenue. I think they found my fascination with the Wild West a bit dull.

Actually, I found life in general a bit dull after the war. I was a colonel in the Rhode Island Infantry and managed well enough in battle. The endless death was depressing, but the action kept me on my toes. How could I go home to ballrooms and debutantes after that? A lot of my fellow soldiers made their way west, and I longed to join them.

I thought maybe I could set up a base here. Build a house—something with a big hitching post outside and lots of antlers inside. The more I thought about that, the more I liked it.

Norbert came from a circus in Virginia. He was a trick pony who came when called, had no issue with gunfire, and really looked the part of a cowboy's horse. A gorgeous paint, I wanted him the moment I saw him. Since we started riding west, however, he became somewhat less enthusiastic.

I ran into Jeb in Illinois, just before crossing the Mississippi into St. Louis. It was a nice reunion in a hotel tavern. Jeb had been down on his luck since the war ended. He'd been an excellent rifleman and missed the action, so he'd decided to go out West and try to make a new life for himself. When I mentioned that I was going to Texas, he leaped at the chance to go with me.

I liked the idea of having a partner for the ride. I told him about my interest in cowboys, and he managed to control his amusement. Apparently, I'd been well-known in my unit for all the dime novels about the Old West that I read. I'd be lying if I said I didn't have a couple in my saddle bag even right now.

The morning wore on, and I made my way downstairs to the dining room to meet Jeb for lunch. The room was filled with normal looking folks, much to my disappointment. I was about to ask my server where the cowboys ate, when I spotted my target.

Marshal Figgins was a large, muscular man. He strode into the dining room like he owned it, taking a seat at a table for two near the window. The table should've been occupied—it was the best spot in the crowded place. That's when I noticed a large placard on it that said, *RESERVED FOR MARSHAL FIGGINS.*

No one spoke to him, I noticed. No one called out or waved in a friendly way. Everyone averted their eyes. Figgins removed his gun belt and slammed it on the table loudly. The people closest to him flinched. A server appeared immediately— a young woman with red hair tied up efficiently. She was the only one who didn't seem afraid of the huge man with the large, dark mustache.

Figgins murmured a few words, and she nodded and rushed off to the kitchens. He then leaned back in his chair and stared out the window.

I was completely absorbed. The history on Figgins was a violent one. Marshal Beau Figgins had spent ten years terrorizing half the Texas territory. He killed Indians at will—women and children too—because he thought they were unnecessary. He was known for his fast draw and his penchant for cheating in duels by placing snipers throughout the town. Most of his prisoners never made it to the jailhouse because they were killed "resisting arrest."

In fact, Figgins had become his own law. The governor and his appointed judges couldn't rein him in. Oh sure, they had some power, but he was stronger, smarter, and meaner than they were. All of this made him the perfect target for me.

My thoughts were interrupted as an argument broke out at the table next to me. Two men in derby hats and spats stood and shook their fists at each other, disagreeing about the bill. I watched as the manager rushed over to quiet them down. He whispered something to the men and then nodded nervously at Figgins, who was now starting to look at them with interest. The two men paled and immediately sat down, apologizing to those around them for disturbing their lunch.

I watched as Figgins fixed them with his gaze for a moment longer before turning back to the window. The men paid their check and fled as fast as they could.

"What just happened there?" Jeb asked as he sat down. He'd had a bath and a shave and bought some clothes. His hat looked a little larger than mine…or maybe it was my imagination. He looked good, really like a cowboy and less like a former infantryman from New England.

I filled him in on the disagreement, and we ordered lunch.

"I checked on…the horses," he winked at me. I'd warned him not to mention Norbert by name in public. "Thought I'd look around town and find out what the prospects are this afternoon."

"I'm going to the saloon," I answered as a huge plate full of meat and potatoes was set in front of me. Jeb nodded as if he approved of my plans, and we tucked in to eat.

After lunch, I got directions from Prudence to the saloon. She didn't seem to approve, or maybe that's just how she treated everyone.

Figgins was still eating, and I wasn't ready to follow him just yet. I needed more intelligence before I could draw up my plans. And the best place for that would be the saloon. To say I was excited to be going to a real, Wild West saloon would be a gross understatement.

"What'll it be?" A jolly, balding man with mutton chop sideburns grinned at me as I settled at the bar in the wonderfully named Diablo Saloon.

"Whiskey," I said, savoring each syllable. Mother would be unnerved. We didn't drink whiskey at the club in Newport. But I wasn't in Newport, and I was going to have whiskey.

"Not from around here?" the barman asked as he poured me a glass of amber fluid.

"Nope," I said as brusquely as I could. The key to being a good cowboy was in being mysterious. The mysterious stranger was the one everyone was always interested in.

"In town for long?" Muttonchops pressed.

"No," I answered, tossing some coins on the counter and turning my back to him. I heard the scrape of his hands retrieving the money, and he asked no more questions. I grinned. I'd pulled it off!

"What're you smiling at?" a tall, thin cowboy with a nasal voice asked me from the table a few feet away.

"Nothin'." I stopped smiling and touched the brim of my hat. This was getting better and better! Mother would be furious at me for my abuse of English, but she wasn't here now. I really needed to get her out of my head if I was going to be a cowboy.

"Leave 'im alone, Rocco." Rocco's buddy cuffed him on the head. "Now, are ya in, or ain'tcha?" He pointed to a pile of chips in the center of the table, and I realized a poker game was in progress.

Rocco pointed at me. "Ya wanna buy in?" Something in his voice was threatening, or at least, I hoped it was.

I narrowed my eyes to show them I was not someone to be trifled with.

"Prolly too steep for ya," Rocco sneered. "It's five dollars ta buy in."

I tried to control my excitement as I slowly made my way to the open chair at the table. I sat down and tossed five dollars on the table. I said nothing, because this was how it was done in the stories.

Rocco's friend introduced himself. "Name's Hank." He pointed to the man on the other side of me. "That's Axel, and ya know Rocco." Hank and Axel were about the same size and build. Both wore heavily stained hats and thick, bushy brown mustaches. The only difference was that Hank had long, greasy hair, and Axel didn't seem to have any sticking out from under his hat.

I almost exploded with enthusiasm! A real, cowboy poker game with high stakes and guys named Rocco, Hank, and Axel! I couldn't have paid people to dress up and act this out back home…not that I ever did that, of course.

"Name's Rio," was all I said.

We played a few hands, and I made sure not to win too much. I'd played a lot of cards during the war, and I knew men didn't like losing to someone they didn't know right off the bat. I had plenty of money. Money wasn't the goal here. Information was the important thing.

After the third hand, the men realized I wasn't going to cheat or kill them, and they began talking amiably. I joined in a little here and there, and let them know I was just passing through. I bought several rounds of whiskey, and before long Rocco, Axel, and Hank were clapping me on the back like I was an old friend.

"I'm stayin' at the hotel," I said as I picked up my cards in the seventh round. "Had lunch there."

Rocco grinned, "Didja see Miss Penny Philpot?" He nudged his friends with his elbows knowingly. "She's got hair like a copper penny. Real purdy gal."

I nodded, feigning interest in my cards. I was a bit sad because I had to throw away another straight just to keep things friendly. I discarded two cards and asked for replacements. "I saw her. Very pretty. She was waiting on the marshal."

Rocco's smile faded quickly, and Hank and Axel frowned. They looked at each other for a second. I didn't prompt them, I just waited as Axel slid me two more cards and I added them to my hand. Damn. Now I had a royal flush.

"Stay away from that marshal, friend," Rocco said quietly. He looked from left to right. "He's bad news."

I raised my eyebrows inquisitively. "I got that impression. In fact, your friend, Miss Penny, seemed to be the only one who wasn't afraid of him."

Hank and Axel exchanged looks before Axel turned to me. "The marshal's sweet on Penny. He's asked her ta marry him six or seven times. She always says no."

Hank nodded. "There's no one braver in this town than Miss Penny."

"I fold, gentlemen," I lied as placed my cards face down. "I just can't seem to catch a break today."

Rocco slapped me on the back and laughed. "I gotta say this, yer a good loser, Rio."

I smiled and motioned to the barman for another round. Hank dealt the next hand.

"What is it, if you don't mind my asking," I said casually, "about this marshal that I need to avoid him?"

Rocco looked at me. "If yer jest passin' through, make sure ya keep yer head down. Marshal Figgins owns this town."

"Owns it?" I asked. "Owns the property?"

Hank shook his head. "No sir. He don't have nothin' but his big house at the end of the street. He kinda owns it in a 'nother way."

"What do you mean?" I dropped one card and held up a finger to Hank, asking for another card. I had nothing in the hand, but I had to make it look like my luck might be starting to turn. I may have been enjoying this a bit too much.

Axel piped up. "He's the boss. He can shoot ya just fer lookin' at him funny and git away with it."

"Really?" I asked as I slid my new card into my hand. "How is that legal?"

Rocco shook his head sadly. "We've buried two judges, and the last one retired five days in. No one cares about what happens here."

I raised my eyebrows. "Why don't you leave?"

Hank shrugged. "Where'd we go?" The other two nodded in agreement, and that seemed to be the end of the conversation.

I didn't press—afraid that would be suspicious. These men were getting liquored up and soon would be useless. I felt a buzz, but that was about it. I had a very high tolerance for alcohol. After losing yet another hand, I thanked them for the game and excused myself. They waved me off good naturedly, and I paid the barman for my tab and left.

It was getting late, and I remembered that Prudence had said dinner was at six. I headed back to my room to clean up and then made my way back to the dining room for dinner.

A different clientele had filled the room this time. Well-dressed men and women took up every table but one—the empty table by the window that still bore the reserved sign.

I guessed that the customers in the evening were guests of the hotel…travelers. Over lunch this must be a popular spot for the townies. I wouldn't get much information from these people, so I just enjoyed my dinner.

The marshal didn't show up. I supposed he either ate at home or was just out killing people. The small bit if information I'd been able to glean so far matched the information given to me about the assignment. Now I just needed to learn more about his movements. It seemed to me that Figgins wasn't going to go down easy, and I was the outsider here.

"Would you care for some cobbler?" A sweet, soft voice intruded on my thoughts. I looked up to see the face of Miss Penny Philpot staring down at me.

She was beautiful. The word "pretty" didn't really do her justice. Large, blue eyes, pale skin with a smattering of freckles across the nose, and wavy, flame-colored hair. She smiled warmly, and I forgot all about cowboys and six shooters.

"That would be nice," I said somehow. She nodded and left, returning almost instantly with a dish of cherry cobbler. I thanked her, and she went back to the kitchen. I tried to read more into it but got nothing. It was immediately clear to me why the marshal had pursued her.

For the rest of the dinner, I tried to catch glimpses of Miss Penny Philpot as she worked her way around the room, greeting customers, serving cobbler, and shining like a beacon of flame-haired loveliness.

I really needed to focus. I wasn't here to court a woman. I was here to kill a bad guy, preferably in a showdown at high noon.

"Sorry I missed dinner, Colonel." Jeb joined me at the table and sat down.

"Not a problem," I said. "But please stop calling me Colonel. The war is over, and I'd rather you called me Rio."

Jeb nodded, and Miss Penny Philpot returned to our table to take his order. I stopped thinking entirely. I couldn't stop staring at the way she smiled...the way she nodded and thanked Jeb for his order...the way she breathed...

"Wow," Jeb said softly as I watched her walk away. "You've got it bad."

I tore my gaze away from the retreating Miss Philpot and turned to him. "What?"

"You couldn't stop staring at her," Jeb said with a grin.

All the air seemed to rush out of me. "I was terribly rude, wasn't I?"

Jeb laughed. "I don't think she minded, Col...I mean, Rio."

"Really?" I sat up a little straighter in my chair. "How do you know?"

"Just a feeling, Sir." Jeb took a sip from his glass of water and sat back.

"You don't have to call me 'Sir,' Jeb. The war is over, and ranks don't matter anymore."

Jeb nodded. "I know. Old habits are hard to break."

We chatted for a few moments until Penny brought his dinner, when I stopped thinking and focused intently on her. I was rewarded with a lovely smile before she left to check on another table.

Jeb had found an interesting prospect for work. A rancher outside of town needed a foreman and was partial to former Union soldiers because he'd lost two sons in the war. I listened politely and tried not to focus on the redhead who was distracting me.

After dinner, we said our good-byes and made our way to our rooms for the night. This business of being a cowboy had worn me out, and I slept very soundly.

At breakfast the next morning, I was a little more reserved when Miss Philpot appeared. What was it about her that turned me into a brainless twit? I was here to do a job, and pursuing a woman who had turned down the most powerful man in town seemed foolish.

Jeb didn't come down to eat, instead meeting me on the stairs to say he was riding out to the ranch for the day to inquire about the foreman position. That gave me a whole day free to find out all I could about Marshal Figgins.

Felony, Texas was not a large town. There was the main street, intersected by four other roads, each with a couple of streets and back alleys all their own. I decided to leave Norbert in his stables and walk.

The day was hot and getting hotter. Dust swirled in the air every time someone stepped off the boardwalks and into the streets. I guessed this was better than mud, but I was completely coated with dust before half an hour was up.

Most of the legitimate businesses were on the main street—a dry goods store, a dentist/barber, and the hotel with its restaurant and the saloon were bookended by a bank at one end and a very large house at the other.

I stopped in the dry goods store and bought a few toiletries, inquiring politely about the large, two-story house at the end of the street.

A young woman with brown hair pulled severely back in a bun, looked nervously around the store before answering.

"That's the marshal's house, mister. Take my advice and don't get too close or ask too many questions." She was then shooed away by a thin, balding man I assumed was the manager. He curtly asked if there was anything else I needed. I got the distinct impression he wanted me to leave. I touched the brim of my hat and gathered up my purchases and left.

After returning to the hotel to drop off my items in my room, I headed back out for more exploration. While getting change at the bank, I asked about houses for sale in the area. A pinched looking man frowned and said I had to build if I wanted anything around here. I asked who had built that large house at the end of Main Street. He shook his head and closed his window.

I had better luck at the stables as I checked on Norbert. My horse was happily eating a bucket of oats which had fresh hay next to it. I swore his eyebrows went up when he saw me, as if to say, *I'm fine. Go away.*

Two young boys were holding down the fort. They spoke animatedly about the town and its most fearful resident.

"And whatever you do, mister, watch out for the marshal!" the boy with red hair said as he hopped from one foot to the other.

"Yeah!" the taller kid with blonde hair added. "He lives in the biggest house I ever saw," He pointed in the direction of the house. "And nobody lives there but him and his servants! Can you imagine that? A big house for just you!"

"He doesn't have any family?" I asked as casually as I could. No family meant a few less grudge holders after I killed him.

The redhead shook his head. "Nope! Just him!" The boy started to dance around the stables. He looked a bit like Miss Philpot, but maybe that was just because they shared the same hair color.

"What's your name, son?" I asked.

The boy grinned. "Percy! Percy Philpot! And I'm seven years old!"

This information startled me. Did Penny have a son? Or was he a younger brother?

"You stayin' at the hotel, mister?" the other boy asked. When I nodded, he said, "Percy's sister, Penny, works there. You probably seen her." He hoisted his thumb to his chest. "I'm Ned. My dad runs these stables. Percy's my cousin."

"I help!" Percy giggled, before beginning to run in circles. Clearly the boy had too much energy.

"I see." I was a little rattled by this new information. But why should I be? I wasn't courting Penny Philpot. Okay, so maybe I harbored the fantasy that she would ride into the sunset with me when this was all over, but now I knew she had family here.

I tossed the boys each a coin and asked them to take extra care of my horse. Norbert snorted as if he were laughing at me, and then buried his snout in oats.

As I walked out into the street, I had this strange feeling I was being watched. Casually I looked around me but saw nothing in the blank faces. My instincts have never been wrong before. I ducked into an alley and waited.

"Didja see 'im?" A cold voice traveled a little ahead of its owner.

"Naw," came an equally gravelly reply. "Just disappeared-like. Figgins said we wuz to rough 'im up. Teach 'im a lesson."

My spine turned to steel, and I prepared myself to fight. These two men were talking about me, I was certain of it.

A man came into view, and I punched him in the throat before he saw me. He collapsed in a heap, spitting and clutching his neck.

"Whut the..." The second man came around the corner, and before he could get to his gun, I laid him out with an uppercut to his bristly, unshaven jaw.

I dragged the bodies into the alley and stepped out onto the street, making my way back to the hotel. It was lunchtime, and I needed to think.

I was sitting at a table in the dining room a few minutes later, concentrating on what had happened.

"Now then," a soft voice said over my shoulder, "what exactly do you think you're doing, asking questions and stirring up trouble?" Penny Philpot was standing over me, holding a pitcher of water that after a knowing glance, she poured into the empty glass in front of me.

"Excuse me?" Her words and her presence had caught me off guard.

Penny shook her head. "You need to be careful when asking questions in this town...Mr...."

"Bombay," Jeb said smoothly as he pulled up a chair next to me. "His name is Rio Bombay."

Penny smiled. "Nice to meet you Mr. Bombay. And you are...?"

"Smith. Jebediah Smith, at your service, ma'am." Jeb nodded.

"How did you know I was asking questions?" I interrupted.

"My little brother told me. Apparently, he's quite taken with you. Calls you the Mysterious Man," Penny said as she filled Jeb's glass. "He likes your horse too. What's his name?"

Jeb winked at me, and I hurried to cut this conversation off. I was thrilled that Penny's brother thought I was mysterious, a feeling that would be somewhat tarnished by a horse named Norbert.

"I was just asking about this place. Seems like a nice town to consider settling down in," I replied.

"Hmmm..." said Penny." Well don't ask about the marshal. He's a bit touchy about that sort of thing." She looked me right in the eyes, and I saw that she knew about the fight in the alleyway.

Miss Philpot took our orders and left for the kitchen.

"What exactly did you do this morning?" Jeb asked.

"Nothing," I tried to be casual, but it wasn't easy. I sipped from my water glass to stall.

Jeb looked at my hand, then at me. "Been in a fight, have you?"

I put the glass down and looked at my knuckles. Damn. I should've worn my black gloves.

"It was nothing." I examined my hands. "A couple of drunks tried to rob me in an alley."

Jeb sat back and looked at me for a long moment. He was a fairly handsome man. I wondered if I had a rival for Miss Philpot. I brushed that thought aside. I wasn't here to court Penny, and Jeb wasn't that kind of man.

Our lunch arrived, and we ate in silence. This gave me time to think. Word spread a bit too fast in this town. Fast enough for the marshal to send some goons after me, and fast enough for my waitress to comment on it. Gossip wasn't necessarily a hindrance. In this case I was sure I could make it work for me.

"How did the job interview go?" I asked Jeb once the dishes were cleared and coffee was poured.

Jeb pushed his chair back and regarded me thoughtfully. "I don't really know. I thought it would be one thing, but it turns out to be another entirely. The rancher runs a tight ship, I'll give him that. But I just don't think I'm cut out to be his foreman. I'm not sure I could treat the men who worked for me like that."

"Like what?" I asked.

"Well, he's pretty strict with them and doesn't trust them at all. I'm used to the trust and respect we had in the army in the war. I don't think I could oversee men like this guy wants me to."

I nodded. "Things are different here, that's for sure."

At that moment, Marshal Figgins walked in and seated himself at his table. Jeb followed my line of vision, and together we watched as Penny Philpot emerged from the kitchen, took his order, and left his table.

"I've heard a thing or two about that marshal," Jeb said softly. "He avoided the draft and rode with Quantrill's Raiders. Even those bastards kicked him out because he was too cruel."

I whistled quietly through my teeth. Quantrill's Raiders were bad news. If they'd kicked Figgins out, he was even worse than I thought. And I didn't think that was possible.

Jeb leaned in toward me. "So what are you really doing here Rio?"

I couldn't tell him, even if I wanted to…which I did. Bombay code forbids it. And that was too bad because Jeb would've been useful in this situation.

"I'm just trying to fulfill a little fantasy, Jeb. That's all. And it seems I've stirred up the marshal's interest."

Jeb nodded. "And the marshal sent a welcoming party." If Jeb knew the truth, he didn't let on. "Maybe this isn't the kind of town I'd like to live in."

"And that's too bad," I replied, watching Penny bring the marshal his lunch. "I kind of liked the scenery."

Jeb insisted on spending the afternoon with me. He seemed protective, and I understood that. An idea was slowly forming in my head, and I thought I could involve Jeb without actually involving him.

We went back to the saloon and found a table in a corner. That was perfect because it seemed appropriate to me that the mysterious stranger (aka me) in town would sum up the saloon from his quiet corner. I think Jeb was onto me, but he said nothing. He was going to let me have my fun, and that made me a bit sad.

Bombays were allowed to have friends, as long as they weren't involved in the family business. As a result, many of us were loners or just stuck to family for our close friends. I had a few of those…a female cousin who lived in Atlanta and another cousin in Florida, but that was about it. Being a Bombay was a lonely business.

Jeb and I talked about the war, reminiscing about the men we'd known. It was a different time then. I'd always felt like I'd gotten away with something when I'd signed up to fight. Bombays weren't supposed to take sides. We weren't supposed to kill people unless it was for money.

The Bombay Council had urged me to do what others have done in this situation—pay someone of a lower class to fight in my stead. I couldn't do that. The very idea of sending someone else to die in my spot was repulsive to me. So, I convinced the Council that my fighting could be useful to the Bombays. In fact, I carried out a number of contracts during the war under the cover of being a soldier. It worked out in the end for them, and I'd done my part for my country. Everyone won.

I was thinking about all of this when a knife whizzed past my ear, embedding itself in the wall just inches from my head.

"Over there," Jeb said in a second as he pulled out his gun and rose to his feet.

I joined him with my gun in my hand (and was a little excited about this) when I noticed a scrawny man standing not a few feet away, actually shaking in his boots—something I always assumed was just a saying.

"Oh!" he pleaded. "Sorry, mister! That was an accident! I swear!"

Accident my ass, I thought. "See that it doesn't happen again, or you'll find enough holes in yourself that your mama could use you to strain beans," I snarled as I holstered my gun and sat down. Okay, maybe that wasn't the best turn of phrase, but I think he got the point.

Jeb did the same. "You know that was no accident."

I nodded. "No, that was too good a throw." I had to work a little to pull the knife free of the timber. "It was in deep, about two inches. You don't throw that hard unless you mean to kill a man." I liked the way I'd said, *kill a man*. It seemed so authentic.

Jeb rubbed his jaw and said, "So you have a new enemy in town."

"Marshal Figgins." I nodded. "Apparently, it doesn't take much to make him nervous."

"So," Jeb nodded toward the knife in my hands. "What are you going to do about it?" He looked kind of excited. There was an adrenaline rush men who'd seen combat experienced at the first sign of a fight. I could see how Jeb wouldn't enjoy being a foreman on a ranch.

"I'm going to wait," I responded, "and see what happens next."

It didn't take long. As we walked out of the saloon, a man rushed me. I stepped to the side and then kicked him off the boardwalk and into the street. My assailant jumped up and ran off.

In front of the bank, another man came out of the alley and tried to grab me from behind. Jeb knocked him unconscious and dragged his body back into the alley. In fact, the two of us found ourselves literally fighting our way back to our hotel. No less than five men tried to accost us, and all five ended up face down in the street.

"That was fun!" Jeb said, rubbing his knuckles once we'd made it inside the hotel. Prudence narrowed her eyes at us from behind the counter and called us over.

"You have a letter," she said curtly, frowning as though she disapproved of me receiving mail. She handed me an unmarked, sealed envelope, then gave us a look that told us to leave the counter.

The restaurant was set for tea, so Jeb and I went in there. It was mostly empty, so we took a table as far from others as we could manage. Penny brought us two tea cups and saucers and a tiered tray with sandwiches and scones. While this didn't seem very cowboy-like, we were hungry from beating up so many men. Jeb and I devoured the food.

"Are you going to open that?" Jeb said as he wiped the last of the crumbs from his lap.

I held the envelope up to the light. There wasn't any paper inside…just some sort of powdery substance.

"I don't think so," I said as I folded the envelope and tucked it into my jacket. "It's got poisoned powder inside."

Jeb choked on his tea. "Poison? You really are popular! Just what kind of questions have you been asking?"

I filled him in on my morning—making it look like I'd just been enquiring around town—which is what I'd hoped it looked like to the townspeople. Unfortunately, some of those folks had been quick to talk, and Marshall Figgins was turning out to be the most paranoid man of all time.

Jeb sat back in his chair. "Well, it seems like things are escalating rather quickly. By nightfall they'll just be shooting directly at us."

"Why don't you just leave?" a soft voice said behind me. Miss Penny Philpot stepped into view.

"Oh!" I said, looking around to see that the restaurant was now empty. "Sorry! I didn't realize how long we'd been here."

To my complete amazement, she sat down at our table. "No, that's not what I meant," Penny said. "Why don't you just leave town?"

"Because I just got here," I answered, settling back into my chair. "And I don't like being attacked for no reason." I left out the part where I thought I wouldn't be a very good cowboy if I cut and run at the slightest bit of trouble. I didn't think she'd appreciate that.

She looked at me curiously. "You've beat up half the town this afternoon. I wouldn't want to see anyone else get hurt."

I wondered if that included me.

"Not my fault," I insisted. "Why do you care about the thugs who would attack an innocent stranger?"

Penny sighed. "They aren't that bad, just stupid. The men who live here are more afraid of Marshal Figgins than they are of you. It's tomorrow you need to worry about."

"Why's that?" Jeb asked. He seemed a little too interested.

"Because that's when the marshal's old gang gets here," Penny said simply, adding nothing useful to that information.

"So why are you here?" I asked. "If Marshal Figgins is such a bully who can call in professional goons to threaten a traveler, why are you still living here?" It was a fair question that also allowed me to find out more about this lovely woman.

Penny looked tired all of the sudden. She looked down at her hands before looking at me. "I came here to teach, Mr.

Bombay. I was a war widow. After my husband and father died, I brought my brother out here to find work as a school teacher."

A school marm! A real-live school marm! This couldn't get any better!

"So why aren't you teaching, Miss Philpot?" Jeb asked, and that's when it occurred to me he was right. We'd seen her at breakfast, lunch, tea, and dinner. Clearly she wasn't in a charming, one-room schoolhouse out on the prairie.

"Because there aren't enough children here," was Penny's reply. "As soon as families move here and realize how dangerous this town is, they leave. There's only my little brother and his cousin. Marshal Figgins forced the town council to quit paying my wages, saying it was a waste of money." She looked angry.

"Why would he do that?" Jeb asked. "Seems to me you can't have growth in a town if you don't have a school. You need families to live here so you have a solid, second generation of citizens."

Penny looked around before answering. I wondered if she was even allowed to sit with us. I didn't want her to lose her job over me.

"Because a school teacher can't be a married woman. There are state regulations about that." There was a fury in her blue eyes that I found almost arousing.

I finished her thought, "And the marshal wants you to marry him."

She nodded, a little shaken that I'd figured that out.

"Gossip goes both ways, Miss Philpot," I said.

Penny stood and smoothed her apron. "I think you should consider leaving tonight, Mr. Bombay." She hurried off before I could press her to see if she was concerned about me.

"Well." Jeb stretched, flexing his fingers in front of him. "I think I'd better take a nap before dinner so I'll be ready for all that hand-to-hand combat that follows you around this place."

I nodded and stood. "Yes, me too. I'll come to your room, and we can walk down here to dinner together."

Jeb saw me to my room with a wink and a stifled laugh. I closed the door and lay down on my bed to think. There was a lot to think about. I tried to focus on the job at hand first, but Penny Philpot kept filling my head.

I felt sorry for her. She wouldn't have liked that, but I did. I'd lost many good men in the war, some of whom had families. Was she one of them? I tried to remember if any of my troops had mentioned a redheaded goddess.

It didn't really matter. A war widow deserved respect regardless. She'd been very brave to uproot all that she knew to come out West and work to support her brother. In fact, it made me feel a little small. Penny came here because she had to. I came here to play cowboy like a spoiled, little kid.

And then Marshal Figgins tried to control her future, whether she liked it or not. You couldn't do that to a Bombay. We were a very wealthy family from very old money. How out of touch was I that it never occurred to me my men's widows were now on their own to raise their families and support them? I felt instant shame over this. I would definitely have to do something about that.

Mother was always involved in charities. I would set up a foundation and have her run it. She'd love that. In spite of her love of society, my mother was very supportive of women's issues.

Marshal Figgins was going to die. I'd make sure of that. What kind of a man bankrupts a school teacher so that he can force her to marry him? He was a very bad man, and I needed to kill him. After all, he was already trying to kill me. It was only fair.

Penny was right—the men he'd been sending after me all day weren't up to snuff. But tomorrow…tomorrow he was bringing in reinforcements. It was interesting that I'd only been in town twenty-four hours and, after simply asking a few questions around town, found myself the target of this man. I could take care of myself, but how many other innocent men had been murdered to temper his incredible paranoia?

I could use that. Figgins' fear of strangers could be exploited to my advantage. *AND*, I could have the showdown at high noon I'd always wanted—which made me very happy. It wouldn't look like a contract killing at all—just a duel, instigated by a mysterious, world-weary traveler who'd had enough of Marshal Figgins. It was perfect.

But the problem was that Figgins was a cheater. He'd most certainly set up these men coming in tomorrow to ambush me once I'd won—which of course, I would. My record with a pistol was flawless, and he didn't know that. Figgins was known for using others to do his dirty work, which told me he wasn't that accurate with a gun. Or worse, they'd try to kill me before I fired. That would suck.

So how to deal with these other men? That was the real problem.

There was a knock at the door, and Jeb asked if I wanted supper. I grabbed my jacket, and together we made our way down to the dining room.

Penny was busy, since every table was full. Every now and then, though, I was rewarded as she caught my eye and smiled. I smiled back when I could, and then I noticed that someone in the room was not smiling. In fact, he was staring at me with a fury I could not mistake.

Marshal Figgins was sitting at his reserved table. And he'd noticed my attention to Miss Philpot. He also noticed her smiling at me. I stared back, practicing my menacing cowboy squint. *It begins*, I thought.

"You really must like trouble," Jeb said quietly as he watched me.

I nodded. It would be wrong to deny it. The marshal's jealousy did speed things up a bit. Maybe we could get this duel out of the way tonight, before his reinforcements arrived. I was just as good a shot in the dark as I was in broad daylight.

The problem with that idea was that I hadn't done anything for him to try to arrest me. And he hadn't done anything for me to challenge him to a gunfight. Sigh. Why did everything have to be so difficult?

"Up for a drink?" I asked Jeb.

He nodded. "Wouldn't miss it for the world." He cracked his knuckles as we paid the bill. No one was waiting for us outside this time. That was somewhat disappointing. I liked a little action before a showdown. I think Jeb wanted something to happen too. Instead, we made our way to the saloon unscathed.

We'd just sat down at a table with our whiskey when Rocco, Axel, and Hank came in and joined us. I made my introductions all around, and Jeb seemed to fit in nicely. It was only a matter of minutes before the cards came out.

Rocco dealt the cards as Hank leaned forward. "Word on the street is you got yerself mixed up with the marshal, Rio."

"Yup," I said as I rearranged my cards. "I don't think he likes me much."

Jeb hid a grin behind his cards but said nothing.

Axel shook his head. "Well nice knowin' ya."

Rocco kicked him under the table loudly enough for me to hear. "Just play yer damn cards, Axel."

There was something going on here. I waited for the next hand before speaking.

"I hear Figgins has men comin' in tomorrow. That can't be all for me..." I feigned innocence, and the men laughed.

"He's got some business at the border, I heared," Rocco said solemnly. "But I wouldn't put it past him to try and kick yer ass a'fore they leave town."

Hank and Axel nodded. This seemed to be a done deal. Take out the mysterious stranger—which is me—first, and then ride out of town.

"When are they leaving?" Jeb asked.

"Afternoon," Hank said. "But they'll try and teach you a lesson first." He nodded at me.

"They'll *try*," I said. "Does Figgins always go after visitors this way?"

All three men nodded and then looked back at their cards. Jeb wisely lost a couple of hands before slowly building a winning streak. They seemed a little put out about that. I folded and made the excuse to approach the bar for another round of drinks.

Mutton Chops, the bartender, eyed me warily as he poured out five whiskeys. He was avoiding my eyes so successfully, I decided to talk to him.

"Somethin' wrong?" I asked gruffly.

He set down the bottle and looked at me. "I just think I'm looking at a dead man, friend." I had to admit...I liked how he said that. It seemed so authentic.

"So you know how it's gonna go down, then," I said, instead of asking. The bartender nodded but offered no information.

"Fine," I said as I carried all five shot glasses back to the table. *Fine.*

The game ended after a few more rounds, and we chatted about the weather and other useless things. The bar was emptying out, and I wondered why. It was early yet in the evening. Something was happening.

I had my answer soon enough. Marshal Beau Figgins strode through the swinging doors and went straight up to the bar, demanding whiskey. Mutton Chops glared at me as the marshal swallowed the shot and demanded another. I did nothing.

Jeb sat back in his chair, relaxed but with his hand near his pistol. The three at our table began nudging each other nervously.

Figgins swallowed his second shot, then came over to our table and loomed over us.

"Rocco," Figgins acknowledged. "Hank, Axel. Who are your new friends?" His voice was very deep. It was the perfect cowboy voice. Too bad it was wasted on a slime ball like the marshal.

Rocco stuck out his chin, defiantly. "This here's Rio and Jeb, Marshal." I had to give him credit. Rocco didn't know me from Adam. He could've saved his own hide and just handed us over. But he didn't. He stood up to Figgins a little. Not much, but a little. I liked that.

"Rio Bombay and Jebediah Smith," I said with a tip of my hat. "And you're Marshal Beauregarde Figgins…The Scourge of Texas."

The marshal laughed. It was a long, slow, menacing laugh that made Rocco and his friends jump to their feet and flee the bar. Figgins slid out Rocco's chair and sat down in it.

"Why are you in town, Rio Bombay and Jebediah Smith? Maybe it's time you left." Figgins fixed me with a stare that summed up his entire career of cruelty. I returned his stare with my cowboy squint. Jeb just looked amused.

I answered him. "This seems like a real nice town to settle down in. Maybe meet a woman and start a family." I didn't need to say more. The way his eyes widened and his nostrils flared told me he knew I was talking about Miss Penny Philpot. I'd struck a nerve. Just as I'd wanted.

Jeb didn't answer—he knew the question wasn't really directed toward him. He just waited to see what would happen, his hand never moving far from his holstered gun.

"Well," the marshal said as he regained his composure. "You wouldn't like this town. There aren't many available women."

"What about that lovely redhead at the hotel?" I asked as casually as I could. "She seems unattached."

I could see the steel forming in Figgins' eyes. He was very angry now. And angry men did stupid things. That's what I was counting on.

"You stay away from Miss Philpot, boy," Figgins spat. "And you think long and hard about getting out of town by morning."

I put on my best innocent expression. "Why, Marshal? I haven't done anything to warrant this kind of hostility." I thought I heard Jeb's throat tighten as he suppressed a smile.

The marshal stood and very, very slowly and loudly, slid his chair in to the table.

"Maybe I'll see you tomorrow then?" he said tightly.

"Tell you what," I answered back. "Let's make it high noon. On Main Street."

An oily grin crossed the man's features. He relaxed a little and nodded. "Sounds good."

I watched as he walked out of the saloon and then rose to my feet. Jeb joined me.

"Well, I guess no one will give us any trouble tonight." Jeb sighed.

"Nope," was all I said as we made our way back to the hotel.

Penny sat down at our table at breakfast and begged me to leave town immediately. While I was happy for her concern for my wellbeing, I told her this was something I had to do. Jeb and I discussed some thoughts about the upcoming gunfight before he left me at the door to my room.

I spent the next couple of hours mentally preparing for the fight. The whole town knew what was about to happen. I could hear people talking beneath my window all morning. I cleaned my gun and double-checked my ammunition. Everything was in working order. Now I just had to wait.

Penny Philpot took up most of my thoughts. She was a unique woman. One I hadn't experienced before in the cultured salons and tailored lawns of Newport. Penny was beautiful, resourceful, courageous, and smart. And I had fallen for her.

I had no idea if she felt the same way about me. I'd like to think she did. That she'd pack up her little brother and run off with me after the showdown. But I wasn't sure. This was a woman who'd already lost one man. It was highly likely she wouldn't want to put herself through that again.

I needed to drop this line of thinking and focus on the upcoming fight. After all, I was here to play cowboy and do a job for the Bombays.

And what would I do with Penny and Percy Philpot anyway? I couldn't just ride back into Newport with a frontier bride and her little brother. I couldn't stay here either, after killing the town's marshal.

A knock at the door brought my thoughts back to the task at hand.

"It's time," Jeb's voice said through the door.

I rose to my feet, put on my new silver spurs, gun belt, and hat, and left my room for the street below.

The sun was blazing above us as Marshal Figgins and I squared off at opposite ends of the street. I was a bit disappointed that he wasn't wearing spurs. He was supposed to wear jingling spurs! If he lived, I'd have to show him the novels in my saddlebag. But then that was silly, because he wasn't going to live.

We were only about fifty paces apart, and I could see the hatred burning in his eyes. We were really going to do this. I tried to look menacing, but in all honesty I was very happy. A real cowboy gunfight at high noon! I'd be a legend back home.

Well, okay, so my mother and sister would most likely roll their eyes, but still…

I looked around and spotted Penny and Percy standing on the boardwalk outside the hotel. Her face was impassive, but she held her little brother tightly against her. Jeb was nowhere to be seen, as expected. He had other work to do.

"When the clock strikes noon, we draw and shoot," Figgins shouted, pointing at an enormous clock on the bank.

I nodded, suppressing my glee—this was so exciting! We had fifteen seconds to go. The clock's second hand seemed to tick so loudly I felt it in my blood. Ten seconds to go…seven…six…five…four…

The marshal's eyes narrowed, and I realized he was going to shoot early. Once a cheater…

Three…two…

A bullet whizzed by me, nearly taking my hat off. I whirled to my right and took out two gunmen who were poised to shoot from the alley. I had four shots left. A rifle cracked behind me twice, and I looked up to see Jeb smiling at me from the top of the hotel. Two more men with guns in their hands fell forward from the next alley on my right.

I heard the click of a pistol's hammer on my left, and I turned and shot one more man who was coming at me from the hotel. Another rifle crack, and one more man at the end of the street fell.

"Don't move, asshole." I couldn't believe I'd fallen for the distraction—this is a huge Bombay no-no. While I was being shot at (and early, mind you—cheater!) Marshal Figgins had grabbed Penny Philpot from behind and put a gun to her head. I steadied my pistol, but it was difficult to get a clean shot. Penny stood still as the marshal hid behind her, the coward. Percy looked up at his sister in fear.

"I'll blow her brains out! I will!" the marshal snarled. I looked up at Jeb, but it was clear he couldn't get a good shot either.

"Let her go!" I shouted. "This is between you and me!" It figured he'd hide behind the woman he'd wanted for so long. The tired, old, *If-I-Can't-Have-Her-No-One-Can* story. There was no style there, just brute idiocy.

"Drop yer guns!" He motioned with his pistol at Jeb. "Both of them!"

I dropped my gun and nodded to Jeb, who laid his down and held his hands up. My mind began working through alternate plans, but the bastard didn't let Penny go. A real fear started to fill me. This wasn't fun anymore. I couldn't let him kill Penny. But what to do next?

I was just thinking about that when Percy screamed, "NORBERT!"

What? He knew the name of my horse? How embarrassing.

A loud whinny filled the air, and Norbert thundered around the corner. Everyone watched as my horse rose up on two legs and started walking on them! He turned around in a complete circle on only two legs. I was hypnotized and a little mortified. Everyone else was stunned. No one could take their eyes off my horse.

Everyone, except for Percy, who brought his heel down hard on the marshal's instep, before shoving Penny aside and going right for the Figgin's groin. Percy's foot connected, and the marshal dropped like a sack of flour.

"You little bastard!" Figgins howled as he pulled his gun and aimed it at Percy.

I fired. The bullet went clean through his forehead, dead center. As his body hit the ground, I ran to Penny, and she fell into my arms.

"Are you hurt? Are you okay?" I said over and over until she assured me she was fine. Percy danced around us in the street, and Norbert went back to being his usual, boring self. I ignored the few whispers of, *"Norbert? Really?"* and just continued holding Penny. It was over. It was all over.

Penny, Percy, and I left town a few days later. I'd decided Texas wasn't really the place for us and thought maybe we could settle in Denver. Penny agreed to marry me, and I adopted Percy as my own. Norbert acted like nothing ever happened.

We built a large house in a nice neighborhood of Denver. Penny started a school, and Percy attended. Mother started that foundation for war widows and orphans. She hired widows of men from my old unit to run the foundation. I liked that.

Jebediah Smith was named the next marshal of Felony, Texas. And since Figgins was dead and had no kin, the town gave Jeb the marshal's big house.

I gave Jeb my stack of western novels. I didn't need them anymore, and he had a lot to learn about how things were supposed to be done in the West. Funny how he never thanked me for that.

With his new job and house and future, I was happy that Jeb had finally found his calling.

And in Miss Penny Philpot and her brother Percy, I'd found mine.

Caspian Bombay
Rome—44 A.D.

He'd really done it this time. Gaul Bombay had gone rogue. And I had to hunt him down and kill him. And he was my brother. Scratch that. My *idiot* brother.

I stood before the Elders, itchy in my new wool toga. While I love a new toga as much as the next girl, I took little pleasure in this one now. What was going on? No one had ever gotten another Bombay as an assignment before. This was unreal. Or rather, it *was* real, and as Gaul's sister, I'd have to deal with it.

"There's no point in arguing with us, Caspian," my grandmother intoned from the dais. Tall and thin with a long nose, I always thought she looked a bit like a regal stork of sorts. Well, one who wore too much makeup and had the power to decide who lives or dies, that is.

"We've made up our mind and cannot be moved." That was the truth. No one argued with my grandmother. She was notorious for cutting you down and making you feel like an infant. But that never stopped me before. I was a bit of an idiot myself.

I stared at the parchment in my hand. "But we've never killed one of our own before!" I protested. The Bombays were an ancient family—we'd been around *forever*. You couldn't just make up new rules after all these centuries of tradition, right?

Grandmother shook her head. "I know that. But we cannot have your brother going around killing people who aren't on their assignment list. The poet Cinna was the third and last straw. We have no choice."

The other Elders nodded in agreement. There would be no more discussion, mainly because I believed they were all a little afraid of Grandmother too. In frustration, I stuffed the parchment into my toga and left.

Back at home, Father turned the document over in his hands, as if it didn't really exist. I couldn't blame him. It was quite a shock. Technically, Bombays aren't supposed to tell other family members who their targets are—it made *plausible deniability* a bit easier. But this was new, so I decided there wasn't precedence for it. Of course, the Council might just decide to hunt me down too, but that was a risk I was willing to take.

"But why?" he said as he held it up to me, as if I hadn't gone over it again and again with him.

"He's an example," I said quietly. "This is a new rule, starting now. If any Bombay runs renegade and starts killing people outside the Council's orders, the penalty is death."

In a weird way, part of me totally got that. The Bombays hadn't gotten as far as we had in this business by straying from the assignments. Gaul was an ass who always did what he wanted. And recently he'd killed whomever he wanted. He thought being an assassin allowed him to kill with impunity— but he knew the rules didn't run that way. And now, they were making up new rules because of him.

He was like that as a child with small animals. Our parents never knew what to do with him. They maintained his training and hoped it would make him a good assassin. It did, I suppose, if your victims are starlings or fish.

Father dropped into a chair and buried his face in his hands. Of course he was upset. His only daughter had to kill his only son. But he was a Bombay. I was certain his feelings were at war with logic here. Thank the gods Mother was dead. I don't think she could've handled it.

Not that she ever handled it well. Marrying into the Bombays was not easy. You had to agree to raise your children to be paid killers. Still, there were benefits. We were very wealthy, and Mother'd had a serious sandal habit.

But you never had to worry about money or security when you were married to a Bombay. Bombays were politically connected and protected. Still, Mother'd always had a fragile mind—the wrong flowers in a vase would set her off, and there was that one time when a lizard looked at her funny. We'd had to replace half the staff that day when all was said and done. When the fever took her a few years ago, I suspect we were all a little relieved in a sad way.

"I should talk to them..." Father said quietly.

I shook my head. "I tried. Your own mother gave the orders. Their minds are set."

I waited for him to collect his thoughts. Who could blame him? No Bombay had ever dealt with something like this before. Well, okay, there was that one time, a century ago, when Mykonos Bombay went a little berserk and killed a bunch of politicians using nothing but a pair of pliers—but people were kind of forgiving about that for some reason.

"Father," I said softly, hating the words I knew I had to say. "This has to be done. You know it does. Maybe we've always known it. Gaul has been...difficult...most of his life."

After a few moments, he stood up and nodded. Then he left me. Knowing Father, he'd lose himself in his miniatures hobby. At present, he was recreating the Battle of Troy, complete with a tiny Achilles and blood-soaked Hector. I used to point out that he was stretching history a bit whenever he'd throw in a herd of rabid badgers or giant, carnivorous plants—but that always fell on deaf ears. He'd be in his workshop for days. It was time to prepare.

Gaul hadn't lived with us for over a year. He'd moved out, and we rarely saw him except at holidays (He always turned up for a gift, the bastard.) or family get-togethers—only because they were mandatory. But over the past year, we'd heard about his exploits.

There were men who beat on the door in the middle of the night, demanding we pay for his gambling debts. (And a few who didn't survive the booby traps we had there—it had taken me a week to disable them all.) Common prostitutes would approach us in the market and show us bruises Gaul had given them. (FYI, be careful how you approach a Bombay on the street—that woman had a hard time accepting my apology through a broken nose.) And then, the murders had started.

The first was a criminal—someone we would normally kill on contract anyway. The man had hustled Gaul, cheating him out of his money and a large quantity of wine. (The money was meaningless to Gaul, but I heard it was some really choice wine.) Gaul beat him to death in a public bath house. There were many witnesses. The authorities decided to look the other way. Father had hoped this would be a one-time thing.

It wasn't.

The Elders called us to meet with them after Gaul's second victim—a young peasant girl who had wandered into town and into Gaul's clutches. She was found with her throat slit in our back yard holding one of Gaul's prized diadems. There were no witnesses, and Gaul was actually at the meeting, insisting he was innocent. That's when the doubt began to settle in the Council's mind.

Now, he'd had the poet Cinna murdered by a mob at Caesar's funeral. It had looked like an accident. After all, a totally different man named Cinna was one of the conspirators in Caesar's assassination. But the crowd turned on the wrong guy.

Several people remembered Gaul inciting it, insisting it was the conspirator Cinna and whipping the mourning mob into a murderous frenzy. The poor man was torn apart. Two people said they saw Gaul on the edges, laughing. I'd wondered what he'd had against the poet.

Cinna was a bit of a perverse freak—his poems were about incest between fathers and daughters, but he didn't deserve to die like that. Some of the witnesses swore that Gaul appeared all over the place, disguising his voice each time to make it sound like a lot of people were calling for Cinna's death.

People really are stupid, and it doesn't take much to get them whipped up into a murderous rage. It was, as mentioned, at Caesar's funeral and all, and folks were still a bit touchy about his assassination. It would be irresponsible for me to fail to mention we had nothing to do with Julius Caesar's assassination. A public scene with senators going all stabby? Too stupid for words.

Anyway, after Cinna's death-by-mob, there was nothing else for the Elders to do. They had to set Gaul up. We would lose all credibility if our employers thought we would just kill whomever we wanted. And I was the Bombay assigned to do it. Why? Because Gaul wouldn't see it coming.

I was surprised to discover my feelings were vague on doing this. He was my brother, after all. Shouldn't I be more upset? Then again, he always bullied me—tormented me. And I really believed that he had killed that peasant girl.

Besides, who didn't want to kill off their brother now and then? The only difference was most people saw reason and didn't follow through with it. I, on the other hand, had been ordered by my family to strike the deciding blow.

No, the Council was right. Gaul was a danger and embarrassment to the Bombays. He was an error in the fabric spun by the gods, and he had to be unraveled and corrected. I steeled myself for this job and decided that the less Father knew about it, the better. I made a note to try to find him a bunch of miniature meerkats for his diorama. That might cheer him up.

Later that night, after packing a bag with a few things, I left the house and made my way into the streets of Rome. I slipped quietly through the crowds, unnoticed, working my way toward the red light district. That would be where I'd find my brother. The sooner I got this over with, the faster Father could recover. At least, that's what I'd hoped.

The streets of Rome at this late hour were filled with beggars, prostitutes, politicians, and thieves—all basically the same thing in my opinion. No one wanted to be "seen" here, so no one saw me.

I liked to divide my assignments into small, achievable goals. Unlike other members of my family, I tended to get overwhelmed easily. This was a problem when I was younger, resulting in some very botched assignments. I would like to point out that I completed each and every one of them—the Council, on the other hand, would probably say that I "lacked focus." I don't truly understand that because, regardless of the fact that the target may have ended up in two to four pieces, or maybe died a little bit too publicly, or the poison maybe ended up melting the victim's face off accidentally, there *was* a body in the end, and it was most assuredly dead. Anything else is just nitpicky, really.

It was my father who came up with the idea of piecing out each assignment into smaller, easier to digest chunks. Take it one step at a time…don't think about the next step—just do the first thing on your list. Once that's complete, move on to the next, and so on. *The gladiator in the arena can only kill one lion at a time. So take it lion by lion,* he liked to say. It worked out pretty well for me, and my assignments—now with my new and improved *To Do* lists—worked out easier.

Gaul loved to exploit this weakness of mine. He'd tease and cajole until I was so freaked out I couldn't see straight. Then I'd figured how to deal with Gaul using the same idea. Gaul had a terror of mice. I'd put a live mouse in his bed every night he tormented me. If he didn't stop, the mouse got larger and more vicious until it was a very bitey rat gnawing him awake. See? Lion by lion! Works every time.

I never had to go beyond the rat, and I'm not sure what I would've used if I had…an irritated mongoose with an unfortunate skin rash maybe? Well, it didn't matter anyway because this twenty-four-year-old woman had finally convinced her asshole big brother to leave her the hell alone.

My goal for tonight was to find an inn and bed down. This would be my headquarters from where I would run my surveillances. I kept the picture of a small, quiet room in my head until I found the perfect spot.

The Odalisque Inn was on a side street and catered to a more discreet clientele. Mainly it seemed that these were senators who wanted to conduct business that would upset Mrs. Senator. The rooms were tiny but clean, and the dining room was full of dark, private corners. *Perfect.*

I unpacked my things and lay down on my bed to think. Here was where I'd come up with the next step in my plan—find Gaul. Finding him and killing him outright wasn't totally out of the question. When you're a Bombay, you take every opportunity you can. But opportunity was a fickle mistress, and I'd say that ninety-nine percent of the time planning was called for.

Tomorrow, I'd start figuring out exactly where I was in relation to my brother. By afternoon, I'd start nosing around the kinds of places my brother would frequent. I didn't think I'd find him that soon and factored that into my plan. The key was to accomplish each step until I reached my goal. I really wished we could use papyrus—I'd feel so much better with a large chart I could spread out. Unfortunately, that sort of evidence would be dangerous lying around, and the Bombay Council forbids it. They had a weird distrust of the stuff.

I committed the next step to memory. Satisfied that I was set for the next day, I drifted off to sleep.

I waited until mid-morning to emerge from my room and had a simple yet satisfying breakfast at the inn. I'd disguised myself as a young man, which was fairly easy to do. Roman clothes weren't much different for men and women except in color. My flat chest and, let's face it, dull features made it fairly easy to pull this off. I had a very expensive wig made years ago that allowed me to stuff my hair under it. Unlike other Roman women, I was not blessed with thick hair.

That's right, I was plain. I wasn't a looker like my mother, and I didn't have my father's handsome features. My parents always worried about this (and Gaul was merciless), but I always sort of embraced it. I liked being an assassin. Being average looking made things so much easier. No one could remember my face. I didn't stand out.

Unlike my female cousins, I didn't care about getting married or even having lovers. Okay, so maybe it would be nice to fall in love someday—but I wasn't obsessed with it or anything. I liked who I was, and I liked living at home and looking after Father.

It was still late morning when I slipped out of the inn, keeping to the walls as I worked the streets in a circular movement. The brothels and gambling dens wouldn't be open yet, but I had to get my bearings. Making note of the side streets and alleys that connected to my hotel, I radiated outwards until I'd exhausted the red light district. Gaul wouldn't be awake yet, wherever he was. There was very little chance I'd run into him. Still, I had a small drawing of him to show people, should I need it. It was a good likeness of him. Art was kind of my thing when I wasn't killing people. Even assassins needed hobbies in the down time between jobs.

Once I'd made a map in my mind of the area, I headed back to the inn for food and rest. I had completed step two— figuring out my surroundings—and it gave me a strong sense of satisfaction. But I needed some down time to digest it all. Back in my room, my mind again wandered to the task at hand—killing my brother for my family.

I was getting used to the idea now, and that bothered me a little. No matter how much I scoured my memories, I found it difficult to come up with a reason why Gaul should continue living. To my surprise, I realized now that the Council was right. How long had it taken them to make this decision? As harsh as Grandmother was, I'd like to believe it wasn't an easy choice.

No, Gaul had forced their hand. It was what any other family would be faced with if harboring a murderer. Except that other families could turn the killer in for justice to be done. My family had their own thoughts about how to handle it. We took care of it ourselves.

Would future generations hate me for what I now knew I had to do? I hoped not. The image of my brother killing that poor, helpless girl loomed heavily in my thoughts. Allowing this to go on would only make things worse for all of us. What he'd done was wrong. Monstrous. And I believed I was ready to do my job.

I needed to head out again and figure out where Gaul was staying. I tied my purse onto my belt, stowed the drawing of my brother into my toga, and ventured back out.

The trick to making inquiries is to make the person you ask forget what you asked, and that you asked it, immediately after. This was not easy to do. Money helped loosen lips, but it also made you memorable. Show too much money, and it made you a memorable target. Too little, and word spread that you didn't know what you were doing. It was a seemingly impossible task but one we were trained for. I liked these "invisibility" lessons as a child. It didn't work on a group of Bombays, but, on any street in Rome, I could ask directions and make you forget you'd even given them to me.

I had to get back to work. Time was on my side. Gaul didn't know about the order against him and likely wouldn't find out for a bit. So my next goal was to figure out where he might stay and the places he would most likely be.

I started with the brothels, hoping I could recognize the women who'd accosted my father and me in the streets, complaining of abuse by Gaul.

"Hey boy!" a woman with brashly bleached blonde hair called to me. I nodded and slouched over to her.

"Looking for some company kid?" Up close, the woman was slathered with garish makeup in order to cover a seriously ugly face. I wondered if that worked for her.

I shook my head. "No ma'am. I'm looking for someone. I have a message for him from a senator."

That gave the woman pause, and she nodded. The word "senator"' meant "be discreet and forget I said this." I shoved my drawing of Gaul toward her trying to emulate a clumsy youth.

The woman shrank back. "Oh. HIM," she said with an ugly sneer. "I don't do anything for him. He's a nasty one. Try the gambling house." She pointed out the way and shrank back from me with a shudder. Another victim of Gaul. The prostitute would try to forget me like a bad memory as soon as I left. *Good.*

I headed toward the gambling house. The shadows of the afternoon were lengthening against the white, marble pillars. Gaul would be on the prowl soon. I needed to spot him from a distance. He'd certainly recognize me. And that I couldn't have.

No matter what happened, I couldn't forget that Gaul had had the same training as I did. He'd notice someone following him. That was how we were taught. He may be fearless, but he wasn't stupid. Most of our victims had no idea a contract had even been taken out on them until we snuck up behind them and bashed them over the head. This time, the prey I was hunting was more aware than usual. I'd have to be very careful.

The gambling den was in an open building, and I circled it before entering. There were several exits, of course. People would want to have a number of escape routes should they be caught in the act by parents, spouses, or someone they owed money to.

I was wary. The job wouldn't be this easy. It would be unusual if Gaul were actually inside. Bombays didn't rely on coincidence or serendipity. In fact, we didn't trust those things because most of the time, they'll kill you. I waited a few moments and entered.

Noise assaulted me as I moved inside—people shouting insults, placing bets, making bawdy jokes. Cruel remarks aimed at me and anyone else bounced around the atmosphere. It was a cold and unforgiving place. *Perfect.*

I skirted the walls, trying to get my bearings. So this was what people did when they wanted to throw away their money. Red-faced men full of wine argued with each other as cheaply made up prostitutes plied their trade. I didn't see Gaul on my first pass, and that was okay. I wasn't really prepared to do anything. I had no knife or other weapons, but killing him here would be fairly easy. Tempers flared all around me as people lost their money and their heads.

I was just getting ready to leave when I heard shouting coming from a small room I hadn't noticed before. I crept to the doorway and peered inside.

There were only two men in the room. A short, portly man in purple senatorial robes, and the man who was beating the crap out of him...my brother, Gaul Bombay.

"I don't have your money!" the fat man gasped between blows to his head. He was in pretty bad shape. A couple of more punches might kill him.

Gaul sneered, "Then I'll kill you, old man!" He pulled back his arm, and I saw the trajectory of his blow. Gaul was going for a kill shot to the throat. Without thinking, I grabbed his arm and yanked him out of the room.

My brother spun on me with a furious look. It took a few seconds for him to realize who I was. Then someone down the hall began screaming, and I knew it was time to go.

"This way!" He roughly grabbed my arm and dragged me out a side exit and into the street. We didn't stop running until we came to a narrow, dead-end alley with a nondescript door. Gaul opened the door and pushed me inside.

"What are you doing here, Cas?" His voice was filled with naked hostility. Anyone who didn't know him would be terrified. And, years ago, that would've included me.

"Piss off, Gaul!" I shrugged loose of his grip. "What the hell were you doing back there? You were going to kill that man. He's a senator! What's wrong with you?"

Gaul narrowed his eyes at me, sizing me up. He said nothing as he went to a cupboard and pulled out a bottle of wine. He poured a glass for himself and drained it quickly. I looked around and realized that he lived here. There were few items that Gaul was never without—his lucky chisel (Don't ask.) and a bronze cup he'd had since he was a child. These were sitting on a shelf not far from me. I also noticed that he'd pilfered one of Father's miniature badgers and had decapitated it.

Other than that, the apartment was small but clean. Why did he live here, off this anonymous little alley? He had enough money to buy a villa.

"That," Gaul finally said during the break that it took to pour himself another glass of wine, "is none of your business. What I want to know is why you're here in the first place."

I rolled my eyes. "Well clearly," I said pointing at the single glass of wine, "it isn't for your hospitality."

"Is it Father?" Gaul's eyes flashed with anger and then went cold. He asked, almost bored, "Is he dead?"

I felt my anger swelling. He was such a bastard. If Father was dead, he clearly didn't care about it.

"No," I said evenly, "Father isn't dead. Not that you care about us."

Gaul shrugged. "I just thought maybe there'd be an inheritance or something."

That's when it hit me. The small, hidden apartment. Beating a man to death (well, trying to) over money. Gaul was broke. And he was hiding out from the law. It was inconceivable to me that he had burned through all of his funds. Maybe the Council had cut him off?

"You're broke," I said as a statement of fact. "You've gambled and whored away all of your money. That's why you live here."

His eyes flickered with mild surprise. "Why yes. You've figured it out. I have nothing."

He continued to pour himself more wine, ignoring the fact that I was something of a guest. "The fucking Council has cut me off. Those bastards. I really should kill them all."

I froze to the spot. I looked into his dead eyes, eyes that had always frightened me and worried my parents, and realized he just might do it. Gaul said it casually, but in my heart at that moment, I knew. Gaul was thinking about wiping out the Council.

"You wouldn't!" I said, wishing I hadn't. Of course he would. Why did I even say that?

My brother nodded. "I've thought about it. No one would miss those dried up prunes anyway."

I could kill him now, I thought. No one would be able to trace it back to me. The Council would be pleased. His body wouldn't be found for days. Gaul had so many enemies, the authorities wouldn't even try hard to solve the case.

"Maybe you'd want in on that action?" Gaul was grinning evilly at me. "Maybe you'd want to be the one who plunges the knife into Grandmother's heart? She's never been that nice to either one of us."

He was baiting me, and I tried not to let revulsion show on my face. Gaul wasn't just tormenting me like he did when we were kids. He was trying to decipher my loyalties with a dangerous trap. If I reacted negatively, he would probably try to kill me and take whatever money I had. If I responded positively, chances were he wouldn't buy it.

Gaul was on his guard here. Trying to take him out right now would be almost impossible. It would be two Bombays fighting against each other—two Bombays who had trained side-by-side and knew each other's strengths and weaknesses. I'd walked into a trap.

The only advantage I had was that Gaul didn't know about my assignment. The disadvantage was that now I knew, beyond a shadow of a doubt, that my brother would not hesitate to kill me or any of us for his own gain.

"I'm leaving." I shrugged—trying to re-create my nonchalant actions when he'd annoyed me in the past. The trouble was, I was shaking. "You're a dick, and I'm gone."

It took everything I had to turn my back to him and walk calmly to the door. My senses were heightened to the highest level of awareness. Somehow, I made myself put one foot in front of the other until I was out the door and out of the alley. Then, I ran.

Back in my room at the inn, I paced the floor, shaking with rage and fear. Why hadn't Gaul attacked me? He'd practically laid out a plan to kill the Council, and I'd rejected it. Didn't he know I was dangerous?

Hmmm…maybe not. Gaul's arrogance had always seen me as his useless little sister. Maybe that was why I'd been able to leave? If that was the case, could I exploit that to my advantage?

And what about the Council? I needed to warn them. They'd be angry that I hadn't finished him off on the spot. But then, they weren't there. If they'd seen his eyes…

I needed to calm down. And I needed a plan that would be more than just one step…

"Father?" I shouted once I crossed the threshold to the house. There was no answer. I ran through the home, checking every room. Nothing. My heart was pounding. If my brother so much as touched a hair on our father's head, I'd kill him with my bare hands.

"Caspian?" Father emerged from the courtyard, looking bewildered. "Where have you been? I've been worried!"

I hugged him and made sure he was all in one piece. "I had to run out. One of my friends was having some trouble. It's sorted."

Father nodded absently and then said, "Well it's all right now! Come out to the garden—we have a guest!"

I sighed. Company was the last thing we needed right now. I needed to get Father to leave the house for a while until I took care of Gaul. Maybe I could talk him into a little trip—leaving immediately. There were rumors of a zoo in Carthage. I could tell him they have some weird new animal he could introduce into his dioramas and offer to help him pack. Hell, I could make up an animal, and by the time he got there and realized I lied, this whole mess with Gaul would be over. I started to sketch out a creature in my mind as we walked. Something that could spit poison perhaps. He'd like that.

As we walked to the terrace, I tried to come up with excuses for why this guest should leave so I could send Father away. I was working on a doozy of an excuse where malaria was making the neighborhood rounds when I came face to face with my brother. Gaul was standing in the garden, an evil grin on his face.

Father smiled. "It's going to be okay, Cas. I told Gaul about the misunderstanding with the Council. He's going to straighten things out."

My heart stopped beating. Father told Gaul about the Council's edict? Did he tell him I was the one who was supposed to carry it out? This was worse than anything I could've imagined.

"What?" I asked Father. "You told him what?"

He nodded. "We don't have to worry about it anymore. Gaul has assured me that he will explain everything, and things will go back to the way they were. Isn't that wonderful?"

I'd misjudged my father's mental stability. The man had snapped. And now, he'd helped Gaul move forward with his idea of killing the Council.

This was all my fault. I shouldn't have told him about the assignment. Bombays had rules for a reason, and now I understood why we didn't tell other Bombays about our assignments. And that reason was staring at me with murder hiding behind his placating eyes. It was all an act. A deadly and evil act.

"So, Caspian," Gaul said nonchalantly. "I guess you had come to warn me, then? That's why you came to find me?"

He said those words, but I knew he didn't believe them. And I realized that now my Father and I were also on Gaul's kill list.

My brother walked over and casually draped his arm around me with a big smile. I shrugged it off. Who was he trying to fool? We weren't one big happy family. In fact, very soon, I was going to try to reduce us to a family of two. If I could.

"There's a Council meeting in a few minutes," Gaul said. "Cas and I will just go over there and settle things."

Oh crap. It was the first night of the week. This was the night the Council met to review business. Of course they'd all be there…Grandmother, Athens, Asia, and Syria. Granted, all four were accomplished assassins, but all four were also very old…nearly fifty years in age!

There was no way to warn them. I'd have to figure something out along the way. Which meant I'd have to wing it. Which was something I didn't do well.

Gaul clamped my hand in his and squeezed painfully. "We'll go together, dear sister. I don't want you wandering off, now, do I?" He dragged me out of the house before I could respond. I'd have to think faster than that if I wanted to make it through this alive…with Gaul dead.

"You know, Cas," Gaul said casually as he dragged me down the street. "I really have to thank you for this opportunity. You're giving me the chance to end the Bombay Family once and for all. You deserve some of the credit, I think."

I said nothing because I was thinking furiously, trying to come up with a plan. And unless I did so, I'd be dead too. But my brain was muddled. I had trouble putting thoughts together. I felt that old panic creeping up my spine.

It took us exactly ten minutes to reach the Council chambers. Julian, Grandmother's right hand slave, admitted us with no problem. I didn't try to warn him because he was unarmed, and Gaul would've surely killed him. I liked Julian— and he didn't deserve to die like this.

"Caspian?" Grandmother rose from the dais when she saw me. The sight of Gaul didn't cause so much as a flicker on her face. "What's this?"

Gaul shoved me roughly aside, and then gave a deep bow of deference. "Grandmother," he said, "you're looking well."

Grandmother narrowed her eyes. The rest of the Council stood there, wondering what was going to happen next.

"Thank you, Gaul. I just had my hair hennaed. You're looking rather slimy yourself."

I suppressed a snicker. Grandmother wasn't one to pass up a good insult. My humor was short-lived when I remembered that not only was Gaul there to kill them, but I had just demonstrated that I'd failed at my assignment.

Gaul spread his hands and shrugged. "Well we can't all be serpents like you, now can we?"

Grandmother arched her eyebrows at this but said nothing. She turned to me.

"Caspian? Why did you bring your brother here? You had your orders."

Oh great. My grandmother had just outed me. In front of my target.

Gaul's expression was confused for a moment, but he recovered quickly. "Oh. I see. You sent my own sister to kill me." He tut-tutted. "Not very nice. The Bombays have never killed one of their own before."

"Yes, well..." Grandmother said. "You set a rather unfortunate precedence for it. I'm afraid you signed your own death warrant."

Gaul flushed at this, his rage showing. "You can't assign me to someone! I'm a Bombay! You cut me off from my money! Who do you think you are?"

Grandmother rose to her full height. She looked regal, like a goddess—well, one of the not-so-crazy goddesses that is. "I am on the Council of the Bombays. And this," she motioned to her sister and cousins on the dais, "is the full Council. And we decide who lives and who dies." She shook her head slowly. "And this, Grandson, is not your lucky day."

Gaul charged the dais, leaping up the steps, and raised his fist at Grandmother. She deftly stepped aside, and, as he ran past her, she tripped him.

"You need to control your anger," she said as Gaul fell to the floor.

Gaul pulled a knife from his belt and ran at her, slashing furiously through the air. Grandmother countered by shoving his knife arm away and kicking him in the ass until he fell off the dais and landed at my feet.

"Are you quite done?" Grandmother asked, sounding bored. I had to admit, it was pretty badass. Grandmother 1, Gaul 0.

"I WILL KILL YOU!" Gaul screamed and charged for the dais again. I had no doubt he would try. Eventually his youth and strength would wear down the old woman who was giving him a beating.

Without thinking, I tore off the belt I was wearing and looped it around Gaul's neck. He was brought up short and fell backwards onto me. I tightened the belt, and he dropped his knife, his fingers clawing at the belt now cutting off his air supply.

Grandmother and the others watched calmly from the dais. They were studying me, waiting to see if I would do it. I'd never intentionally had an audience for my work before. It unnerved me.

But I had no choice. Gaul was writhing and spitting like an animal. Letting go now would mean he would keep coming at us until he or we were dead—just like he'd charged the dais and Grandmother, over and over.

Gaul's skin was turning purple, and he was beginning to lose consciousness. I looked at the Council. Their calm demeanor was sickening. But I had an enraged and murderous animal in front of me. I had no choice.

My arms were strained, and I thought I might lose my strength at any moment. But I continued to hold on. Tears began streaming down my face. I was weeping for my family. Weeping for the Council. Weeping for myself. And weeping for Gaul.

I waited a few minutes after his struggling stopped, just to make sure he was dead. When I was convinced, I let go of the belt. I rose to my feet and dropped the belt on the ground next to my brother's body. After giving the Council a withering look, I turned and left the chamber.

I did not go home. I couldn't face Father after what I'd done. Instead, I somehow found my way back to Gaul's small, rented room. Taking a blanket from the bed, I curled up on a divan and went to sleep.

The Council offered Father and I retirement from the family business at the next meeting, and we eagerly accepted it. They made it clear that this wouldn't happen for others who had to take out their own family, but they thought it was a fitting reward for me being the first and for Father having to lose a child. Grandmother begrudgingly congratulated me on a job well-done. It was weird.

Somehow, we were able to move on with our lives. Father hired me an art tutor named Janus, and to this day I spend most of my time drawing. The art tutor is pretty cute—in a sort of professorial way and we seem to be hitting it off. I'm not making any promises, but maybe I might be interested in a little romance after all, especially now that I'm out of the family business.

Oh, I still consult for the Bombays. Turns out there are other family members that have the same problem with tasks that I do. Grandmother asked me to work with them, and occasionally I have to travel to meet with distant cousins and show them the *lion by lion* method. They seem very grateful, and it's a relief to see that others have the same problem focusing.

Father has, oddly enough, found some fame for his diorama work. Turns out people like the little scenarios he makes, and the fact that the little stadiums are often filled with toga wearing storks, and the arena features plants attacking each other doesn't seem to matter. I think the storks kind of look like Grandmother.

But maybe that's just me.

Aberdeen Bombay
Richmond, Virginia—1856

"I'm boooooooored, darling," Troy Bombay whined from his chair as he tossed aside the newspaper. His immaculately clad leg dangled recklessly over the arm of the chair, in definite danger of being obscenely wrinkled. "What time is the party?"

"Keep that up and you'll get frown lines," I said. Well, I more like wheezed. Siobhan was torturing my tender flesh into the confines of the latest corset from Paris. Just as I tried to inhale, my maid took advantage of my breathless state to squeeze a fraction of an inch more out of my lungs. And I was paying her to do that.

"Someone has been overdoing it at the buffet," Troy mumbled quietly.

"I heard that!" I shouted in short, restrained gasps. "Remember that you're next, Auntie India." That would take the wind out of his sails if he were a normal man. But my cousin Troy loved dressing as a woman to be my chaperone. In fact, I think he enjoyed the pain of the corset a little too much. But that was something I never asked him—mainly because I didn't really want to know the answer.

Siobhan said nothing. She was an excellent maid and never commented on our weird arrangement. Of course I paid her well. That may have had something to do with it.

Troy rolled his eyes. "I'd bet my waistline is smaller than yours today."

I tried to growl, but it is difficult with no oxygen in your lungs. Instead, I shot him a look that hopefully said, *Knock it off or I'll tell the other Bombays that you impersonate your mom.*

My name is Aberdeen Bombay, but I prefer Abby. My cousin, Troy Bombay, prefers Auntie India. And that works well for me because as an orphan in a southern town, I would not gain acceptance into society if I were a young woman living alone. And I lived for these parties. No one parties like southerners. No one.

Oh yes, and we're assassins. I probably should've mentioned that. Troy and I come from a long line of assassins. The Bombay Family has been in business since Ancient Greece, and everybody born a Bombay works in the field.

It was my late mother who was the Bombay before me. A tried and true Yankee, she somehow fell in love with a southern boy from an old family. And then they had me.

"Do you think that little tramp Carmella will be there?" Troy wiggled his eyebrows at me.

I shook my head. "After the way you humiliated her at the Green's party last week? Never!"

Troy grinned wickedly. "All I said was that she shouldn't wear that décolletage in public."

I narrowed my eyes at him. "No. You said she looked like a painted harlot who had no business pretending to have cleavage. And you *said* it in public."

Troy giggled. "Oh, that's right. I did say that."

I rolled my eyes. "I don't know why I ever agreed to this whole Auntie India charade."

"Sure you do," Troy said. "Because you wouldn't get invites to all the best parties if I wasn't here."

"If Auntie India wasn't here," I corrected.

Troy was suddenly engrossed in the newspaper again. "Didn't I say that?"

I actually lived in hotels. My parents were deceased, and as soon as my father passed, I sent my newly inherited and immediately freed slaves north to live. It might have been a tad impulsive to sell the family plantation, but there was so much wicked history there that I simply couldn't keep it. It was only after the fact that I'd realized I had forgotten about some of our victims being buried there. Hopefully, that wouldn't come back to haunt me later.

Slavery had been an issue with me. My father never understood that, and, to my consternation, Mother never fussed about it, and she was a Yankee. On my tenth birthday, in fact, I asked for my father to free my personal slaves. To my amazement, he did. Then I immediately asked for a paid servant because how could I manage without one? He responded by throwing his arms up in the air and exiting the room. Mother gave me Siobhan. She'd been with me ever since.

So, equipped with an Irish, *paid* servant and my cousin, Troy Bombay, and no plantation to live on, I lived in hotels. This one, The Washingtonian, being my particular favorite. The lifestyle suited me, and I still had someone to take care of me.

My father was from a very old, southern family that had settled at Jamestown in 1609. He was proud and obnoxious, to say the least. We had our disagreements, but in the end he was my father after all. And I was the typical southern belle—in love with dresses and parties and plantation mansions. It made it difficult being an assassin, but I'd learned to adapt, just like my family has for centuries.

My mother, on the other hand, was a Yankee and a Bombay. The very essence of an independent-thinking woman, she'd disdained the frippery and frivolity that went with a southern life. But she had loved my father—for reasons I'll never understand.

It's actually an acceptable southern tradition for the man to occasionally take his wife's last name. Mostly this is due to seeing the end of the family name on the horizon. Men are so terribly sensitive about their family names, don't you think? At any rate, the Rhett family had done it—so had many others. It always surprised me that my father had agreed to it. But then, you had to if you wanted to marry a Bombay.

I was fifteen when they had died in a bizarre carriage incident. I'd always suspected foul play, but the Bombay Council came down from New York City and checked it out and found nothing unusual. I personally haven't trusted a herd of goats to this very day.

My Auntie India and cousin Troy had moved here and taken care of me for the next two years, looking after things until I was able to do so on my own. It was they who introduced me to living in hotels. Moving up north where most of the Bombays lived was completely out of the question. Northerners are soooooo serious and dull. And their parties! Dreadful!

Auntie India returned to Massachusetts, but Troy stayed because he too loved the parties. Unfortunately, having a male relative living with me was considered quite scandalous—which meant I wouldn't be invited to these lovely, aforementioned parties. So Troy became Auntie India—with his mother's assistance and tutelage, provided he didn't tell the rest of the family.

Now in my nineteenth year, I was becoming a bit long in the tooth by marriageable standards, but that didn't stop me from having several suitors. I flirted and teased but mainly ignored them. They were after my fortune of course, and I simply didn't have time for that.

Besides, I was having too much fun! Why tie myself down to some boozy old colonel or some silly-headed plantation owner's son who did nothing but laze about and party? Okay, so *I* lazed about and partied, but that didn't mean I wanted the same thing in a mate.

"Darling." Troy lounged in an overstuffed chair in my room as I got ready for the picnic. "Tell me you aren't wearing that tired old thing!" He pointed to the blue and white dress on the bed.

"Dearest cousin, that *tired old thing* just arrived from Paris yesterday, so be a darling and do shut up," I answered him. "When are you getting dressed? We have to leave soon, and I can't go to the party without Auntie."

Troy suppressed a yawn so it wouldn't mar his delicate features. "I'm already in my corset. Once Siobhan is done stuffing you into yours, she'll go to work on me."

Siobhan said nothing, as if helping a man dress in drag was an everyday occurrence in Ireland. And maybe it was, for all I knew.

"Do you think that silly Susanna Thornton will be there?" Troy asked. "I really do hate her. Always tossing those ratty curls like she's all that."

I giggled. "I doubt it after the tongue-lashing you gave her at the Franklin's party last week. What was it you said exactly? That her horsehair coat looked better on the original horse?"

Troy rolled his eyes. "I think she was wearing the horse's teeth too…poor dear." Troy always ended a slam with "poor dear," as if it forgave him for his sharp tongue.

"And still you get invited to all the best parties," I sighed.

"People *love me*, darling." Troy pouted. "I just say what they're thinking anyway."

"Miss Abby, ma'am?" Siobhan was helping me lace up my corset. The Buckinghams were having a barbeque, and it was THE event of the month. I ate early, so I wouldn't eat at the party. If I did, my corset would surely burst open.

"What is it Siobhan?" I asked in short bursts of breaths as she tugged hard on the laces. She would have made an excellent torturer under Torquemada. That made me a little proud.

"There's a packet for you in the hall. It was just delivered. Had one of those red wax seals on it. I thought you should know."

Oh. An assignment. I breathed out, and, unfortunately, Siobhan took advantage of my breathing out to tighten the corset. Now I couldn't breathe in. Well, as they say, fashion is pain…gorgeous, gorgeous pain.

"Well…you'd better…bring it…here then," I said after a few attempts at breathing. Siobhan nodded and left the room. She returned in moments with a large, brown envelope with my name on it and the blood-red crest of the Bombays sealed in wax. She excused herself. The maid had been with me enough to know she wasn't allowed to see the contents of the envelope, and she never pried. She really was an excellent servant.

Troy rose daintily to his feet and giggled like a toddler who'd just figured out where the hidden candy was. "I'm going to steal Siobhan now." He nodded and followed the maid out of the room. He knew an assignment was private. He also knew I would tell him anything, and he'd get the details later.

I cracked the seal and opened the envelope, spilling the contents onto my bed. Oh sure, I could've left it until after the party—but what if my target was attending? After all, half of Richmond would be at the Buckingham's this afternoon. Never let an opportunity pass you by. That's what Mother always said during my training, and I've found that to be true in almost every situation.

A drawing of a handsome, young man stood out among the files. He had short, dark hair and a darling set of sideburns. His eyes seemed to be looking right at me. The notes in the margin said they were green. That should make him easy to find.

"Carter Livingstone Sperry," I read quietly. It really was too bad. He was such a handsome man. Oh well.

Apparently, Mr. Sperry was in Richmond, visiting from California. He was staying, where else, with the Buckinghams. He'd surely be at the picnic today. Serendipity! A kill AND a barbeque!

I stuffed the rest of the file back into the envelope and moved it to my suitcase, where I had a false bottom hidden. Tucking the assignment inside, I decided I needed to pick a hatpin for the occasion. That was one of my favorite ways to kill someone at a social engagement. Hatpins were so perfect— functional and pretty and left very little mess (which is very important when wearing the latest fashions). The holes were undetectable most of the time—which meant I could enjoy the rest of the party and make a clean getaway.

I didn't know what Sperry had done to warrant me killing him, and I didn't care. I stopped reading the reasons why in the files long ago. I'd realized that the Bombay Council always had good reasons for dispatching someone. Why waste my time with more reading than was necessary?

Our targets were always villains. Always. There was simply no point in questioning it. So I didn't. Instead, I summoned Siobhan and told her I'd need a hat.

She picked out a simply *lovely* straw hat with a blue ribbon that circled the brim and tied under my chin or fetchingly around my neck. The maid then handed me a long, mahogany case, and I opened it.

"The sapphire, I think," I said as I selected a very long and very sharp hatpin. The head of the pin was a large sapphire, encrusted with diamonds. It was a personal favorite because it went with my eyes. It is always beneficial to coordinate one's accessories with your best feature. And if it was lethal, all the better.

Siobhan finished dressing me. Once she styled my hair, I added the hat and pierced the hat and hair with the pin. Now I was ready to have some fun and kill someone naughty. It was the perfect day.

Troy joined me an hour later dressed as Auntie India. He looked positively gorgeous in an emerald green dress with matching bonnet.

"*You* are *not* wearing that hat!" Troy pointed his matching parasol at the straw hat on my head.

I stuck my chin out. "I am too." Really! Troy could be so snooty about fashion sometimes. Like he was an expert or something.

He shook his head and his wig's shiny, black sausage curls bounced appropriately. "You are *too old* to wear *that hat*."

I whacked him on the arm with my own, blue parasol. "I am not. I'm nineteen. Just on the borderline. Besides," I pointed to the sapphire pin, "I need it for this. I have an assignment."

Troy's eyebrows rose. "I will be completely *humiliated*!" Troy always talked in italics. You could hear the words bending to the right as he spoke them. "They will blame *me* for not *insisting* you wear a bonnet!"

"No, they will think nothing of the sort." I pulled my shoulders back to show I was serious. "Or we can tell them I insisted."

Troy/Auntie India whipped out his lace fan and fanned himself/herself quickly. "I *don't* like it."

"I don't care," I answered. "It's just a hat."

He/she gasped in horror. "It is *not* just a *hat*! It is so much more than that! I can't think of a worse scandal!"

I giggled. "It would be worse if I didn't do my job." He knew that. If you failed at a mission, you ran the risk of being hunted down. That would mean Troy would have to go back home. No more parties. And no more dress up.

Siobhan joined us. "Your carriage is here." Then she turned on her heel and left. She probably couldn't get away from us fast enough.

In the carriage, Troy tapped me on the hand with his fan. "So, are you going to *tell me* about the job?"

"Carter Livingstone Sperry," I answered. "He's staying with our hosts and, from the drawing, is quite a dish."

Troy shook his head sadly. "That just doesn't seem right. Why can't we have more *ugly* vics? Like in Savannah. Remember that?"

How could I forget? Savannah, last year, Troy helped me take out a pair of twin slave traders. Ugly twin slave traders. It really should be a crime that if you're that ugly, there shouldn't be an exact copy of you. Both men had eyebrows that not only came together in the middle of their forehead, but also formed a sort of caveman overhang over their eyes. I won't even tell you about the teeth and warts. It wouldn't be decent.

"I seem to recall that we had a little trouble in Vicksburg. Something about wet gunpowder?" I asked innocently.

Troy scowled. "Am I to be *tormented* by that one mistake forever? I forgot I'd hidden it in my wig. When I washed it, the powder got *wet*. You need to get over that."

"I don't think I ever will," I said. "You should've gone as Troy, not Auntie India. I had to strangle one of those brutes with my bare hands! It took weeks to grow those fingernails back!"

Troy looked at my hat. "Well, my dear, now that you have your *age-inappropriate hat*, no one would ever notice your fingernails."

I rolled my eyes.

"So." Troy grinned. "What's it going to be? The razor bladed fan? The sharpened whalebones in the corset? The poison in the locket? Or the pistol inside the cage crinoline?" My cousin listed my weaponry as accessories.

"None of them." I smiled and tapped my hat pin.

"Ah. *That's* why you're wearing the wrong hat for your *age*." Troy nodded, happy to get one more dig in.

The driver pulled up in front of a large, plantation house and helped Auntie and me out of the vehicle. As he drove off, I linked my arm through Auntie India's (Once we were in character, I wasn't allowed to even think of him as Troy.), and we opened our parasols and joined the party.

"Oh damn," Auntie said softly in her fake falsetto voice. "Colonel Potter is here."

Sure enough, the short, fat colonel was quickly waddling toward us. I suppressed a giggle. Colonel Potter had met Auntie India at the holiday party at the Cantwells last year. Somehow, he'd fallen in love with her and was making it his life's work to pursue and woo my dear, widowed Auntie. Troy hated the old, overweight officer, but I thought they were darling together.

"Miss India!" Colonel Potter swept low before us in an obnoxious courtly bow. His bald spot caught the sun and blinded us. Beside me I felt Auntie shiver.

"And Miss Abby!" the man quickly added. "You are both such a vision to these old eyes!" He wrestled Auntie's arm from mine and placed her hand on his forearm. "Come with me, my dear! Your niece won't mind, will you, Miss Abby?"

It took all I had to suppress a smile. "Of course not, Colonel Potter! Why my Auntie was just saying on the ride over here how much she was looking forward to seeing you today!"

Okay, it was a bit much, but I was still stinging a bit from the *too old to wear that hat*. My cousin glared at me over her fan before being dragged off by her suitor.

"Abby!" I turned to see Winifred Buckingham coming toward me. I raised my hand and waved. I loved Winifred. She was my cousin on my father's side, and we were very close. It's unusual for Bombays to spend time with family on the non-Bombay side, and we are discouraged from having friends outside of the family. Wini was my connection to the south—my connection to the world I insisted on being part of. We hugged each other, and then she led me around the side of the house.

"I have been waiting for you!" Winifred was the very embodiment of over enthusiasm. There was nothing that made this girl upset and everything made her happy—kind of like a hungry puppy inside a smokehouse. "We have a new guest that I'm simply mad for you to meet!"

"Oh? Really?" I pretended. Of course she meant my assignment—Carter Livingstone Sperry. But she had no idea that I knew that, so I played along. I liked the idea of getting this over quickly so I could truly enjoy the rest of the party.

"He's a distant cousin from California! Can you believe that?"

"That he's a cousin or that he's from California?" I teased.

Winifred laughed. "Both darling, both! Anyway, his name is Carter Livingstone Sperry, and he's a gold prospector! He's found an entire mountain made of the stuff!" Wini smiled broadly. An only and overly spoiled child, she was a very pretty girl with strawberry blonde hair, green eyes, and freckles. I wondered if green eyes ran in her family.

"So he's wealthy." I sighed with boredom. It never failed to amaze me how these ridiculously rich southern belles were so smitten by a man with money. How dull.

Winifred looked at me with faux shock written in her eyes. "Must you be so gauche, Abby? What's wrong with a wealthy man anyway? You will need a husband to look after you sooner or later. Why not one with money?"

I shook my head. "Surely you haven't forgotten that I don't need money or a man to look after me, my friend. I can take care of myself. And I have Auntie India."

Winifred shook her head. I'm sure I scandalized her. Most of these women thought I was completely mad. Who wouldn't want to be married and settled?

"Well he's handsome and charming too," Winifred ventured a little more carefully. "You simply must meet him!" Her puppy-like enthusiasm returned in abundance, and she took my hand and ran for the door of the house.

The Buckingham's home was larger than the White House. And I knew because I'd been. To the White House, I mean. It was years ago, but I was able to help Mother take out a member of the French Foreign Minister's staff who was there to kill the president. That was my introduction to the elegant simplicity of the hat pin as a weapon.

Wini and I stepped off the front porch onto the inlaid, tile floors, and I looked around. The extreme gaudiness of her home never failed to embarrass me. How did the Buckinghams live like this?

Pink and green marble from Italy clashed wildly with a huge, mahogany staircase and banister. The wallpaper had giant, gold fleur-de-lis dripping down the walls behind a crystal chandelier that took up half of the ceiling. I'd often toyed with the idea of saying something to Wini about this obnoxious display of wealth, but what good would it do? Troy often referred to it as Satan's entryway into Hell. I thought maybe he was right.

We stopped beside a giant, stuffed bear, posed on his hind legs as if he was going to attack us for humiliating him this way.

"Now let me see." Wini tapped her chin with a well-manicured forefinger. She was so lucky she didn't have to strangle anyone with her bare hands.

"Where did Carter go off to?" She finally finished her question to herself and then squeaked like a spaniel as she dashed off, dragging me behind her, toward the library.

We opened the huge, oak doors to the library and sure enough, found ourselves face to face with Wini's soon to be dead, distant cousin.

"Carter!" Wini cried out as she pulled me towards my victim. "I want you to meet my very best and oldest friend, Miss Aberdeen Bombay!"

Carter Livingstone Sperry rose to his feet, and I could see that he was quite a bit taller than I. I would probably have to plunge the hat pin into his ear when he was sitting down. Yes, that would be the best way to do it.

He took my hand in his and drew it up to his lips for a kiss. "The pleasure is mine, Miss Bombay." Carter's voice was deep and smooth as silk. What an oily bastard. It wouldn't be difficult to get him alone for the fatal blow. Men like this took whatever conquests they could get.

"The pleasure is, I assure you, all mine, Mr. Sperry." I managed to scrounge up a blush as he gently let go of my hand. Now all I had to do was get rid of Wini. I didn't really want her around when I killed her cousin. She didn't seem to know him at all, but, still, discovering that your best friend is an assassin would be a major shock to the poor girl, and I'd probably have to kill her for knowing that.

"Oh Wini!" I gushed. "He's darling! Absolutely darling!" I was quite good at flattery, and Mr. Sperry had the good grace to smile.

I turned to my friend. "You simply must find Auntie India so she can meet him! Do be a darling and run off to find her! She's with Colonel Potter by the buffet, I'm certain."

Wini cocked her head to one side with a quizzical look on her face. Of course, I was asking for a scandalous breach of protocol, asking to be left alone with a man I didn't know. But I needed to get on with it so I could enjoy the rest of the party. I figured I could lay Sperry out on the sofa to make it look like he was napping. It would be hours before anyone realized he was dead. Whoever came into a library during a barbeque anyway? My fingers twitched for the sapphire hat pin, lodged in my hair.

"But Abby," Wini pouted, "I can't leave you alone in here with Carter!"

I nodded dismissively as I laid out the plan in my head. I'd invite Sperry to sit with me on the sofa—that would eliminate my need to carry him and bring him down to my ear level. I could carry a man—but it would devastate my dress. And that was *not* happening.

"Oh darling!" I waved her off. "This is your cousin! I'm certain he is a complete gentleman. We will be fine. I promise you." I pictured the whole event playing out in my thoughts. We were only a few feet from the sofa. I'd bat my eyelashes and flirt shamelessly while removing my hat and pin. It would be over in moments. I toyed with going through the eye socket—but sometimes the eyeball popped which would make it easier to declare foul play. Going through the ear was far harder to detect, but it was nearly impossible with a man's full attention on you. I could always go up through the nose into the brain…

"But we'll be scandalized!" Wini squealed. "Simply scandalized!"

I frowned at her. She was making a tremendous fuss. All she had to do was leave the room for a while. I would need to distance myself from the body as soon as I'd killed the man, but I could say I went looking for Wini and Auntie myself when they didn't come back soon enough. It would be easy if Wini would just do what I said.

"Wini! It's me, Abby, you are worried about! You have nothing to fear. We will be fine."

Wini looked from me to the now amused Carter Livingstone Sperry. The cad didn't even try to protest. He wanted to be alone with me. And he would pay for that.

"It's not just you, Abby." Wini actually began wringing her hands. What was wrong with the silly girl? "It's my family. No, I simply cannot do it. We shall all go look for your aunt." She turned to beam at her cousin. "Isn't that right, Carter, dear?"

I stared at her. Okay, fine. It wouldn't be the first time plans in the middle of a hit had to change. There was no point insisting on doing it my way because it would stick in Wini's memory if I did.

"That is fine, my friend," I soothed. "There is no need for you to get so upset!"

Wini smiled and stepped closer to Carter. A huge smile spread across her face. "I do apologize, Abby! It's just that I'm so terribly excited!"

"About what?" I asked casually, starting to work on a new plan for Carter's demise.

"The reason I was so worried about a scandal wasn't for you," Wini said. "It was for us."

"Us?" I asked. Maybe I could get him alone in the evening. The Buckinghams had several acres of woodlands on their property. The body wouldn't be discovered immediately. That was probably a better plan.

Winifred smiled and put her arm around her cousin. "Yes, us. You see, Carter and I are engaged to be married! Isn't that simply divine?"

It took everything I had to force my lips into a sincere smile. My diaphragm pushed my voice up and out past my lips. My legs felt like they'd grown roots and were holding me to the floor, and my stomach was spinning inside of me.

"That is wonderful news!" I managed somehow.

Wini pulled me into a crushing embrace. "Oh darling! I'm so glad!" She pulled back and searched my eyes. "I wanted you to be the first to know! Daddy insists on announcing it at noon. I didn't want you to hear that way!"

"What an honor that you wanted to tell me first!" My throat burned as I spoke each word. "May I tell Auntie India your joyful news?" I wanted to get out of there. Leave that library and the house. I wanted to find my cousin and our driver and head back to the hotel.

Wini nodded before hugging me again. "Of course you can, silly! Just make sure she doesn't breathe a word of it to anyone else before Daddy makes his announcement!"

I nodded and fled the house. My best friend was marrying my victim. I dodged other guests as I worked the perimeter of the barbeque, searching for Auntie India. I finally found her, surrounded by other matrons who were laughing hysterically at something she'd just said.

"Auntie! There you are!" I said breathlessly. It was dreadfully hot out, and racing about in a corset had not been a good idea. I turned to the women surrounding my cousin. "Will you excuse us, ladies? I really must ask my aunt a very important question!"

The other matrons nodded and then looked at each other warily. I knew that the minute we left them, I would suddenly become the subject of their gossip. And I didn't care.

Once we were a safe distance away, Auntie pulled her arm out of mine and hissed, "What's gotten into you?"

"I met my vic," I said, taking a moment to compose myself.

"So?" Auntie shrugged.

"It's bad," I said. "Really bad. I'm not sure I can go through with this."

Auntie's eyes grew wide. This was serious. A Bombay never backed down from an assignment. "What do you mean? Do you need my help?"

I swallowed. "No, I mean neither of us can go through with it. Not today, at least."

"Don't be silly, Abby," Auntie's falsetto changed back into Troy's baritone. "We're here. The vic is here. There are about one hundred other suspects to confuse things and several places to ditch the body."

I realized what my cousin was saying. She thought I'd lost my nerve.

"It's not that. None of that," I said. "It's worse."

Auntie resumed her falsetto as a woman walked past us. We nodded at her and waited until she was out of earshot. "Worse?" Troy's voice returned. "How could it be *worse*?"

"Carter Livingstone Sperry is now Winifred Buckingham's fiancé. This isn't just a barbeque—it's an engagement party," I said quietly.

"Oh," Troy whispered. "That *is* worse."

I nodded as my cousin whisked me away to a quiet, shady spot beneath a magnolia tree—far from the other party-goers. After resuming Auntie's voice and persona, she waited for me to start breathing normally again before offering her help.

"I could do it."

I looked at her. "You could do what?"

"I could kill him for you." Auntie whisked out her fan and began fanning herself madly as if she felt the vapors coming on.

I shook my head. "Neither of us can do it. We can't kill Wini's fiancé."

Auntie stared at me for a moment and then looked around to see if there was anyone nearby who could hear. "Do you want to go home? I could make up some excuse? Maybe that you're *terribly* embarrassed because you wore a hat that is *too young* for you?"

"We can't walk out. This is Wini's big day. Besides, I think we need to get to know Sperry a little better." I kicked at a tree root. "Oh dammit! Why didn't I read the file? Then maybe I could talk some sense into Wini—tell her what a bad man he is!"

Auntie's jaw dropped open in the most unladylike way. "You didn't read the *file*? How could you *not read* the file?"

I started to feel a little defensive. "I never read the file. Who has time to waste on doing that?"

"You should always read the file, darling. That's why they give it to you." Auntie's voice was incredulous. She acted as if I'd just told her I didn't put on that seventh petticoat layer or had poisoned kittens.

I threw up my hands. "They're always bad. Always. I trust the Council on that. Why should I question it?"

Auntie shook her head. "It's not that. You should *always* be aware of your target. You need to know their background, interests, and motivations. It helps when things go *wrong*. Seriously! Didn't your mother train you right?"

"I know that!" And I did, too. I just…well I…it's just that…Dammit! I knew what I was doing!

"Sweet pea," Auntie said soothingly. "You'll have to do this the old fashioned way. You have no time to run home and read the file. You're going to have to get to know Mr. Sperry. Here. At the barbeque."

My mouth opened and then closed. Get to know my vic? Was she crazy? I didn't get to know my vic! It was far better just to swoop in, kill them, and then be done with the deed. Get to know him?

Auntie nodded as if she could read my thoughts. Damn.

"There you are!" Wini's voice carried across the well-manicured lawn. "Abby! I've been looking all over for you!" Attached to Wini's arm was the man in question. Carter Livingstone Sperry.

"Miss Aberdeen," he removed his hat and bowed. "And who is this charming creature with you? Your sister?"

Auntie smacked him on the arm with her fan. "Oh you *are* a charmer, aren't you?" She turned to Winifred. "My dear, please introduce me to this simply *dashing* young man!"

Winifred made the introductions, and I watched as Sperry bowed over Auntie's hand. Auntie made a complete fool out of herself fawning all over him.

"What is the matter with you?" Wini whispered in my ear. "You just ran off! And on my special day!"

Auntie turned and glared at me, and somehow I found my voice.

"I am so sorry, Wini!" I gushed with as much sincerity as I could muster. "I wasn't feeling very well. It's my own fault—I really should've eaten before we left. I'm quite famished."

It was a silly excuse because I wasn't at all hungry. But it was all I had, and I hoped it would get me away from Wini and

Sperry for a few moments to think. I couldn't keep my thoughts straight.

I'd never had a personal connection to an assignment before. Well, there was that one time when I'd had to kill Wini's governess. (She liked to murder the children in her care with poisoned oat cakes.) But that was a fluke. This was something different. I barely knew Sperry and would normally have no problem plunging my hat pin into his eye. But Wini was a different matter. She finally had her little fairytale engagement. And I was supposed to ruin it for her. Of course it would certainly ruin the party to have the guest of honor murdered.

"Carter!" Wini cried out. "Please escort Abby to the buffet and make certain she eats! I simply have to run and find my parents to finish the arrangements for our announcement."

Wait…what?

"No," I started to protest. "I cannot take you away from your fiancé at your engagement party!" I looked at Auntie for help, but she gave none.

Instead, she took Sperry's other arm. "We shall *all* go *together!*" With a triumphant look she usually reserved for our waist measuring competitions, Auntie pulled Sperry away toward the other side of the house.

I followed limply, wondering if I could get away with killing Auntie too. It would have to be something gory so it would muss up her lovely face. She'd hate that.

"Well aren't you *just* adorable!" Auntie exclaimed as she and Sperry walked around. Her falsetto was cracking. I toyed with pulling her wig off. Instead, I caught up.

"I am looking forward to expanding my holdings," Sperry was saying once I slid my hand through his other arm. He nodded to me before continuing. "I'm planning on buying up land north of California. There's more mining to be done up there."

Auntie responded with a ribald cackling that could be heard in three counties. I looked for Colonel Potter. Maybe I could tell him she was considering accepting his proposal and preferred autumn weddings.

"So you're the man who will take our *beloved* Winifred away from us?" Auntie said loudly so I'd hear. That got my attention. Of course Wini would leave Virginia when she married! Why hadn't I thought of that? That might just be enough for me to want to kill him.

"How long have you and Winifred known each other?" I asked, I hoped, casually. It just occurred to me that they barely knew each other at all. That gave me a glimmer of hope. Wini would be sad, but she probably wasn't in love, and she did look rather fetching in black. She'd make an attractive widow. I'd need to wait until after they were married. And of course, her holdings would double in size. She'd be the catch of Richmond, maybe even the whole South! Why, I'd be helping her!

Sperry grinned at me, showing a row of neat, gleaming white teeth. I pictured a great white shark. This might be easier than I thought.

"Well we've known of each other's existence for years," he said slowly. "But I haven't seen her in a long time. We did begin a correspondence a few months ago. That would be how we got to know each other. She really will make a wonderful wife."

I tried not to shudder. The way Sperry said *wife* made me think of trophies. Wini deserved better than that. I needed to help her.

"Have you selected the wedding date yet?" Auntie asked, whipping her fan open and coyly looking at Sperry over the top. She was every bit the coquette. I wanted to kick her but thought that might look a bit strange.

"Why wait?" Sperry asked. "I go back to California in a few days." He looked around before smiling at us conspiratorially. "Can you ladies keep a secret?"

Auntie giggled and I simply nodded.

"We are planning to get married today! At this very party!" Sperry smiled, looking smug.

"But...but you'll deny Wini her perfect wedding day!" I blurted out, not very ladylike either. This just wasn't done! Every southern belle longed for a huge wedding! How could he take that away from her?

Sperry patted my hand condescendingly. "Yes, I know. You ladies like white lace and lots of attention. But I have a business to run. I need a wife, and we need to do this immediately. Wini understands, I assure you."

He used *my* pet name for Wini! The bastard! Who did he think he was? I was ready to kill him right now.

Auntie drew his attention away from my fuming. "Of course you need to get started *right away*! No time like the present!"

Sperry laughed. "You are so right, my dear. I need to get that little filly home so she can start her wifely duties!"

To say I was horrified was an understatement. This repulsive man needed to die. There was simply no way around it. I couldn't kill him before the wedding. In fact, I probably should wait a few days just to make sure everything was legal for Wini. Aberdeen Bombay was back in action. I just needed to bide my time.

Sperry led us through the buffet. I had to take more food than I would normally eat because of my earlier statement on being weak with hunger. After parking me and Auntie on a bench, my target left to find his bride-to-be.

"Could you be more ridiculous?" I asked Auntie.

She glared at me. "I'm afraid I don't know what you mean." She speared an olive with her fork and chewed on it thoughtfully. "I wondered if you were *ever* going to snap out of it. I *literally* had to do everything."

I did not hit her. A lady never hits her chaperone. Instead I dropped a spider on her plate and watched as she screamed. She really screamed like a girl. Isn't it funny how an assassin—a trained killer—can be terrified of spiders? I'd bet she wished she'd never told me that.

I waited for Auntie to regain her composure. Assassins are very patient people as a rule.

"Well *that* was uncalled for!" Auntie said with a deadly look.

"We have to get back on track," I said, ignoring her. "What are we going to do about Vic?"

"I'd been thinking about that while you were looking for a spider" Auntie said. "I think we need to allow Winifred her wedding day and night. Killing her fiancé before that would just be *mean*." She wiggled her eyebrows at me, so I knew that putting a spider on her plate was mean too.

I nodded. "Yes, I agree. If we wait a couple of days, Wini will be a very wealthy widow. She might as well get something out of that."

Auntie looked at me. "Don't you think she'll be upset?"

I did. Maybe not as upset as she'd be if she was truly in love with Carter. More like I-broke-a-nail upset. "Yes. But that gives us time to figure something out."

A young slave girl came up to us to tell us we needed to gather for a special announcement on the front lawn. Auntie and I handed the girl our plates and made our way to the front of the house.

On the marble front porch, framed by huge, marble pillars, Winifred stood next to Sperry, beaming like a blushing bride. Her father, my uncle Daniel, held a glass of champagne aloft.

"My dear friends!" he shouted. "Today I have a very special announcement! My darling daughter, Winifred, is betrothed to my dear cousin's boy, Mr. Carter Livingstone Sperry!"

A roar went up from the audience, and I turned to Auntie. "Everyone seems very fond of using his middle name, don't they?"

Auntie leaned in and whispered, "This is your territory, my dear. I *always* thought the way you people throw names about was weird."

Uncle Daniel continued, "And as a special surprise! The lovely couple is going to get married right here! In one hour!"

The party goers cheered as Winifred and Sperry were spirited away by the family.

The same slave girl who took my plate earlier appeared at my elbow. "Miss Abby," she said quietly. "Miss Winifred would like you to help her get ready."

Auntie frowned. "What about *me*? Can't I go *too*?"

I shook my head. "You have a job to do, Auntie India." I leaned closer and whispered into her ear. "I need you to try to find out what anyone here knows about our vic."

Without waiting for a response, I took off in the direction of the porch and entered the house. Wini's room was at the top of the stairs on the right. Her mother, Aunt Josephine, opened the door to let me in and hugged me warmly.

"Isn't this exciting Abby?" She squeezed me extra hard before letting me go. Aunt Josephine was a petite woman who could crush a horse if she had a mind too. She managed to squeeze me tighter than my corset did.

"And so unexpected! I had no idea!" I proclaimed with faux happiness.

Josephine nodded. "I know, it does seem rather sudden. But when Carter made his intentions known we thought, 'why wait'?"

I pressed my aunt. "I didn't even know Wini and Mr. Sperry were that well acquainted!"

"Oh, they barely know each other!" Josephine giggled. "But they will have plenty of time to get to know each other later." She then pulled an exaggerated pout. "I will miss my little girl though. He's taking her off to California in a few days! I'm simply devastated."

I patted Aunt Josephine on the hand and mumbled some condolences. If they were so happy Wini was getting married, why were they upset that she was leaving?

"There you are!" Wini pushed her mother aside and hugged me. "I need you to help me get ready! You are my maid of honor, after all."

Under any other circumstances, I would love to hear this news. My head would be spinning helping with wedding plans, getting a new dress to wear, and anticipating the parties that would happen from now until the wedding. But today was different when you consider I had to off the groom before he took his bride away.

Aunt Josephine and I helped the house slaves strip Wini down to her corset and begin to build her foundation clothing. A lovely, white lace gown dripped from a hanger—presumably Wini's wedding dress. I had so many questions to ask my cousin, but how to manage that?

"Wini," I said as I helped with her fifth petticoat. "Were you surprised to hear of Mr. Sperry's proposal?"

Aunt Josephine shot me a look, but then went back to fussing with a veil she was sewing onto a garland of magnolia blossoms.

Wini nodded absently. "I was, in fact. I didn't even know that Carter remembered me! But it's so exciting, isn't it Abby? Imagine me! A married woman!" Winifred actually pirouetted across the floor, landing in her mother's arms in a rain of giggles. They were a very close family. Winifred was an only child. Of course they'd be upset to see her go.

It made me wonder why they agreed to it. There were plenty of eligible bachelors here in Richmond and all over the Commonwealth of Virginia. Bachelors who'd stay close by so Wini would always be in her parents' lives. But they agreed to Sperry's out-of-the-blue proposal. Well, maybe they were just happy to see Winifred married. Or maybe her enthusiasm made them happy. Or maybe they were one of those families that liked intermarrying each other. I really didn't care about that. I had a job to do.

"And don't forget, Wini," Aunt Josephine said. "You must carry my mother's handkerchief. For luck."

Wini hugged her mother with tears in her eyes. "Of course I will!"

As I watched them, I started to get a little teary. Wini's departure would be a difficulty for Aunt Josephine and Uncle Daniel. Of course I was planning to kill her husband before he could take her out of town, but still, they had to be sad.

"I'm so happy you could be here, Abby." Josephine squeezed my hand. "I wish your father were here." Then she bounced out of the room, mumbling something about finding her blue parasol for the bride.

Now I was sad. Aunt Josephine and my father were also orphaned young. My grandparents had left each of them wealthy enough to get along in comfort, and Josephine married very well. Uncle Daniel had the largest tobacco plantation in the Commonwealth. And when they died, it would all go to Wini. Her dowry would be enormous.

Wait a minute…

There was a sharp knock on the door. I answered to find Auntie India standing there, her face flushed with activity. Did she run up those stairs? In that dress?

"Wini," I called to my friend who was having her corset tightened. "Could you excuse me for a moment?" I took advantage of her breathless state to slip out of the room. I pulled Auntie into a small sitting area off the main corridor.

"I *have* to tell you something!" Auntie said.

"I have to tell *you* something!" I replied.

"Sperry is after her money!" We both said simultaneously. This was followed by us frowning simultaneously. It was like looking into a mirror image of myself who was also a man.

Auntie held up one finger to cut me off. "Me first. Sperry's prospects are not what he says they are. He's broke and needs money to keep his gold mine going."

I nodded, "Everything was rushed. Wini had no idea he wanted to propose, and he wanted to get married right away! Wini's an only child. When she dies, all of her parents' money will go to Sperry!"

We stared at each other for a moment before saying in perfect unison, "He's going to kill Wini!"

When two Bombays come to the same conclusion at the same time, it's bound to be true. Sperry needed Wini's family money. But loans from Uncle Daniel wouldn't last forever. He needed more than that. He might not kill Wini immediately or even in the next few months. But he would kill her.

"I really wish I'd read that file," I mumbled.

"So we have to take him out," Auntie said.

I nodded. "Only now, we have to do it before the wedding."

"Or Winifred will inherit Sperry's debts too," Auntie finished. I hadn't even thought of that.

"You have to go in there and stall Winifred. I'll go finish my assignment," I said.

Auntie shook her head. "No, *you* go in and stall, and *I'll* finish your assignment."

"Not a chance," I said to her. "I'm supposed to be the maid of honor. My disappearance will hold things up a bit. You have to find a way to distract the bride."

"Damn it." Auntie bit her lip. "I hate it when you're right." With a sigh, she went to Wini's door. She stood there for a moment and then looked at me and nodded. After a quick knock, she went in.

Now, where would Sperry be? He wouldn't have to do much to get ready. I'd have to find him quickly and get the job done. I'd also have to dispose of him. Yes, that was it! Make it look like Sperry had run off—jilted Wini at the altar! It was cruel but far better than having Winifred married to this monster.

But where would I find him? I searched the house but couldn't find anyone who knew where the groom had gotten to. Very carefully, I slipped into the kitchen and out the back door. Soon, Wini would launch a search party to find her missing maid of honor, so I couldn't take the chance of anyone seeing me.

Have you ever tried to hide while wearing a hoop skirt? You cannot press flat against a wall, and climbing, running, or even walking fast is impossible—especially with the addition of a corset.

Carter Livingstone Sperry was nowhere to be found. Nearly everyone in attendance had moved to the front of the house after being told the wedding would take place on the porch. I managed to skirt the perimeter of trees, which shredded my dress. Surveillance was not easy when you were a well-dressed woman in the South.

Branches tore at my hair and scratched my face. By the time I emerged from the trees behind the house, I looked every inch a disaster.

Instead of facing the other revelers in this state, I located a small path that would eventually lead to the tobacco barn where I could straighten my appearance and think. No one would be there at this time—the slaves were all working at the party, preparing food, setting up tables and chairs, and serving.

The barn door was slightly ajar, causing me to pause outside. Bombays are a suspicious people—something learned from entering one too many buildings where the door had been left open, I suppose. After waiting outside a few moments, and hearing no sound from within, I decided to go in.

The spicy scent of dried tobacco leaves hung oppressively in the hot, dusky air. I started to work on repairing my hair. I couldn't remain here long if I didn't want to smell like tobacco. It took longer than usual, because my damn corset made it difficult for me to raise my arms and breathe at the same time.

Once my hair was in some semblance of order, I started to clean up my face with a handkerchief. How had I gotten so dirty? The dress was beyond repair in some places. There was nothing to be done about that. I tried to rearrange the fabric to cover the worst tears, but people would notice. I'd have to come up with an answer for that.

"Ahem..." A deep voice to my left caused me to jump. I landed in a defensive stance and realized with a start that I didn't have my hat, which meant I didn't have my hatpin. Both were sitting on Wini's bed...where I was supposed to be. Damn.

"I am sorry to disturb you." Carter Livingstone Sperry stepped out of the shadows. "I thought no one would be here, and I'd have a few moments to myself before the wedding."

"You should've announced yourself!" I pulled out of my defensive stance.

"What happened to you, Miss Abby?" he asked with a leer. "A bit of a tussle with some young man in the woods?"

My face flushed hotly. "How dare you imply such a thing! I was not compromised in any such manner!" What a bastard. How did Wini think she could marry such an oaf?

He raised his hands in a mock attempt to fend me off. "I meant no disrespect. I was just curious. After all, you are supposed to be helping my betrothed prepare for her nuptials."

I looked at him for a long moment and decided to dispense with the southern belle niceties.

"I'd personally rather she didn't marry a man like you. I don't really care for your sort."

Sperry's face grew dark. He grabbed my wrist roughly. "I don't care what you think of me. You'd better not come between me and my bride."

I yanked my wrist from his grasp. Did you know that the thumb is the weakest of the fingers? If someone grabs your arm, pull in the direction of their thumb. You'll get free every time. We are taught that as toddlers. Bombays start early.

"Winifred deserves far better than you," I said quietly. "She deserves a man who really loves her and wants her. You, I suspect, are more interested in her inheritance."

Sperry lunged at me, but I dodged out of the way. I wanted to bring my knee up and force his balls into his throat. But that would be very silly in a hoop skirt considering you couldn't see what the legs were doing at all under there. So instead, I punched him in the throat. Hard. I heard his trachea splinter.

Sperry stumbled backward, clutching his throat in surprise as he gasped for the air that would not come. He dropped to his knees, his body shaking as it struggled to get oxygen. Within seconds, the man fell dead at my feet.

That happened faster than I thought it would. I'd thought it would take a while to lure my vic to someplace where we could be alone. That I'd have to plan some way to catch him unawares. That I'd have to work hard to kill him. None of this seemed to be the case. Sometimes, you just have to punch your vic in the throat. That's all it takes and often all you have time for.

I looked around the barn for some sort of place to dispose of the dead man, but found nothing. If only there'd been a bottomless shaft or something. I trod back and forth on the boards, looking for a loose one to stash the body under. Nothing.

The wedding would be starting soon. If I didn't get rid of the body of the groom, they'd find it with me standing over it looking like I'd just been mauled by a badger. I had to think quickly. And fast.

"Abby!" Auntie India burst into the barn and stopped when she spotted Sperry at my feet. She looked me up and down.

"What on *earth* have you done to your gown? I *cannot* be *seen* with you like this!"

"Really? That's what you're going to give me a hard time over? My dress?" I asked.

Auntie grinned for a moment. "Well, I *was* going to complain that you didn't wait for me. But that seemed a *bit* narcissistic."

"How did you find me?" I asked.

"Everyone said you were running around in the woods. They also *chastised* me for allowing you out of my sight, and a few said some *unkind* words about me being a lazy chaperone— which I thought was *completely* unnecessary. I thought about the layout of the plantation and guessed you were here. And I was *right*."

I sighed. "Fine. You were right. Now help me get rid of Carter Livingstone Sperry."

It was sad, an hour later, seeing Wini in her wedding dress, weeping openly in front of everyone. It was sad that she thought Sperry had ditched her on her wedding day. It was sad that it took Auntie and me twenty minutes to find that old, unused well and dump Sperry's body into it. We threw in a dead pig on top for good measure. That way, when the smell hit, they'd most likely just bury the retired well. And it was sad that I'd ruined my dress from Paris manhandling a dead pig.

People were in such a state of shock that Wini had announced her engagement and been jilted at her own wedding all in the same hour that very few people noticed my ruined dress. Aunt Josephine turned everyone out in order to comfort her daughter in privacy.

Back at the Washingtonian, once Siobhan had gone to bed for the night and Auntie India had once again become Troy, we opened the file on Sperry together.

The Bombay Council had been right. As they always were. Sperry was the worst sort of man. In his lust for gold, he'd allowed an unstable mine to collapse, trapping and slowly killing ten miners inside. Gambling debts had become overwhelming, and he'd taken to seducing and killing a wealthy widow for her money. Once that ran out, he'd decided to come home and woo his cousin Winifred.

"And that's why you need to read the file the Council sends," Troy admonished when I'd tossed the papers into the fireplace. "You wouldn't have second-guessed yourself today if you'd just read the file."

I was exhausted and depressed. In one day, I'd managed to crush the hopes of my best friend who only wanted a husband

and family. And while she almost married a monster who would've killed her, I still felt raw and empty.

"You did the right thing." Troy patted my hand gently. "Wini will find someone else."

"I know." I leaned back in my chair and stared at the flames as they devoured the sordid story of Carter Livingstone Sperry.

"Maybe I need a little change," I finally said.

Troy sat straight up. "Ugh! Please *don't* say we are going up north! I don't want to see Mother and the others right now."

I shook my head. "I was thinking of something else. Maybe a grand tour of Europe?"

Troy perked up. "Will there be parties?"

I nodded. "Yes. And you don't even have to be Auntie India if you don't want to."

"Can I be someone else?" Troy pouted.

"How about if you are just you? The dashing and wonderful and witty you?"

Troy looked at me sternly. "My darling, I am *always* wonderful and witty, whether I am a woman or not. No, you *need* a chaperone. I think I'll come up with someone else. A sister perhaps? Or a cousin this time? I *do* hate playing an older woman."

"Okay. You can be my sister," I said. I'd always wanted a sister.

Troy nodded. "Yes, your *younger, prettier* sister. Who has a *smaller* waist and wears hats that are *appropriate* to her age."

I sighed. I guess I could live with that.

Dublin Bombay
Moray, Scotland—892 A.D.

"You have to go to the Orkneys. We have a target for you," Uncle Rome said as he tossed another greasy bone to the dogs at his feet. He sucked on his fingers before wiping a slimy hand across his tunic.

I shook my head. "I don't want to go to the Orkneys. No one does. It's cold there, and they have Vikings." And I meant it. Vikings were a pain in the ass—always bludgeoning this and stabbing that. Nobody wanted them and yet there they were, like an infestation of fleas…well-armed fleas that wanted to kill you.

And you want to talk about cold? In winter, the Orkney Islands were frigid and damp, leaving your bones aching with the question of, *Why in the hell are we in the damn Orkneys?* The fire crackled to my left as if it too wanted me to stay.

Uncle looked down his nose at me. "You say that as if you have a choice. You don't."

He was right. I might as well have been arguing with the wind. The cold, bitter wind that blew down from the Orkneys.

Currently, the Bombay Family was comfortably ensconced in a large, warm castle. After defeating a rather scruffy tribe of Picts (another group who are very stabby and bludgeony—but with worse manners) to claim the land, we'd settled in. Sure, the Picts had been tough to remove, but the Bombay Council had wanted a northern stronghold. This was it.

Sharing a castle with family wasn't a trial so much as it was a challenge. A challenge to keep us from killing one another. And we faced this challenge every day. Not an easy task when every member of the family is a trained assassin. I, myself, was eyeing the fireplace poker and wondering how many ways I could kill Uncle Rome right now. Currently, I was entertaining a method that involved fire and a soft part of his body that I will leave to your imagination.

"You will leave at once," Uncle continued, tearing off a hunk of bread. "You must kill Sigurd the Mighty. You have two weeks."

"Two weeks?" I complained like a girl—I'll admit that. And it was not very becoming for a twenty-two year old man, but I was hoping it would work. "Two weeks to get there, establish some sort of ruse, and kill him? Are you mad?" It probably was not a good idea to piss my uncle off. At more than thirty stone in weight, he could probably squash me at will. In fact, that was his modus operandi when it came to killing the bad guys—he basically sat on them until the breath left their lungs. Completely charmless and unimaginative if you ask me.

"Off with you." Fortunately, I caught him while he was eating. This meant he'd be at the table for a while at least. I'd be gone before someone was required to help him out of his chair. It was an event—usually involving the whole family. Other families have interesting and dare I say, fun, traditions. Ours involved levering a fat man out of various forms of furniture.

"Stupid Uncle Rome. Stupid Orkneys. Stupid Sigurd the Mighty," I grumbled all the way to my room. I didn't mind killing people for work. I just wasn't a fan of Vikings or cold weather. Well, at least Vikings I could kill. There weren't enough wool socks to keep me warm and dry where I was going.

My idea of a good time was playing chess in front of a fire with a flagon of warm mead nearby. Not that there were any good chess players in the family. There weren't. Any.

You'd think that strange, wouldn't you? A family of assassins and none of them but me played chess. I think it's weird. We got the game a few years back from a cousin who'd travelled to Persia. So far, I was the only one who'd taken it up.

Strategy is important, I think. For a very long time, Bombays have planned out assassinations in ways that left us undetected. Planning a killing took skill and creativity—like in chess. Why couldn't they see that?

"Going somewhere?" My little sister Iona stood in the doorway, grinning. She'd just turned fourteen and, like most women, thought she knew everything. By the way, she did. It was incredibly annoying.

"Up north. To the Orkneys. To take out a Viking," I groaned. *Vikings*. Not only did I have weather to deal with, I had to kill a Viking.

Not that it was hard to do so, mind you. Vikings were relatively easy to kill. You just needed to make them mad. From there, you just outwitted them. And I spoke their language. Again, I was the only Bombay who'd been interested in learning the other languages when we'd relocated up here from Northumbria to the north of Hadrian's Wall. Why was that?

Iona plopped down onto my bed. "So, how are you going to do it?"

"I don't know," I said honestly. "I'll figure it out when I get there. Do you know anything about Sigurd the Mighty?" My history of the northeastern islands was a little, well, deficient. But Iona liked political intrigue. *Women*.

"Oh, him," she said in a bored way. "He's Earl of Orkney. Kind of an idiot. His brother gave him that title and then abandoned him. The brother didn't want to be in the Orkneys either."

"An idiot is good," I said as I stuffed a shirt and a couple of hoods into a sack. Maybe this would be so easy I could just ride up there, gut him, and be home before anyone was the wiser. I eyed the ongoing chess game in the corner of the room. I had an important move to think about. Even though I was just playing against myself.

"You can't just walk up to him and kill him," Iona said, her voice heavy with sarcasm. "These are Vikings you're dealing with. You have to finesse it somehow."

I rolled my eyes. "Really? You're saying it's more complicated than that? I don't believe it."

Vikings thought with their weapons: strike first, and then remember you needed to ask the dead guy something. Realize you just killed the only guy who could give you this information. Take his goat and find someone else to kill. Repeat.

My sister ignored this. "I think there's some sort of border dispute going on there near Caithness. Something with the Magnate of Moray. That's where you should start." She tapped a finger to her chin as she stared into space. After a few seconds, she shrugged. "Anyway, good luck!"

I grabbed her arm as she was about to bounce out of the room. "I think you should come with me. You could help."

Iona grabbed my hand and twisted, throwing me neatly to the floor. All air had abandoned my lungs and she stood over me, hands on her hips as I gasped like a fish on the icy, stone floor. I really should put a nice warm rug in here.

"Why should I help you? Why would I go there? Besides…some Viking warrior might try to rape me or carry me off and make me a slave. Why would I want that?"

I wheezed as I climbed to my feet. "Like anyone could take advantage of *you*." I brushed the dust from my clothes. "Besides, I was thinking more of you traveling in disguise."

A flicker of interest glimmered in my sister's eyes. She liked disguises. As a child in Northumbria, she often moved through the streets unnoticed as an urchin, or was kowtowed to as a princess. Dressing up was her favorite thing and a weakness I could easily exploit.

"Really?" she asked with enthusiasm. Upon seeing my interest, she toned it down and started pulling at a string on her dress. "Why would I be interested in that?"

"Because you love costumes and you love intrigue," I answered. I was really warming up to the idea. Having someone else along would make the time pass quickly too, even if it was Iona.

"Okay. I'll do it." Iona smiled. Either she was bored, or she wanted a break from wrestling Uncle Rome out of his chair. "What will I be? A Pictish princess? A warrior girl? A Viking shield-maiden?"

"A boy," I answered.

Iona sulked from the back of her horse as we picked our way through the muddy forest. She hadn't quite gotten used to the idea of being my boy servant. She'd had to bind her breasts and put her hair up under a hood. For some reason, Iona had gotten a bit girly and man-crazy in the last year, and she was not enjoying this disguise as much as I'd hoped.

"Not too far now," I said for the tenth time today. "Moray is nearby. I'm pretty sure of it." Actually, the only thing I was pretty sure of was that I'd forgotten to bring a map. We'd had to ask people all along the road if we were going in the right direction. I'd made Iona swear she wouldn't tell the other Bombays when we got back. That would be humiliating.

It had been a three-day's journey from home to get this far. A cold, wet drizzle glazed the branches of dead trees, and, in spite of our heavy wool cloaks, we were soaked through and chilled to the bone. Iona had been moody and silent the whole way, so I spent my time thinking of my next chess move. I really was stuck with this one because both of my rooks were cornered. Maybe I'd get an idea along the way.

At least we'd been able to stay at various farms and inns. They were rough, and they were few, but having a night to hang our wet clothes in front of a fireplace had been a benefit. Money wasn't really a problem for us, and it did most of the talking. There were few travelers who could afford to stay at these places. Hot food was another plus. Although if I ate one more eel I was pretty sure I'd snap. What was it with these people and eels?

"Are you still sulking?" I asked my sister. "You should be getting into character."

Iona nodded and said in a dead voice. "Fine. I'm Oxnar—your servant boy. I'm thirteen. And we are on our way to the northern islands to see your father. Who is a fisherman." She threw her hands up in the air. "That's the best you could come up with? A fisherman? How many fishermen's sons can afford a servant? And why in the hell would we go visit him in winter? *I* should've made up the backstory. I'm far better at it than you."

I shook my head. "You have to keep things simple. A fisherman's son is unimportant. The people of Moray won't feel like they have to bow to or even acknowledge us. They will forget us once we've gone."

Iona shook her head. "What about the servant thing? How can you explain that?"

I sighed. "I told you. I'm now a cloth merchant of some small reputation. You are my apprentice." I tried hard not to roll my eyes. That would've made her angrier than she already was, and I didn't need that.

"Whatever!" Iona threw her hands up again, before slouching into sulk mode.

"You there!" a voice cried out ahead of us. I squinted into the piercing rain to see a figure form out of the mist. A young man, about my age I'd guess, stepped forward, wielding a large stick. Sticks were a favored weapon of these parts. They literally grew on trees.

"Yes?" I asked casually. We'd encountered many people like this on the road—most of them beggars and thieves. I reached for the axe I had hidden under my cloak.

"Where do ya think yer goin?" The man thrust a stubborn chin up at us. His hair was red and unruly, but his clothes were intact and not worn out. I decided he was a guardian from a local farm or something similar.

"To Moray to spend a few days resting our horses before continuing up north," I said, looking him directly in the eyes.

The young man looked from Iona to me. He seemed to be struggling with a thought. I let him. There's really no point in giving someone too much information.

"I'm Taran," the man said, and I realized he was much younger than me—closer to Iona's age. "My da is the innkeep in Moray. You kin stay with us." And without waiting for my reply, he took hold of Iona's horse and began leading us up the trail.

My sister raised her eyebrows at me, and I knew she was wondering if this was an ambush or a trap. Her hand went to her short sword she kept hidden beneath a cloak. I shook my head and she nodded. We might as well follow Taran. If he was telling the truth, then we'd have our place to stay. If he was lying, well, he'd be dead soon. It didn't really matter.

The horses moved slowly through the muck that sucked at their hooves as the rain began to come down in freezing sheets. Loud, sharp cracking sounds filled the still, rain-muffled air as the coated tree branches snapped beneath the weight of the ice. I hoped Taran was right. We needed to find shelter quickly.

I studied the back of the boy as he walked, his right hand still gripping the rope of Iona's horse. How had I misjudged him so easily? This was clearly a boy. The illusion that made me think he was a man was subterfuge. It must have been his stance and his attitude. The boy had developed it to deter the wrong sort. It made me like him immensely.

We pulled up to a two-story, half-timbered building with a thatched roof.

"This is it," Taran said. "I kin take yer horses around back and see to em."

Iona and I climbed off the horses, and I tossed the boy a coin. He looked at it, and his eyes grew wide. A smile crossed his features making him look younger than ever.

"Tell Da you want the corner room," Taran said with a wink. "That's the best one." And with that, he was gone.

The door complained heavily as we entered the inn. The main room was filled with people sitting at rough-hewn tables and benches, but it was warm from a roaring fire, and the smells of stewed meat and baked bread made me sigh in relief.

A grizzled but friendly-looking old man met us and handed our soaking wet cloaks to a thin, frowning woman. "Taran brought ye?"

"He did," I answered. "He told us to ask for the corner room."

The man nodded. "He must like you then. Just so happens it's not bein' used." He motioned to the tables filled with people. "None of these folks are staying here. They just like the food." I noticed the thin, frowning woman start to smile at this. She must be the cook, and this was a compliment of importance to her.

"Well it smells as though we are in heaven," I said, bowing to the woman who let her guard down enough to widen her grin. "My compliments, madam. My boy and I are famished."

I glanced at Iona and saw that she was staring at a platter of meat and bread on one of the tables. The old man guided us to a table closest to the fireplace, chasing off a couple of men who were sitting there but not eating. They spat on the floor, but left without a fight.

"Name's Deort," the man said as we sat down. "How long will ye be with us?"

"Two or three nights," I answered, handing him a couple of coins.

Deort's hand closed over them, but his eyes never looked at the money. He nodded. "That'll be good." He whistled, and the thin, now smiling woman brought us a tray full of food and two cups of beer.

"When yer done, I'll show ye to yer room," Deort said before leaving us to our dinner.

Iona took a bite and rolled her eyes heavenward. "Oh my God. This is the best thing I've ever tasted. Ever."

I knew that was a lie. Our cook at the castle was talented. But we were cold and wet, and that made this tavern a glittering castle.

The meat was succulent, and the bread was crusty and warm. We ate in silence, savoring every morsel. We'd made it here, to Moray. The worst part of our trip was over.

"What's our next move?" Iona said quietly as she shoved the now empty trencher away and wiped her mouth on her sleeve. She belched, and I was proud of the fact she was really getting into her role.

I looked around the room. These were villagers, not visitors, Deort had said. We'd need to get some information. If the Magnate of Moray was involved in a dispute with Sigurd— this seemed like the logical place to start.

"Work the room. See if you can overhear any gossip," I said. Iona nodded and slipped away from the table.

"How was yer dinner?" Taran appeared at my elbow with a wide grin.

"Hit the spot," I said. "Are we the only ones staying the night?"

Taran nodded. "Yeah. Everyone jes comes 'ere fer dinner." He pointed at a couple of men the next table over. "They work for the magnate." Taran puffed up his chest. "He comes here a lot."

"After the dinner I just had, I can see why the most important people come here." My words had the desired effect— Taran lit up with pride.

"I keep tellin' my da that. Maelbrigte the Tusk always comes here."

"Maelbrigte the Tusk?" I asked.

Taran nodded. "The magnate. They call 'im The Tusk on account of his teeth sticking out." He pointed at the door. "And there he is!"

A man, his face shielded by a hood, stood in the doorway. He didn't look like anything special—average size and height. A cheer went up at the table next to me, and the man in the doorway slipped off his hood.

If Taran hadn't prepared me, I wouldn't have been unable to stop staring. Maelbrigte the Tusk was aptly named. The ugly man had shaggy, dark hair that went in a number of surprising directions out over one, thick black eyebrow. His eyes were wild, as if he was mad. A broken nose sat frankly between them. But it wasn't his strange appearance above the lips that startled me.

Maelbrigte had two, huge teeth in the front that stuck nearly straight out from his face. I'd never seen anything like it. A wild boar would find himself confused if confronted with this man.

"Don't stare," Taran said quietly. "He don' like it when yer stare."

I pulled my eyes away as Maelbrigte made his way over to the table filled with his men.

"I see why he's called The Tusk," I said softly.

Taran nodded. "He looks mean, but he's a good man. He's fair, an that's more'n yer can say fer most."

"I've heard rumors on the road that your magnate is involved in a dispute with a Viking?"

Taran spat on the floor, his face contorted with disgust. "The Earl of the Orkneys." He spat again. Apparently Sigurd rated a double spit. "He ain't the earl of me! He's a bastard. That's what Da says."

Trying to seem as if I really didn't care, I asked, "Why?"

"Vikings. They don' belong here," Taran said.

Deort called his son away from me, and I was left with my thoughts.

Iona appeared in front of me. "We got lucky. Sigurd is coming here in two days' time. And he won't be alone."

That got my attention. "Really? Why?"

Iona grinned. "There's to be a fight. A forty-on-forty-man battle. To settle the border dispute."

A forty-on-forty was interesting. Basically, the magnate and the earl would each bring forty men to the battle, just to keep it fair. Whoever won the battle won the dispute. Actually, I was a little surprised that the magnate had agreed to it. Vikings were talented fighters in a group. They could just chop away at people with axes until there was no one else to chop. After which, they'd look confused and go find some goats to steal.

I shrugged. "Why not just let Sigurd be killed in battle then?" Did we even need to be here, I wondered?

"You need to make sure the job is finished," Iona answered. "We can't leave until we know for sure Sigurd is dead."

That was a good point—but I wasn't about to say it to my sister. Chances were, the Vikings would come out on top here. I needed to make sure Sigurd did not survive this battle.

We once again gave our compliments on the dinner and followed Deort upstairs to our room. To my surprise, it was a large, corner room with two small beds and a blazing fireplace. After bolting the door and shuttering the one window, Iona and I disrobed and hung our clothing in front of the fire.

The things we'd brought were wet, so they too went in front of the fire. My sister and I wrapped blankets around our bodies and sat on our beds, mulling over what we knew and what we still needed to know.

"We should check this town out after breakfast," Iona said. "We can get a lot of gossip in the market."

I nodded. "All we have to do is make sure Sigurd doesn't leave here alive. I can volunteer to join Maelbrigte's forty fighters." I'd had a great deal of battle experience. Up here in the Pictlands, you just needed to step outside your front door to find it.

"I can help with that," Iona said. "As your boy, I can fight with you."

"No. I'd rather you didn't. You're just here to help me. I need to carry this assignment out." And that part was true. It was my job. But I also didn't want her to get hurt. It was better if she stayed out of the fray.

Iona frowned. I knew that look. That look meant I was in for it.

"I'm a trained killer too, Dublin. I can handle myself." She was angry with me.

"I know that." I struggled to figure out how to placate her—considering my next move from every angle. I missed my chess board. "What I meant was that I want you to stay on higher ground. Watch the whole field. If Sigurd makes any attempt to run away, you can go after him if I can't."

Iona smiled and nodded. She really was too easy to manipulate. Maybe I needed to teach her chess when we got back. She'd shown no interest in it previously, but my sister needed to learn strategy.

"I'll go to the bakery tomorrow and get us some bread," Iona said. "You need to make friends with the magnate."

"Good idea. By the way, did you get a look at the man?"

"Not really but I heard about his teeth. I was wondering how he eats like that." My sister shuddered a little under her blankets. "Why doesn't he just have them pulled?"

"Because maybe that's all he has," I answered. Teeth were important. Once you lost them, you were stuck eating broth or, in the case of my grandparents, having others pre-chew food for you. Which is why I brushed my teeth every day with a bristled twig. The others made fun of me sometimes, but my sister and mother used it, and we still had all of our teeth.

Sleep got the better of us. Our bones were weary but finally warm, and we settled into the straw filled mattresses and were out quickly.

"Dublin! Dub!" Iona's voice startled me awake, and I sprang from my bed, ready to fight.

My sister laughed. "You might want to put some clothes on." She pointed at my nudity, and I scowled as I walked over to the fire and retrieved my stiff but dry clothes.

"I thought there was trouble," I grumbled.

Iona giggled. "No, I was just waking you up." She'd already folded her clothing and was dressed.

"What time is it?" I asked.

"Oh, it's still pretty early," she answered. "I just didn't want to miss breakfast." Iona took a deep breath, and that's when I noticed the tantalizing smell of fresh baked bread in the room.

Deort's cook, who turned out to be Eithne, Deort's wife, greeted us with a smile and led us to a table. In minutes, she'd brought out a plate of bread, cheese, and apples. Once again, the little tavern room was filled with people. Iona and I ate heartily. We weren't going to be hungry again until we left.

It was a cold but bright, sunny day outside. Our breath mingled in the damp air. The village was not much to look at in the daytime. There were maybe ten crude buildings scattered recklessly about. People moved to and fro—some dragging animals or children with them. I asked a few questions and soon found myself standing face-to-tooth with Maelbrigte the Magnate.

I was staring. I know it was rude. But I couldn't help myself. The two teeth were even bigger in person. And they seemed to know I was staring at them. I don't know how I knew that…I just did.

"You lookin' fer me?" Maelbrigte said, but I could swear it came from those two teeth. They were enormous.

I forced my eyes upward and looked into his. He had two different colored eyes. The green one, on the left, looked right at me. The brown one on the right, wandered somewhere off to my right. I focused on his eyebrow.

"Yes. I've heard much about you and wanted to meet you in person."

The brown eye focused with the green eye on me for one moment before wandering off again. "That so?" the magnate said. "Buy me a drink then." His hand came up and turned my shoulder back to the place where I'd just come from. I curbed my instincts to toss him to the ground. Bombays didn't like to be manhandled as a rule. But I needed this weird looking man. So I allowed it.

Back in the inn's tavern, Deort clapped two tankards of mead in front of us.

"Who are you?" Maelbrigte asked as he took a large swig of mead. "Why are you here?"

"My name is Rabe. I'm a merchant from the South. Just passing through." I nailed the backstory. In your face, Iona! "I'd heard about the Magnate of Moray. You have the reputation of being a good man. I thought I'd introduce myself."

Maelbrigte's green eye regarded me thoughtfully. It was difficult to say what the teeth were thinking. Their gaze never wavered. "Good to meet yer." He clapped me on the arm. "Sorry yer had ta come at this time though."

I polished off my tankard and motioned for Deort to bring another round. This seemed to please the magnate, and he took another drink.

"Why is that?" I asked innocently. I needed to maneuver him into telling me about Sigurd. It would be too telling to ask directly.

The magnate ran a hand through his stiff, unruly hair, accomplishing nothing. He looked at me again and sighed. "I've got a Viking problem."

"Vikings?" I asked with what I hoped was casual interest. Even though I was starting to get used to the crazy eyes and protruding teeth, it was still unnerving.

"Sigurd the Mighty. Earl of the Orkneys. He's comin' here with forty men." All of a sudden I picked up on the fact that Maelbrigte was weary. He was worried about the battle. Taran had said he was a good man. Maybe he was concerned for his village as well.

"Is there anything I can do to help?" I offered. It was a risky gambit. After all, why would a minor merchant passing through want to help?

The brown eye swiveled in its socket and fixed on me. Obviously, I had his attention.

"Why?" Maelbrigte asked.

"Because I hate Vikings," I answered. "And I'm good with my sword." I let that information lie there for a moment.

He nodded. "That would be kind of yer. I'm short a few men. Most of 'em heard about the Vikings and lit out."

"Give me the details, and I'll be there," I said.

Maelbrigte told me about the forty-on-forty-man agreement. Sigurd had encroached one too many times into Moray. The two men had worked up a deal that each should bring forty men and the results of the battle would decide the terms.

"And just where will that battle take place?" I asked.

The magnate drained the second tankard and rose to leave. I tossed a few coins on the table and followed him out the door. We walked in silence over the frozen mud until we came to a small clearing.

"Here." Maelbrigte pointed at the field. "We wait for 'em here. Day after tomorrow." He ran his hand through his hair again. The man looked miserable. Clearly he had no confidence in the idea of winning the battle.

"Is it just to be man-on-man or will there be cavalry?" I asked.

"We're to fight on foot," he said. "That was the deal. But they'll arrive on horseback."

I looked at him for a moment. "Something is bothering you."

Maelbrigte looked off into the distance—which was something of a relief because I was exhausted trying to figure out which eye to talk to.

"I don't trust 'im," he said simply.

I nodded. You just couldn't trust Vikings. Sigurd might honor the agreement. But he might not. I tried to remember if I'd ever heard of Vikings doing the honorable thing, but I was useless at history. I'd have to ask Iona later.

"For what it's worth," I said, "I'll help do what I can."

Maelbrigte agreed to meet me in the morning to discuss the battle in detail. I studied the field a while longer after he left me. Then I returned to the inn.

Iona was waiting for me in our room. She told me pretty much the same story, and she had a loaf of bread and a bag of cheese. We sat in front of the fireplace and ate while I told her about my visit with the magnate.

"How big is the clearing?" she asked.

"Not big. And it's surrounded by trees and marsh in every direction except from the road leading to the village."

Iona wrapped the remaining bread and cheese in the bag. "You think they're going to cheat, don't you?"

"I don't know what to expect. What do you know about Vikings?" I asked. My sister knew her history and, according to her, everything else.

"They show loyalty to their leader, so it's up to what kind of character he is. Sigurd's a younger brother, so he'll be trying to prove himself. The problem is, the Vikings aren't really vested in this land. They don't think of it as home." She threw her hands up in the air. "It's a crapshoot really."

I nodded. "I'm going to work with Maelbrigte tomorrow. Maybe we can come up with something."

"Can I come along? I won't speak. Please?" Iona looked at me pleadingly.

"Fine." I felt bad for her having to bind her hair and breasts all the time for this ruse. She had to be bored out of her mind. "But let me do all the talking. It would be weird if my servant started spouting history or politics."

She nodded and made an "X" sign over her heart. Yeesh.

The next morning, Maelbrigte joined us for breaking the fast. I introduced Iona as Oxnar, and immediately realized I'd made a huge mistake. I hadn't prepared my sister for Maelbrigte's um, unusual appearance.

The magnate, fortunately, ignored my servant. Iona, however, did not ignore him. I'm not sure I've ever seen a fourteen year old girl stare at a man like that before. Her eyes moved back and forth between each eye and the teeth. She couldn't seem to decide which feature was more worthy of her attention. In moments, she drew in closer, her face just inches from his profile, staring as if he was, well, a man with freakish features.

"Go check on the horses," I said gruffly, trying to distract her. Iona snapped out of it and looked at me. Her mouth opened with the protest she was just about to utter, when she realized what she had been doing. She nodded and fled the tavern.

"Forgive Oxnar..." I apologized. "He doesn't get out much. Never leaves the shop back home." I twirled my finger around at the side of my forehead. "Idiot," I explained.

Maelbrigte stiffened, and then relaxed a little. He probably never got used to the attention. "I didn't even notice he was here."

"Tell me what you have in mind for tomorrow," I said.

"I have forty men now, with you." The magnate pointed at me, his brown eye aimed at his finger. "We wait at the field. They will come. We will fight."

I tried not to sigh. I truly did. Yet another example of how chess would help people like Maelbrigte plan his battles. Granted, this was a small battle. More like a melee actually. But planning was still important. I stood up.

"Follow me," I said as I headed outside. Along the wall to the left of the door was a long bench. I motioned for Maelbrigte to sit, and I picked up a stick and began to draw.

"This is the field." I drew a rough oval. "These are the trees, and this is the road to town." I added trees that looked like X's and a line for the road. I wasn't much of an artist. That was more Iona's area. But she was hopefully off with the horses and not staring at the magnate from a distance somewhere. I really had to talk to her about that.

"I suggest we be ready here." I drew a line at the far end of the field, opposite where the road came in. "That way, we can watch them arrive and arrange themselves."

Maelbrigte nodded. "They'll have horses."

"Yes, but they'll use them for travel only. The field is too small for a cavalry charge, and Vikings aren't keen on fighting from the back of a horse."

We talked for a few hours, discussing his men and their strengths and weaknesses. It was cold outside and overcast, but I didn't feel it. The thrill of strategy took over. Iona joined us at one point and squirmed, trying not to stare at Maelbrigte. Eventually, she began to follow the drawing in the dirt. If she knew better about something, she didn't show it.

"This is good," the magnate said slowly. "I think we have a chance."

I smiled because I got to introduce him to planning. Now if I'd only had my chess board...

"Maelbrigte!" A young boy came running up to us. "There's a problem with the pigs!"

The magnate thanked us and followed the boy away.

"You spent all this time doing that?" Iona pointed to the drawing. "I could've told you that."

"You spent all that time with the horses? Maybe you should take a bath," I grumbled.

"Why didn't you warn me?" Iona asked. "I had no idea he looked like that."

"I do apologize for that. I should've prepared you."

"It was a total shock!" My sister folded her arms over her chest. "I wanted to run and get a pair of pliers to straighten his teeth at least!"

"How would you have handled the brown eye?" I asked.

Iona frowned. "An eye patch, I think. Why?"

I just shook my head. I was hoping she had a real answer because it was very distracting. Then again, maybe that was the point. Maybe he liked it that way.

I changed the subject. "Tomorrow's the battle. Do you remember what I wanted you to do?"

She nodded. "You want me to watch from higher ground. If Sigurd runs off, I go after him." The way her eyes gleamed, I was afraid she was hoping she'd get the chance to take him out herself. That wasn't going to happen though. I'd kill him on the battlefield first.

That night I had trouble sleeping. Iona snored softly, but I was worried. Of course I couldn't tell her that. She'd mock me, or come up with a better way to handle things. I'd have to move out of the castle back home and find somewhere else to live. Women really were impossible.

The problem was that I was getting attached. To Maelbrigte. Buck-toothed, roaming eyed, wild haired, one-eyebrowed Maelbrigte. I could see how Taran and the other villagers liked him. He was a man who worried about his people. But then, why did he enter into such an asinine agreement with the Vikings? Maybe he wasn't all he was cracked up to be.

At dawn, Iona and I ate breakfast. Taran appeared at my elbow.

"I'm gonna fight with yer," he said, a stubborn look in his eye.

"No. You're not," I responded as harshly as I could. Even though boys his age had a history of participating in battle, I didn't want to risk anything happening to the boy.

Taran frowned, crossing his arms over his chest. "Yes I am! I kin fight! Yer need me!"

I shook my head. "Your da needs you. More than the magnate does. You stay here."

"You can come and watch," Iona said.

I glared at her. She had no idea what she was doing. Boys are stubborn and will lie to you. Taran would no sooner arrive at the field than he'd pick up a fallen man's axe and plunge into the fray.

"I don't think that's a good..." I started.

Iona turned to Taran. "I'll be there. You can stand with me." Taran considered this before nodding and running off.

"What are you doing? He shouldn't be there!" I protested.

My sister shook her head. "He's going anyway. You can't stop him. This way at least I can keep an eye on him. You'll be on the field. You can't."

I couldn't argue with her logic. Okay...she was right. There I said it. Demanding the boy stay away would only make him more determined to go.

"Fine," I said at last. "But you'll have to watch him and make sure he doesn't fight."

Iona nodded and went back to her food, smug in the knowledge that once again, she was right.

I paid for our meals and collected my weapons before heading out to the field. No one really knew what time the Vikings were coming. They'd sort of forgotten to set up that part of the deal. How hard would it have been to say, *Hey Sigurd, let's meet at dawn?* Instead we had to wait.

Maelbrigte came first with about twenty other men. The others staggered in, either hung over or maybe they just walked that way. By noon, we had our full complement of men.

A stark, dull sun hung limply in an iron-grey sky. The air was flat and brisk, but at least the mud had hardened overnight. No one spoke much. I surveyed our troops.

The majority were farmers, each holding a favored implement. They were big men, which was good, and Maelbrigte had assured me they were seasoned fighters. I hoped so, for his sake and theirs. Whatever their vocation, it was clear they had no problems fighting. The Vikings were not popular here.

I gripped my axe in my left hand and my short sword in my right. I was anxious to get started. To get it over. To make sure Sigurd the Mighty was dead so I could go back home.

A noise came from the road, and the magnate's troops turned their heads at the same time. One rider on a small horse trotted toward us. He came to the middle of the field and stopped.

"Maelbrigte!" the man shouted as he got down off his horse. "I am here!"

This was Sigurd? Sigurd the Mighty? The man before us was very short. I was considered tall in my family, but Sigurd barely came up to my shoulder. He had a full head of curly dark hair that rose up from his forehead and swooped backwards. Tiny, sharp eyes framed a tiny nose and thin lips. But the worst thing was his voice. He sounded like a squirrel who'd been kicked in the balls.

"Where are your men?" Maelbrigte shouted.

"They are coming," Sigurd cried with a strange giggle. His thin, reedy voice was ridiculous. And he giggled. I should've killed him right then and there for that alone. "You can still back out and turn over Moray to me!" The Viking spread his feet and assumed a haughty pose intended to intimidate. Instead, it gave the impression of a cricket throwing a tantrum. Out of the corner of my eye, I spotted Iona doubled over with laughter. For a moment I thought of joining her.

Maelbrigte shook his head. "You'll have your fight, Viking."

The sound of hoof beats echoed down the road, and the magnate's men formed a line, gripping their spears, rakes, and hoes. I wondered why the sound of forty horses didn't sound more intimidating. It should have.

Then I saw it. A line of horsemen on small horses. Very small horses. Was this a joke? First a dwarf Viking and now dwarf ponies? I watched as the horsemen came in and lined up opposite us. There was something else. The horses seemed to enter the field and move into a line without turning their backs on us. Why did they do that?

The Vikings on little ponyback didn't dismount. Were they going to make an attempt at a cavalry charge, I wondered? I looked up and down the line. Something else wasn't right. I rubbed my eyes. What was it?

"Are you going to fight on yer horses?" Maelbrigte shouted. "That wasn't the agreement."

And that's when I saw it. I knew what was wrong. I pushed my way through the other men to get to the magnate.

"Yer can't change things this way," Maelbrigte continued. I grabbed his arm, and he shrugged it off, intent on yelling at the tiny Viking. "A deal's a deal, Sigurd!"

"Maelbrigte!" I hissed into his ear.

The man turned his brown eye on me. Was I imagining it or were the two teeth sticking out further than before? "What?" he snarled.

I pointed at the riders on ponies. "Look!"

The magnate followed my finger, and his eyes widened when he saw what I saw. Each rider seemed to have an extra pair of legs. There were two men on each horse. Sigurd the Mighty had cheated. He'd brought eighty men to a forty-man fight.

"You need to say something to your men!" I urged as the Vikings began to get off their little horses now. Each rider seemed to double now, and Maelbrigte's men realized that they were outnumbered.

"Give them a speech—inspire them!" I begged. The magnate needed to instill confidence in his men before it was lost.

Maelbrigte turned to his men and began to shout, "I expect each one of you to slay two men today!" And that was it.

No, *Let's get rid of these Viking bastards once and for all,* or even an, *I know you can do it!*

I looked at our troops. They were stunned. Horrified. Yup. We were going to lose.

With a war cry that can only be described as the sound a chicken makes when you step on it, Sigurd the Mighty unleashed his eighty strong Viking force on Maelbrigte's farmers.

I fought alongside them, trying to help them when I could, but it was too much. The Vikings cut them down like weeds. It should be noted that I killed way more than my allotted two men. But it was over before it began. The field was full of bloody body parts. Only myself and a couple of others were still standing when Sigurd called an end to the fighting.

To say I was disappointed was an understatement. Maelbrigte the Magnate and most of the men of the village were now dead. Sigurd the Mighty was still alive. And I hadn't finished the job.

Iona appeared beside me. "That didn't turn out well," she said.

"Where's Taran?" I asked.

My sister shook her head. "He showed up, but I sent him back to the tavern for water and food for the survivors. He didn't make it back in time." She scratched her nose. "Not that I thought he would…"

Bragging, know-it-all kid sister. How did she do it?

We watched as Sigurd walked over to the corpse of Maelbrigte the Magnate and cut off his head. Being that he was a small man, it took him overly long to do this. I wondered if the other Vikings made fun of him.

Sigurd spotted Iona and tossed her Maelbrigte's head. "Tie that onto my saddle, boy!" he squeaked. "I'm taking home a trophy."

I put my arm out to stop her, but my sister just shook her head and carried the magnate's head away.

"The rest of you," the Viking earl tittered, "go back to your fields. Tend my crops and prepare for taxation in the spring." Sigurd giggled insanely, reminding me somewhat of a deranged leprechaun.

Iona joined me, her hands and tunic covered in blood. She smelled faintly of feces. But this field was filled with horrible sights and smells. It would take several baths to wash it all off. We watched in silence as Sigurd attempted three times to climb on his horse. Finally, one of the other Vikings tossed him into the saddle. He swung his leg over, and I saw that it was right next to Maelbrigte's head. The empty eyes stared straight ahead. The brown eye didn't swivel. Not even once. And that made me a little sad.

The other Vikings mounted their tiny ponies and rode off. Then the women of the village came to gather the bodies of those who'd died.

"We need to go after them," I said to Iona. "I'll have to sneak into his camp at night and slit his throat."

Iona smiled and shook her head. "No. You won't. He's already dead. He just doesn't know it yet."

"What are you talking about?" I asked.

My sister just grinned and said, "You'll see."

We followed the Vikings for two days, keeping to the forest so we wouldn't be discovered. On the third day, I noticed that the Vikings were not uprooting camp. They remained at the crook of a small river for another two days.

Iona and I lived off the loaves of bread and the cheese she'd packed from the village. We sheltered in an old cave we'd found, waiting for the Vikings to move on to the coast. But that didn't happen.

"See?" Iona said with a grin. "I told you." She was wrapped in her cloak, trying to stave off the early evening's clammy chill.

"I don't see anything," I growled. The cold and damp were wearing on me, as was the complete lack of activity. What was happening?

"Oh, go see for yourself since you can't sit still." Iona rolled her eyes, and I stood up and made my way out of the cave.

"You stay here," I ordered. For once, she didn't argue.

I moved carefully through the trees, keeping to whatever foliage I could find for cover. There wasn't much. Sticks cracked beneath my feet, and leaves crunched however I moved. My short sword was at my side, and I had a knife in my boot. This was it. I was going to kill Sigurd so we could go home.

Twilight had fallen like a blanket over the forest as I came upon the farthest edge of the camp. Two men were digging a deep hole in the frozen ground. From their swearing, I could see they were not happy to be doing so.

"Why don't we just take him to the coast and do a proper burial at sea?" one of the Vikings asked.

Viking number two shook his head. "He died of the fever. We can't risk catching it ourselves. Olin says burial, so we are doing a burial."

Someone died of fever? That would explain the camp staying put. Maybe the fever would wipe them all out, and I wouldn't have to kill Sigurd.

"It's weird, isn't it?" Viking number one said. "It's like the magnate got his revenge."

What were they talking about? Who did Maelbrigte get revenge on? He was nothing more than a head.

"We're to bury the head too," Viking number two said. "Just in case."

The first Viking shuddered. "Sigurd was a fool. Riding with Maelbrigte the Tusk's head against his leg like that. The Tusk got him alright!"

The two men laughed, and I moved a bit closer. They weren't making any sense. How did The Tusk get Sigurd?

"It's a curse! It has to be!" Viking two said. "Maelbrigte biting Sigurd's leg like that and the wound getting pus so fast! We need to bury them both and get out of here!"

Back in the cave, Iona smiled as I walked in.

"He's dead, isn't he?" she asked with an impressive level of sarcasm.

"Yes. How did you do it?" I asked. My sister already knew she was right. She always was. There was no point in ignoring it.

"Horse shit," Iona said. "From those stupid little ponies. After I tied the magnate's head on the saddle so his teeth would rub on the Viking's leg, I smeared a little horse shit on them. I figured that would work."

"It did," I said as I stood and lifted her to her feet. "And now we can go home."

Iona became nearly impossible to live with. She didn't tell the others in the family that she was actually the one who took out Sigurd the Mighty. But she made it clear she could at any time—especially when she wanted something. I pleaded with Mother to marry her off quickly, but my pleas fell on deaf ears. Mom liked having her around.

That winter was a hard one. A thick blanket of snow made it impossible to leave the castle. Uncle Rome had a heart attack when we tried to extricate him from the privy. It was a relief, really. And now there was more food for us. Mother took his place on the Council.

On a cold, despondent day, I entered my room to find Iona puzzling over my chess set. After pretending she really didn't care for a few days, she finally allowed me to teach her the game. We've been playing all winter long.

And she wins every damn time.

AUTHOR'S NOTE

I hope you enjoyed these stories from the historical files of the Bombay Family of Assassins. As a history geek, I enjoyed writing them. Especially the John Billington story. I'm a direct descendant of this man who came over on the Mayflower and was also the first person hung for murder in the American Colonies—and it was fun killing off my 11th Great Grandpa (in a weird way).

If you haven't read any of the Bombay books, I suggest you start with 'SCUSE ME WHILE I KILL THIS GUY. You can find more information on my website: www.leslielangtry.com

If you have read them all, watch for a special Christmas short story coming out for the holidays of this year: FOUR KILLING BIRDS, which will be part of an anthology by the Killer Fiction Writers.

~ Leslie Langtry

ABOUT THE AUTHOR

Leslie Langtry is the author of the Greatest Hits Mysteries, *The Adulterer's Unofficial Guide to Family Vacations*, and several books she hasn't finished yet, because she's very lazy. Leslie loves puppies and cake (but she will not share her cake with puppies) and lives with her family and assorted animals in the Midwest.

To learn more about Leslie, visit her online at
www.leslielangtry.com

Enjoyed this book? Check out these other romantic
mysteries available in print now from
Gemma Halliday Publishing:

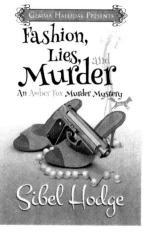

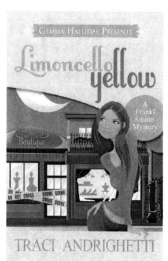

www.GemmaHalliday.com/Halliday_Publishing

CPSIA information can be obtained at www.ICGtesting.com
Printed in the USA
LVOW06s1439150614

390131LV00001B/114/P